Tales from Pangea

THE LOST CITY OF OLD

Book 1 -

Ryan Cam-Tron Cameron

CAM-tron
Studios

Cover Illustration : @bkz_art
Editor : Warren Baumstark-Ullom
Cover Design : Ryan Cam-Tron Cameron
Story : Ryan Cam-Tron Cameron
Art : Ryan Cam-Tron Cameron

ISBN: 978-0-578-36963-1
Tales From Pangea : The Lost City of Old (Book 1)
Ryan Cam-Tron Cameron
CAM-tron Studios LLC, CamTronStudios.com
Camtron954@gmail.com
Self Published, 2022

" For all the dreamers who never give up,
Even when you think no one is watching ...
We see you."

Special thanks
to all my family, friends
and loved ones who supported me
during this journey.

My Mom & Dad, Angela Vedanayakam,
Warren & Haya Baumstark-Ullom,
Aisha Gillette, Carlton Brown,
my auntie's Flo - Ruth & Angela, my brothers
Rolando & Rasheed.
Jasmine, Michael, Nathan DuConge, Darryl
Aikens (Cali), Brendan Salters (Scribe), Miles
Gordon & Jen Dalton, Xavier Miles, Brian
Bondurant, MystiqueRose Publishing, John
Miyasato, David Swisher, my boy Richard
Brandtsmith,
And anyone else I've forgotten.

But most importantly,
I have to give thanks to the Most High
for making all of this possible.

Pangea Map

Treasure Map

Prologue

Staring me in the eyes, *Lockjaw* tossed his pistol into the water, then pulled his large greatsword with one hand, eager to settle the score. We charged simultaneously, kicking up golden coins in our wake. With the water almost up to their necks, *Naji* exclaimed, "Hurry, there's not much time!"

Splitting up, they began searching the confines of the room, desperately trying to find an exit; but the rising water continued to burst through the walls. Within moments it flooded most of the area, forcing them to seek higher ground.

Swinging his golden katana to the left, *Spectre* lunged in with a quick slash. While dodging to the side, *Lockjaw* countered with a hard cleave as their two blades clashed with a loud *Clang*. Harnessing the power of the crystal, *Lockjaw's* muscles suddenly began to bulge. He then used his combat reflexes to predict his opponent's next attack.

While swinging wide, *Spectre* was caught off guard as *Lockjaw* ducked his attack and elbowed him in the stomach, sweeping him off his feet with his blade. *Spectre* crashed into the water with a splash. " Such power! I can feel it pulsing through my veins!" *Lockjaw* roared, as his eyes began glowing in a neon blue.

Ascending the pile of treasure, I tried to intervene with a crippling strike, but was easily countered as he *Lockjaw* deflected the blow, then kicked me off the mound. "We have to stop him before the *Crystal* gives him too much power!" I shouted.

Immediately, *Sasha* fell upon him with a surprise attack. With a dazzling display, her speed allowed her to pierce *Lockjaw's* now toughened skin. However, his sheer determination willed him to backhand her into the water, ignoring the minor flesh wound as they instantly began to reconstruct." Hahaha! I'm invincible!" He yelled vehemently.

With only a yard of breathing room from the roof, we were running out of time. "It's not supposed to end like this!" *Naji* responded.

" Not every story has a happy ending, kid," *Spectre* replied. With less than a foot of air, we treaded water, taking our last deep breaths.

I thought to myself, "How did this happen?" Just 12 days ago I was an average kid, struggling to get by like anyone else. And now here I am. Face-to-face with the deadliest pirate in the sky. So much had happened over the course of the journey, that I almost forgot what led us here in the first place.
To explain, I would have to start from the beginning…

Mom & Dad.

Chapter 1

Millennia ago the planet *Gaia* was a dense oasis, filled with hundreds of *Piku* trees, massive chunks of timber, 1000 feet tall and over 50 feet around. Immense energy from *Gaia's* core pulsed through their roots, covering the planetside with lush landscapes and abundant vegetation.

Upon creation, man quickly became aware of his surroundings and adapted to the environment. In no time, he would spread across the continent of *Pangea*. He later learned of the *Piku* tree's capabilities, harnessing its raw energy into material form known as *Power Crystals*. These luminous blue shards filled with energy were said to power a society for centuries.

However, the people of old were excellent craftsmen and master masons. They used the crystals to create spectacular structures and erect elaborate cities. But as they say, everything has a price. The more *Power Crystals* they harvested, the more trees would wither away, quickly becoming dry and brittle.

Then one day a curious chemist ran some experiments, realizing the crystals held more abilities. Through tapping into their infinite energy he learned to manipulate the cellular process, granting him superhuman abilities. He then discovered how to prolong life at an accelerated rate, or cause it to grow feeble with plague and disease.

The chemist soon gathered many acolytes who devoted themselves to his vast knowledge. Within a year his following had grown into an army that immediately embarked on a conquest around the world, destroying many cities and civilizations in search of the *Power Crystals*. But his insatiable hunger to feed on the energy began to taint and corrupt the chemist. He then forced the master smiths high in the *Forged Mountains* to create potent weapons infused with the energy, thus granting him the title of *Dark One*. As centuries went on, this eventually led to the *Piku* tree's extinction until only one remained.

But as fate would have it, a brave soul vowed to guard that last tree, hoping to put an end to *The Dark One* and his tyranny.

He then rallied all of the other nations and their heroes, for the final battle against evil. The people in the mountains agreed to give their assistance, by forging the heroes weapons as well. Their conscience wouldn't allow them to help *The Dark One* destroy the world. Covered in new armor, that brave man became known as *The Gold Knight*.

The warring armies faced off in a heated battle on the *Green Plateau* for control of the final tree, and the fate of the world. In a valiant display, *The Gold Knight* delivered the fatal blow, wounding *The Dark One,* who somehow managed to flee the battlefield and was never seen again.

After the war, *The Gold Knight* ordered that all the *Power Crystals* and their weapons to be destroyed. With the evil army defeated, he lived out his days on the *Green Plateau,* later founding the city of *Edenia* & guarding the last living *Piku* tree, which was then forever known as *The Tree of Life*...

Flashing forward to the 19th century, piracy was at an all-time high. The leading nations funded privateer expeditions in lieu of treasure, as ravenous bandits scoured the continent. Tales of golden cities and caverns loaded with jewels pacified the impoverished people. Natural resources were scarce and in high demand. The planet of *Gaia* had fallen to war.

Then In 1832, a master mechanic and inventor named *Ferdinand Von Zeppelin*, created the first aircraft - the "*Model LZ1*", *a* steel fabricated boat with a helium balloon above the mast. He later went on to manufacture a line of these ships, mostly for transporting food to the starving nations. But tensions festered on the outskirts of the city, leading rogue buccaneers to unite and form raiding parties. Taking to the clouds, they labeled themselves "Sky Pirates", thus changing the course of battle as we know it.

8 years later *Zeppelin* and his wife *Angela* gave birth to a son, then adopted another. Safeguarded from the lawlessness outside of the city, they raised these children through the rise of an industrial revolution. Then, in May of 1846, *Zeppelin* and his wife were killed in a horrific accident.
Ferdinand Von Zeppelin was *Thomas's* father...

Thomas

Hearing the kettle whistle, I instantly raised my head. BANG! -I was greeted by a swinging light, and a knot on my forehead. Dropping my hammer down to the floor, I descended the 8 foot wooden ladder. My teeth still vibrated from pummeling nails into a thin sheet of metal. Reaching inside my toolbox, beads of sweat trickled from my face. I grabbed a 3/8 drive ratchet. Walking to the underbelly of my unfinished project, I ducked underneath the right wing. Reaching upwards, I began tightening the last remaining bolts before the test run.
The first two attempts had proven useless.

Clink clink clink. Letting out a breath of relief, I wiped my forehead with exhaustion, "This looks better than the blueprint", I thought to myself. Getting things done right the first time was an important philosophy I stood by. My parents always encouraged us to reach for the stars. Walking to the kettle, I poured some water into a copper tankard with a tea bag.

While stirring the sugar, I stepped over bundles of dirty clothes. For the past few weeks, I'd been sleeping in the workshop. Putting in overtime.

Now there she was, the *Model - 1*. Suspended by metal chains she hung from the ceiling, 13 feet from head to toe, with a 9-foot alloy wingspan; open roof bucket seats fully equipped for two passengers, one behind the other. 900 lbs of raw torque. It was a real testament to my late father's genius. Inside her frame sat the first-ever steam powered engine, running completely on water; the first self-propelled aerial machine. I nicknamed it - the Aero-plane. I had found the schematics years ago, while rummaging through some old papers. Just days after my parents death.

My father *Zeppelin* (known to others as *Zepp* for short), was the master mechanic and head inventor at Zeppelin Technologies (or Zep-Tec "The best this side of the *Green Plateau!*"). He was also the lead engineer at the old industrial plant near the center of town, where they manufactured his flying ships, known as Zeppelins. I would spend most of my time here at the Zep-Tec home workshop, tinkering with gadgets until the sun would rise.

My mother *Angela* was a language arts teacher. She loved volunteering at *Deacon Blues* old orphanage and feeding the kids. That was where they found *Naji*, a *Saharian* refugee. He always had a thing for culinary arts, and Mom was always proud of our creations, like that machine we invented to help wash the dirty dishes. Dad called it the "Hydro Augmented Circulator", but it was mom's feminine finesse that helped us shorten the name to "the Dishwasher". She was so ecstatic, she cooked our favorite meals for a week. Without a doubt my father and I were the perfect team…

Until the day of their sixth anniversary.

Father was preparing to take mother on a surprise test flight on his latest invention, the *Model-0*. I can still remember him kneeling in front of me saying,"Son, life is about taking chances, not being afraid to go where others won't. Sometimes obstacles are going to stand in your way, But it's the strong man who faces them head-on. This world can be a dangerous place, but I know you'll do just fine. You and your brother were always quick learners". Reaching into his waistcoat, he then placed his silver compass watch into my hand. Gently grabbing my shoulders he added,"One day, Zep-Tec will be yours. 'Til then, look after your brother. There's nothing like family son. We love you both dearly." Those were the last words I heard him say.

A minute later, they were taking off down a runway and into the air. Awestruck, *Naji* and I watched from below. We were only six then. Like a metal bird, the *Model-0* climbed high above the city of *Edenia*, attracting quite the audience. Making circles over the red-tiled roofs, *Zepp* waved from above. When no sooner had the flight begun, a thunderous burst came from the tail, spewing a trail of black smoke.

Hearing screams from the crowd, *Naji* and I were filled with apprehension. The *Model-0* was now spiraling downward, before finally crashing into a thicket of trees and exploding into a ball of shrapnel. Frozen stiff, my legs trembled with fear as the citizens rushed to the crash site. Moments later, I watched as they retrieved our parent's lifeless bodies from the wreckage... From that day on, I made a vow to carry on my father's legacy.

11 years later, here I stand in front of the same machine that claimed the lives of my parents. This time however, I'm using my own design - the "Dual Hydraulic Converter". After wiping the *Model - 1* down from excess dust and metal shavings, I

climbed the ladder, squeezing into the cockpit. Clad in tanned leather and polished steel I slid into the padded seat, letting my hands glide across the smooth surface of the dashboard, thinking to myself, "This is it. The moment of truth".

Pulling the brown pilot's helmet and goggles down over my combed black hair, I then pressed the engine's ignition button. Suddenly the engine began to turn and sputter, making loud metal ticking sounds. The propeller slowly spun at first, before rapidly picking up speed like a ceiling fan. "It worked!?". I blurted out half-surprised, with my mouth hanging low. Surveying the gauges on the dashboard, I eagerly turned my head from side to side, resembling a chicken. "It works!" I bellowed, raising my hands in triumph.

A voice to my left suddenly responded, "What works!?", shouting over the loud hum from the motor.

Startled, I turned my head. Then noticed an athletic brown-skinned figure standing with his arms crossed, leaning against the doorway.
He carried a large bag on his shoulder, possibly storing his loot. Not recognizing the person at first, I studied him closer. I then noticed his sleeveless loose-fitting jalabiya, with matching white pants cut off above the ankles, silver accessories and woven brown sandals adorning his wrists and feet. It was the shiny bald head and black hilt scimitar hanging from his waist that gave him away. It was none other than my adopted brother.

"*Naji*?" I asked. Shortly after our parents death, we were forced to change schools and then were sent to an orphanage. He had been abandoned by his mother two years prior. Cunning and street savvy, we hit it off. With my brains and his wit, we soon became the best of friends. The orphanage governor was a shady old man named *Deacon Blues* - head of the local missionary. The *Deacon* always had it out for us, often putting worms in our spaghetti for dinner, or sometimes even locking us away in a closet for hours at a time. It's safe to say the *Deacon* was a real douchebag. Then one day *Naji* fell in with a group of thieves and ran away. He would disappear for months at a time, so it became hard to keep track of him. Last I heard, he had left with a group of smugglers, on a ship called the *Centennial Eagle*.

Climbing out of the cockpit with excitement, I repeated. "*Naji*? Is that really you"? Extending my right hand.

"In the flesh." He replied with a smile. Shaking hands, I returned,

"I wasn't expecting you for another week. So, how was the voyage?"

"Not so good. The port authorities caught word of the spice we were smuggling and set up a sting for the buyer, so we had to abort. But we did manage to score some loot from a passing trading convoy. You know, just food and cargo. Nothing unusual-" he spoke then paused for a second, as he looked at me with an anxious grin. Reaching behind him, he pulled from his back pocket a tattered old parchment- "I also found this," he continued, unfolding the paper on top of my wooden workbench. Instantly, I spotted the symbols and dotted lines.

"What is that? A map"? I said.

"It's not just any map. I think it's a Treasure map". He replied.
Showing the sudden disappointment on my face, I squinted my eyes.

"A treasure map"? I replied suspiciously.

"Yeah! One of the traders kept it hidden in a small box, filled with golden coins and jewels. The old fart wouldn't let go of it. When he finally handed it over, he told us that it led to the *Lost City of Old*."

"Wait a minute, the old wives tale?" *Naji* continued,

"One and the same. Once the others heard that, they laughed and pushed him aside. But there was something strange about him. A certain look in his eye... I think he was telling the truth." Turning back towards the *Model - 1*, I told him,

"The *Lost City of Old* is a myth. No one has ever come close to finding a single clue of where it might be". As I walked in front of the plane, I stood, captivated by its beauty. "That was just an old bedtime story they tell children at the orphanage".

Persistent with his theory, *Naji* stepped closer, replying, "I'm going to find it. And I want you to come with me." Walking around to the other side of the plane, I climbed inside the cockpit.

"Haha. Thanks for the offer, but I don't think I could afford a vacation right now. If I don't come up with a new invention soon, I'm going to lose my parents' workshop. They've worked too hard to achieve this. So, sorry but I don't think I've got the time."
Stepping even closer, *Naji* tried to reason.

"That's why you should come along! We could split the treasure 50/50! With your knowledge and my navigation, I KNOW we'll find it. Besides, who better to share this with than my own brother?"
Leaning back into the seat, I answered,

"It sounds like fun, but I've got a lot of work to do," causing Naji to wrinkle his face,

"What is this thing anyway? Another slingshot?"

A few years prior, I attached 2 steel beams to a hydraulic pump fueled by pressurized water. Held together with 10 feet of treated rubber, the test subject (myself at the time) would stretch the rubber cord back, and sit on the chair fastened at the end. With the flip of a switch, the subject would be launched through the air at a 50 degree angle (and myself headfirst into a rose bush). I then wore an arm brace for about a month.

I now explained, "No, it's not another Hydraulic Spring Launcher. It's better than that. This is the *Model - 1*, also known as the *Aero-plane*. The first-ever self-propelled aircraft. Here, allow me to demonstrate."

Standing up in the cockpit, I leaned over the dashboard, pointing to the copper mesh covering the engine." A 6-liter inline engine pumps steam into a cylinder, condensed by cold water. This creates a vacuum in the cylinder, resulting in an atmospheric pressure operating the pistons downward stroke". Using my hands for emphasis, I continued:

"She also sports a Dual Hydraulic Converter. The whole thing runs completely on pressurized water, stored over there in a tank behind the passenger seat. I decided to use soapy water for the hydraulic fluid. You know, to help lube the valves." Sitting back down in the seat, I said. "Using these petals here at my feet, I can distribute water throughout the pipes like a pump. Leading it to a boiler which turns it into steam. The turbines then spin a generator, making enough electricity for the propulsion system."

I began to demonstrate by peddling the gears with my feet when suddenly - BOOM!
A loud burst came from under the engine, followed by a series of metal banging sounds. Shocked by the noise, I reflexively pressed the engine's ignition button, shutting it off. Gray smoke rose from the mesh behind the propeller, slowly painting the roof. *Naji* said,

"I don't think it was supposed to do that."

I stood on top of the seat. Leaning over the dashboard console, I unhooked the latch exposing the engine's guts, fanning the smoke away as it seeped from the pipes. Disappointed by my circumstance, I lamented,

"At this rate, I'll never get it running."

Naji said, "Why don't you come on board with us on this expedition? The *Centennial Eagle* could use your expertise. One of the guys is plugged in with *the Baron*, we could always use an extra hand. Especially since that last group of smugglers tried to run away with his coin. He had them hung from the gallows...If you want, I can vouch for you." -when out of the blue a squeaky voice said,

"The *Baron*? The wanted criminal on all those fliers? You filthy Sky Pirates think you can just sail wherever you want, and steal from hard-working people like myself? It seems with all the fame shooting straight to your father's head, he must have forgotten to teach you both manners. Hmph, I should alert the port authorities and have you both thrown away."

Standing in the garage door opening behind us was none other than the *Deacon Blues* himself. With fingers interlocked upon his chest the frail partly-bald man smiled with a conspiratorial grin, sporting his typical brown robe like a fryer. The mid-afternoon sun rays gleamed off his olive scrunched face.

For years, I was told about my father's genius as a young man. The neighbors were all too excited to lend him a helping hand, until the accident happened. Then they quickly forgot about us, and the Zep-Tec family name. Life at the orphanage after that was a real drag.

Everyone treated us like an outcast, and *Deacon Blues* made sure of that. Despite his strange attraction to my mother, it wasn't hard to see the malice he held towards my little brother and I. He and my father once were the final contestants of a city wide grant for new inventors; the prize was 50,000 coin. But, It seemed no one liked his ingenious idea of a portable bible stand.

My old man used the proceeds to create the floor model of his famous invention. Which later locked him into a business deal with the tycoon *George Stephens*, owner of *Edenia Steel* Mill. *Deacon Blues* didn't know how to take it. And from that day on, his overzealous spite for us orphans was noticeable.

"Who invited you? Trespassing is a crime in Edenia!" I threatened.

Naji chimed in,"Yeah, hard-working people my ass. We all know you're nothing more than a child smuggler. Remember? We were there."

Deacon Blues snarled. "I don't smuggle orphans you ruffians. I save them from their cruel reality. Give them a purpose, a chance at a better life. Here, with the church of St.Paul." He then made a look of disgust, adding, "But you little muskrats never understood the meaning of gratitude, for such a glorious opportunity. By far, you were the WORST my orphanage has ever seen."

"Thanks for the confession, but don't you have a sweatshop to lord over? Why are you even here anyway?" I said.

Then *Deacon Blues* explained. "Why, I'm here on business of course".

"Well thanks but, whatever it is you're selling? We don't want any". I quickly returned.

Deacon replied, "Heh heh heh, on the contrary: I'm here with your final notice of foreclosure for this... 'has been' establishment. It appears the trust fund your father left you has finally been depleted weeks ago. Zep-Tec still owes 100,000 coin on the building, and as an investment, I plan to purchase this DUMP, and turn it into another orphanage for wayward souls."

"What! You can't do that!" I yelled, as he stepped closer handing me the notice.

"Yes, I can. And I will. You have two weeks to gather the funds," He returned.

"Once this new prototype works, I'll be able to manufacture a fleet and sell them. That will cover all the expenses. Please, I just need more time," I pleaded.

With an evil look in his eyes, *Deacon Blues* said, "Well, it sounds like you have your work cut out for you. It would be a shame to see all of your father's hard work go down the drain. You're a smart boy, I'm sure you'll figure something out. Heh heh heh, pity." Turning around, he headed for the exit. "Good day, gentlemen."

After reviewing the paper, I lamented. "What am I going to do? I can't lose the workshop? Zep-Tec is my family's legacy."

Leaning his back against the *Model - 1*, *Naji* said, "Whatever you do, we better do it fast. Two weeks isn't a lot of time."
My mind was racing a mile a minute and felt like a hamster on a spinning wheel. My life as I knew it was about to come crashing down... And fast.

Naji stood in front of the workbench and looked down at the treasure map. Picking it up with a sudden look of discovery, he exclaimed, "I've got it! We can use the coin from the treasure!", pointing to the bold-printed X on the parchment.

"Come on, now is not the time for games. What about *King Raynor*? He's got a lot of coin." I replied.

Shaking his head, *Naji* returned, "Pfft, that jarhead? All he's worried about is fortifying *Edenia's* army."

"Well, maybe dad's old friend *Mr. Stephens* will loan us the coin?" I rebutted.

Naji replied, "I'm serious, what if we found it? We could pay for Dad's workshop? Even the *Deacons* church if we wanted to."

As I looked in his direction I could see the determination in his eyes. Like a fire burning from inside. This must have been the same look he'd seen on the old man's face who had the map.

"Do you think we can really find it in time"? I asked.

"Of course I do! Besides, what else do you have to lose?" *Naji* replied.

Giving his message time to sink in, I accepted his offer.

"All right, let's do it. But we split the treasure 50/50."

Jumping with excitement, he replied.

"Right, 50/50. We better get a move on. Come on, the crew should be at the tavern."

Folding up the map and throwing a tarp over the *Model - 1*, we hurried out of the workshop in hopes of finding assistance.

The city of *Edenia* was elevated into five sections, above the overpopulated *Slums* below. The last known *Piku tree* towered alone at the top, behind *King Raynor's* palace, serving as a lookout point for the city.

The city was surrounded by fortified stone walls 10 ft thick, and about 20 ft high. Arrow slits & murder holes were carefully positioned alongside the guards barracks, in case of random bandit attacks. Canons, heavy catapults, and ballistas were all fixed into the watchtower crenellations to defend against any aerial assault from sky pirates. Nestled above the *Green Plateau*, it was safe to say, *Edenia* was near impenetrable. The city hadn't seen an attack in years.

While passing the massive steel manufacturing mill, we were overshadowed by a fleet of zeppelins, drifting over our heads. All shapes & sizes decorated the turquoise sky. Walking inside the huge open-air building, I navigated around the metal beams used to construct zeppelins. The steel mill's humidity would soon plaster my buttoned shirt to my skin.

Spotting the foreman's office, we made our way across the colossal building. The sound of hammering metal numbed my ears, but I didn't wince; I grew up here.

Upon entering the office, I spotted *Mr. Stephens* sitting behind a wooden desk, scolding an employee.

"I'm sorry I'm late, boss. My bicycle tire had a flat," The worker with brown stuffy hair said.

Leaning back into his chair, the plump *Mr Stephens* replied, "Now son, I don't like excuses. Just make sure it doesn't happen again, or I'm docking your pay, *Sylvester*."

Nodding his head, the worker turned and exited the office. Waving us forward, the short gray haired man said, "Come on in... Wait a minute, I remember you? Your *Zepps* boy!"

Approaching the cluttered desk, I replied. "Yes sir. Thomas Von Zeppelin."

Interlocking his fingers over his belly, *Mr. Stephens* continued in a southern accent. "So, what can I do for you?"

"Well. My father's workshop is about to undergo foreclosure. I know he and you were business partners in the past and we could really use your help. So I came to ask you for a favor, a loan if you will. Just until my new prototype hits the market," I bargained.

Picking up his black top hat from the desk, he placed it on top of his head. Rising from his seat he grabbed hold of his silver cane. Strolling out onto the main floor of the steel mill with us in tow, he gestured grandly and said,

"Now boys, your father and I had a good history together. Hell, he made me a FORTUNE, and I would love nothing more than to fund your noble cause, but I can't. You see, we're also undergoing a new project. It's going to bring local transportation to the surrounding nations. We're talking millions of coin here, boys... I'm sorry, but I just can't." Then he started in the other direction, shouting at another employee.

I said to *Naji,* "Well. It was worth a shot..."

As we walked out from the building, *Naji* returned. "Come on. The tavern is just up ahead."

I could see the *Deacons* church in the distance, two-hundred feet tall with a steeple. The stained white brick building laid under a large evergreen. The city's rust-colored cobblestone streets were winding and wide, allowing the boisterous citizens to go about their daily lives. Guards patrolled the walkways in pairs, wearing silver chest plates with matching helmets and arm bracers. Long swords swung from their hips, rifles dangling from their shoulder straps.

We soon came to a run-down shack, called the *Rusty Dagger,* the local tavern and bandit hideout. You could smell the stench of rum from outside. A torn flier hung from the front of the door, reading :

WANTED for HEINOUS WAR CRIMES and HUMAN TRAFFICKING!
1,000,000 coin bounty for the head of the mysterious *Baron Of The Sky!!!*
Dead or Alive!

But as tempting as it sounded, he was way out of our league.

Stepping inside, it was obvious this wasn't the type of scene a brown-skinned 17 year-old wearing a charcoal waistcoat and nicely combed hair should be. Instantly I attracted cold stares from thugs, vagabonds, and misfits alike.

Burly men decorated in tattoos & battle scars laughed rambunctiously amongst their peers, and under their breaths I could hear the racial slurs posing as comedy. Following *Naji's* lead towards the bar, he turned to me reassuringly,

"Hmm, I don't see them... Don't worry, I got this."

Squeezing past tables full of drunken wild patrons and lusty barmaids, we approached the bar. The hairy overweight barkeep said,

"Well, if it isn't little *Naji* from the orphanage. Boy how you've grown. I remember when you were just a kid pickpocketing the drunks in the alleyway out back. Heh heh, their loss. So, how are you?"

"I'm doing good, *Rej*. But I need some info..." *Naji* replied with a friendly smile.

Rej (the barkeep), picked up a mug and began to clean the inside with a cloth. "Sure, whatcha' need?"

"I'm looking for the *Baron's* smugglers. Have you seen them?" *Naji* said.

The barkeep answered, "As a matter of fact, I did. You just missed them."

"What?! Naji shouted in surprise. "We can still catch them! Come on!" Then quickly zigzagging through the tables, we dashed out of the tavern.

While running alongside *Naji,* he shouted to me, "They must be at the port preparing to leave!"

As we continued across town, we descended into the lower levels of Edenia, racing past warehouses & storage sheds. *Edenia's Port* has 3 piers, each docked with dozens of Zeppelins.

Naji then pointed to the sky yelling, "There they are!" As I then crashed into a fish cart pulled by an elderly man.

Hearing the commotion, Naji slowed down to look behind him. Tumbling to the floor, I sent the fish cart sliding a couple of feet, spilling funky squid and old sardines. Jogging back, *Naji* extended his hand and pulled me upright, while I apologized to the vendor. "Why did you stop? They're going to get away?" I asked.

Turning our heads, we looked towards the pier, watching the small cargo ship known as the *Centennial Eagle* raise into the sky. "Well, there goes our chance," He said, letting out a disappointed sigh.

Dusting myself off, I lowered my head returning, "Sorry bro. It's my fault we missed it... If only there was another way..."

Then, seeing a dozen slow-moving Zeppelins sail across the blue horizon, it hit me. "There is another way." I said with a tone of intrigue. "Follow me..." I added, then started walking in the opposite direction.

Confused, *Naji* tagged along.

Once back at the Zep-Tec workshop, I slipped on a pair of comfy boots and a sturdy belt. I then began piling the bare essentials needed for survival into two backpacks. While I tossed things around the room, *Naji* got the curiosity to finally ask: "Uhhh? What are you doing?"

Stuffing a rolled-up orange tent and 2 bed rolls into a bag, I answered. "What does it look like I'm doing? I'm going to find *The Lost City*."

Stepping closer, *Naji* raised his hands saying,

"Did I miss something? How are you going to do that? The *Barons* smugglers have already departed. And we don't have that kind of coin to charter a Zeppelin around."

Opening a cabinet above the counter with a tool rack, I began shoveling boxes of trail rations and a small copper pot into the bag. Walking over to the closet, I swung it open. Searching through a couple of crates, I retrieved a small pack of flares, and some water skins, dropping them into the bag.

Stepping even closer, *Naji* followed me near a set of tall metal lockers.

"Don't you think now is a bad time to do your spring cleaning? Come on, maybe we can stow away on a cargo ship... Are you even listening to me?"

Spinning the dial on my weapons locker and pulling the handle, I opened the doors wide, revealing all the gadgets and inventions I've created over the years; a sort of timeline if you will.

I grabbed a holstered 4-barrel pistol with a brass magnifying glass scope and a belt of bullets, strapping the holster over my shoulder. Reaching for a short sword, I wrapped its 2-foot sheath horizontally around the back of my waist; against pirates in close combat, I would need something more dependable than a pistol, which could run out of ammunition at the worst time. I then pulled a metal glove from the rack and slid it down over my left hand. Squeezing my palm into a fist, I triggered a spring unlatching a thin sheet of steel. Cascading into a circle like a clock, it began to shape into a small buckler shield. Locking on with white eyes, *Naji* dropped his jaw saying, "Whoa!"

I simply smiled replying, "I know, right!?"

I grabbed a hunting rifle with a square clip attachment and magnifying scope, I threw it to *Naji,* then dumped a few boxes of bullets in the bag before slamming the locker door shut.

While I walked towards the *Model - 1, Naji* asked. "Okay, are we going treasure-hunting or robbing *King Raynor's* bank?" Removing the tarp, I climbed into the cockpit then pressed the engine button, firing it up. Slowly the propeller began to churn as the engine sputtered, making loud clanging sounds. A couple of startling bursts came from under the hood, causing a puff of white smoke to float through the air. Standing inside the pilot seat, I grabbed hold of the chain to lower the Aero-plane. I then began to reel the chain upwards, lowering the *Model - 1* down to the floor.

Sitting down, I pulled my helmet and goggles over my round face, then turned to *Naji,* saying "Are you coming or what"? Over the engine's hum.

"Wait a minute, we're taking THAT thing!? How do you know it's safe!?" *Naji* yelled with terror on his face. I slowly steered the Aero-plane under the large garage door.

"I don't, but, you only live once, right?" I shouted.

Shaking his head, *Naji* tossed our bags into the plane, then climbed into the back passenger seat, putting on an extra pair of goggles dangling nearby.

"I can't believe I let you talk me into this!" He said, as I guided the plane onto our small runway.

"Ladies and gentlemen, fasten your seatbelts!" I said, pedaling the gears as fast as I could. Quickly running out of land, the plane zoomed off the tiny runaway cliff, sputtering once more. Another loud burst then came from the engine, leaving a trail of smoke. The *Model - 1* immediately lost power, and began spiraling downward...

Thomas.

Chapter 2
(13 Days left.)

Plunging off the runway, the *Aero-plane* fell into an accelerated free-fall. As the engine choked, *Naji* began to yell. "I told you this wasn't safe! We're gonna die!" Spiraling downward in loops, we braced ourselves against the plane's interior, desperately trying to regain our balance.

Pulling back on the yoke, I gritted my teeth as my neck lashed from side to side. "Hold on tight!" I shouted, while stomping the pedals that had become stuck. Feeling a vibration from under my feet, the chassis started to rattle vigorously, careening toward the forest below. Straining with all my might, I managed to slowly inch the yoke back, tilting the plane's nose upward. Skimming the emergent layer of the trees beneath us, I could hear the branches as they scraped against the belly of the *Model - 1*.

Suddenly another loud burst came from under the hood, causing the plane to rumble before coughing up smoke. The propeller then finally regained itself and began to pick up speed. Listening to the hum as the engine returned, my heart slowly returned to my chest, as the jerk from the plane darted us forward.

Cautiously ascending, the *Model - 1* pulled above the trees, climbing into the sky. "Just a little more!" I said, biting down on my teeth. Easing back into the seat, I gently relaxed my muscles, while the plane leveled itself out. Turning the yoke, we leaned into a tailspin, gliding through the air like a bird.

"We're flying! It really works!" I yelled with excitement. Looking behind me, I could see the terror on Naji's face amongst the blue sky. Peeking out from the passenger seat he lifted his head saying,

"Are we - Are we dead yet?" Bringing me to a chuckle.

"No, we're not dead. But take a look at the view! It's amazing!" I exclaimed. Slowly sitting upright, *Naji* peered over the side of the plane.

"Unbelievable!" He exclaimed.

From above, the rust covered zinc on the roofs in the slums melted together like a collage. Due to piracy people flocked to *Edenia* in droves, hoping to find security. But once the overpopulation set in, bandits soon found their way into the shanty town known as *the Slums,* which led to more crime and a life of hardship for the people. The king later reinforced the walls to keep them out.

Drifting through the air, I took the plane in a few circles around the city, overlooking the Grand *Piku* tree's gigantic size and splendor. Zipping overhead, I weaved in and out of the large zeppelins cluttering the sky. Dipping low, we swooped above the streets, gaining the citizens attention.

The king's lavish palace oversaw all of Edenia, just beneath the *Tree of Life*. Veering left around the old steel mill then up over the farmers' market, we hovered 10ft above their heads.

"Hahaha! This is great!" *Naji* shouted, shaking my shoulder.

Pulling upwards, I decided to pay the orphanage a visit. Zigzagging through the winding streets and over houses, we sped, eventually coming to the *Deacon Blues* church. Circling overhead in a figure 8, I could hear the children below cheering with excitement. Reaching inside a small compartment under the dashboard, I retrieved a few of my homemade fireworks. Snapping them in half, I triggered the combustion needed to set them off, then dropped them down below.

<Boom-Pow Bang!>

They exploded as a vivid display of sparks lit up the sky, forming many shapes and colors. Watching the children celebrate and admire the gesture, I could spot the *Deacon* standing beside them, wrinkling his face with anger and disgust. We waved farewell, causing the *Deacon* to shake his fist at us before the plane swooped higher.

Soaring back into the clouds, I turned to view Edenia for one last time. It sat on top of a high hill above a grassy meadow. The *Great Flood* of millennia ago had carved everything inside the basin, forming the *Green Plateau*.

"All right, where to first?" I asked *Naji*.

Digging into his pocket, he pulled out the treasure map and unfolded it, scanning his finger from our current location across to the bold red X.

"It says here! We should head East toward the center of the continent!" He read.

"East it is!" I responded over the low hum of the propeller. Going into my pocket, I pulled out my silver compass watch to verify the direction, but the needle spun aimlessly. Ever since my father had given it to me, I'd never gotten it to work properly. Even after countless repairs it still remained faulty. I gazed for a moment at the tiny polished sapphire embedded in the center of it's face. Even though it had never worked, I was unable to discard it because of its sentimental value. It had become my most-cherished keepsake.

32

Hovering over the emerald colored grass of *Pangea*, we were escorted by a flock of curious brown geese. Looking at the dashboard, I was taken by surprise by the altimeter. It read we were 20,000 feet above the ground. It was like looking through the wrong end of a magnifying glass, a first in history. Here we were, piloting an actual self controlled aircraft, and not using helium, like those flabby balloons that carry the zeppelins.

Steering the *Model - 1* across rivers and hilltops, it was a marvel to overlook the landscape. The untamed plains were sparse, with small trees and thin bushes; I could barely make out the oak trees and roaming caribou below. My *Mother* and I used to go bird watching when *Dad* was at work. She taught me all the ins-and-outs about animals and their natural habitats.

Hours later, the orange dusk set in, looming above the landscape like a curtain. After sitting down for so long my neck began to ache and my legs went numb. Slowly stretching out, I said to *Naji,* "This view is great, but who would have known these seats would be so hard on your back?"

"Yeah, I don't remember seeing that in the fine print!" He replied.

Scanning the meters on the dashboard, I noticed that the fuel gauge was falling beneath the quarter mark. "We're running a little low on fuel. Maybe we should take her down for the night, somewhere safe. What do you say?" I said, over the noisy rumbling from the engine.

"Sounds good! I was getting drowsy anyway," *Naji* responded with a yawn. Moments later, he unfolded the map and looked over it from side to side. Pointing his finger over my shoulder, I heard him say, "There should be a small village coming up on your left."

"Roger that!" I affirmed, nodding my head. Tilting the plane's controls forward, we began to descend 50 degrees west. While lowering in altitude, the *Model - 1* burst through a group of pearly stratocumulus clouds. Surveying the brush below, I gazed side to side, searching for a place to spend the evening.

Passing over a bundle of pine trees, I saw rising smoke up ahead. Slowing our speed, I brought the plane into a smooth coast. Coming over a hill, we spotted a tiny cottage-filled town, a settled farm land area with grain and vegetable crops.

"There it is! Take us down nice and slow!" *Naji* said behind me. Gently easing the yoke forward, we continued our descent. Noticing a large pasture outside the small stone wall fence, I decided to land there.

Gliding over the town's square, I could see its citizens below, glaring at us. Bracing for impact, the plane bounced sparingly on the high grass, as the wheels made traction. Moments later we came to a screeching halt, as I pedaled backwards on the gears. Shutting off the engine, I lifted my goggles above my head. Letting out a deep breath of air, I began climbing out of the cockpit. Looking behind me, I noticed a long paved line across the grassy pasture.

Lifting himself up out of the back seat and down onto the grass, *Naji* said, "Woo! That was by far the coolest thing I've ever done. No one's going to believe this! I can't believe that thing actually works...You know... With the near-death experience and all."

"Hahaha! This is going to be huge. We'll go down in history. All that's left to do is work out a few kinks, and should be ready for the assembly line," I replied.

"So, I get to fly it next, right?" *Naji* asked.

"We'll talk about it," I returned sarcastically.

The townspeople showed up shortly after. Excitedly they dashed across the field, encircling us. They crowded around the *Model - 1* in awe; some even felt the fabrics of our clothes. Eyeing the meager appeal of their patchwork garments, I concluded these were common folk, farmers who tilled the land. A little girl with two golden pigtails looked up at me, asking, "Are you guys aliens?"

Naji held their curious stares as he turned to face the crowd. Raising his hands high, he said,
"Greetings, people of this noble town! My name is *Naji Abdul*, and this is my brother *Thomas Von Zeppelin*! We travel from a planet far far away, in search of a great treasure! We come in peace and seek shelter for the night!"

Naji took the crowd captive, eliciting gasps from all around, when suddenly a man with a limp cleared a path through the crowd, making his way to the front. As he came into view, I saw that the round short man sported a long gray mustache and no beard. Over his pale skin he wore a gaudy black suit with a matching top hat, and a gray fur coat wrapped around his shoulders.

"All right, all right, step aside," he said, stopping at an arm's length from us. "Allow me to introduce myself. My name is *Randall Bloomfield*, town mayor. Normally I would give you a warm welcome, but it seems my citizens have already beaten me to it," he continued while extending his hand. "Now if you will, please explain what this... contraption is, and how did you get it here?"

Shaking his hand, I step closer explaining,

"This is the *Model - 1*, a self-piloting aircraft, first-of-its-kind! We flew from the City of Edenia and landed here in your pasture, hoping to stock up on provisions and stay for the night. If it's okay with you, *Mayor Bloomfield."* Raising my hand, I turned from side-to-side reassuring the confused townsfolk, "And no! We're not aliens!"

The townsfolk moaned, perhaps disappointed that we WEREN'T aliens.

Mayor Bloomfield said, "So you two are from *Edenia*, huh? It must be nice living way up there, safe from the raiders and bandits. But either way, anyone who is a guest to *Bloomsfield* is a guest to us all. Gather your things, you can stay at the *Moon Lodge*." Leaning closer he whispered, "The crumble cake is to die for."

Looking at *Naji*, I shrugged my shoulders in confirmation. Grabbing our bags from the plane, I threw the black tarp over the *Model - 1* for the night. We then followed the mayor into town, escorted by a handful of citizens.

Upon entering the second story lodge, I noticed the town's architecture. The smaller homes were made of wood, and overlaid with uneven stones. The roof boards were sealed together with a fairly simple pitch tar. As we came to the front desk, I went into my coin sack preparing to pay, but the mayor stopped me.

"Oh no, it's on the house." With his hands holding the sides of his jacket, he told the innkeeper, "Put them in the best room available. Our small shire doesn't have much to offer but dinner is on me."

"Thank you mayor, that's mighty kind of you. It's not every day two of *Edenia's* noblemen graze these parts," *Naji* said.

"Oh yes, you two are my honored guests. Maybe later you can share some details of your people, we'd all love to hear them!" The mayor ecstatically replied.

"It would be my pleasure," *Naji* responded, as he bowed elegantly. The man waved with a smile then departed.

The Innkeeper, a redheaded girl with cute freckles, began leading us upstairs. The fresh pastries in the dining room tickled my nose. Squinting my eyes towards *Naji*, he could sense my disappointment with the fake backstory he'd told the mayor.

"Two noblemen from Edenia?" I whispered angrily, "What are you going to do when they find out we're nothing more than two orphans!?"

Turning the corner at the top of the stairs, *Naji* returned. "Relax, they're not GOING to find out. We're a couple hundred miles away from home. I don't even think anyone here has even seen *Edenia*." Approaching the room at the end of a hallway, he added, "Besides, we're like celebrities here... I think I might stay a little longer."

Coming to the door of the room, the innkeeper removed the hair from over her right ear before opening it.

"Here we are. I hope everything is to your liking," she said. I can see Naji was preparing to quote something out of a fairy tale again, so I stepped in front of him replying,

"Yes, it's perfect, thank you." She then departed with a smile.

Walking past Naji, I lugged my bag through the doorway. Naji watched, responding.

"What? Was it something I said?"

Throwing my stuff onto the mahogany floor, I face planted into one of the two king size beds.

"Finally."

Naji closed the room door with his foot, then dropped his bag near the head of the other bed. Rolling over, I noticed the crystal knick-knacks and polished cherry wood furniture decorating our large suite. The silk sheets and hand-stitched rug signified that this was a room for *Bloomfield's* elite guests. Grabbing a handful of almonds from a nearby bowl, *Naji* began flicking a couple into his mouth.

"I could get used to this," he said while chewing.

Sitting up, I peered out the window nearby. The bland design of the stone buildings and plainly clothed people outside explained their simple lifestyle. This small town was undisturbed by the hustle and bustle of screaming vendors, or the noise from passing Zeppelins overhead like in *Edenia*. *Bloomsfield* was the epitome of common life. A peasant's bliss I'd never seen before but had only heard, as this was really my first time away from *Edenia's* walls.

"These people live so simple, but they seem happy. Why do you think that is?" I asked.

"Who knows? Maybe they haven't seen any other options?" *Naji* replied, approaching the window and putting his hand on the glass. Looking down below he continued, "Eventually the zeppelins will come, opening new trade routes, then one day more guests will show up, corrupting these people with their influence. Until they lose the morals and values of their ancestors, and never be the same again... It happens to all societies."

"Wow, that was deep. Did you get that from a philosophy book or something?" I asked.

"Nah, I think I'm just hungry. Come on, let's go get something to eat," He answered.

Dismissing the finite possibility of his intellect, I followed him downstairs to the *Moon Lodge's* diner.

Forty minutes later, we were the talk of the town. Gathered around us were the mayor and a few nosy patrons, admiring us as we enjoyed our lamb chop sirloins and seasoned rice. The square dining tables were loaded with an assortment of foods, from baked turnips to chicken pot pie, chocolate pastries to cream carrot cake - all compliments of the chef. Sitting at the table, *Naji* entertained a room full of citizens and thirsty maidens. Laughter filled the air.

"So *Thomas*? What happened next?" *Mayor Bloomfield* said with intrigue lighting up his face.

Eating the white grapes being fed to him by a waitress sitting on his lap, *Naji* cataloged our tale:

"Well, we were then surrounded by five scary bandits on one side, and five ferocious lions on the other. The bandits each held swords pointed at our throats, and the lions were on a leash, showing their razor-sharp fangs. I looked over to my partner here" -gesturing dramatically toward me- "I could see the fear in his eyes as he trembled. So I told him, 'Don't worry, I have a plan.' Then using my basic instincts, I quickly drew my sword and began slashing our way out from their evil clutches. The lions then scattered into separate directions once I gave them a mighty roar. Hours later, we were back on board our aircraft, sailing through the skies until we landed here for the night."

Leaning on the table with one palm pressed against my left cheek, I thought to myself, "Oh brother," slowly taking bites out of my frosted brown crumble cake (which might I add was actually quite scrumptious). Watching the room's reaction to *Naji's* story made my eyes heavy as I fought fatigue.

"Can I have your autograph"? A patron asked during the crowd's applause, causing *Naji* to blush, replying,

"Please, please, you're too kind."

Standing from his seat, Mayor *Bloomfield* said, "That sounds like quite the adventure you've both had," then began to yawn, adding, "Now, if you'll excuse me gentlemen. I've had enough excitement for one day. Enjoy your night." Tipping his hat farewell, he turned to leave.

The wench in *Naji's* lap caressed the back of his head, asking. "So, where are you two going next?"

Pulling the treasure map from his pants, he unfolded it over the table. "Well, we're actually in search of a great treasure. The *Lost City of Old,*" he said.

Instantly Mayor *Bloomfield* stopped in his tracks, then turned around. "Did - did you say the *Lost City*?" He asked.

Nodding his head, Naji returned. "Yeah? You've heard of it?"

Mayor *Bloomfield* returned to the table saying. "My grandfather *Ryan Bloomfield* told me that story when I was just a boy. He was an archaeologist who claimed to have once ventured into the *Lost City*. Succumbing to greed, his team leader ended up stealing my grandfather's journal, which contained all the information on finding the treasure. Although my grandfather somehow found his way back home, the expedition had claimed the lives of the rest of party... may I?" He motioned towards the map and Naji handed it to him.

Studying over the map, the mayor exclaimed, "My God. It WAS true!"

Immediately gaining my attention, I rose from my seat asking. "What was true? Do you know anything about it?"

"Very little. He spoke of magnificent buildings and streets decorated in jewels. An old tribe once dwelled there, deep within a dangerous jungle, as legend has it... Although, the treasure was never found," Mayor *Bloomfield* replied.

"Any idea where it might be, this jungle?" I asked eagerly.
Putting his hand on his chin, Mayor *Bloomfield* looked at the map in deep thought.

"Hmm, I do recall him saying something about a floating island. He referenced it to a paradise but that's all I can remember," he explained.

"Thank you Mayor *Bloomfield*, for your help and the kind hospitality," I said.

"Oh it's nothing. After that wonderful tale of the perilous adventures you both endured, it's an honor to have you stay with us tonight." The mayor responded.

"Heh heh, right. Perilous adventures," I repeated, while sternly looking at *Naji*.

The mayor then said, "All right folks. Let's leave our guests alone so that they can get some rest." The crowd then groaned as they slowly began to disperse. With a smile *Naji* waved goodbye to them, while shaking a few hands along the way. Shaking my head I looked him in the eye with disappointment, then headed for our room.

Once upstairs, I prepared for bed then fell into the velvet soft mattress the back of my head slowly sinking into a fluffy pillow. I imagined this was what clouds felt like. Removing his sword's sheath from around his waist, *Naji* dropped it to the floor next to his bed, then climbed under his covers.

"Floating island? Where the hell are we going to find one of those?" I said.

Wiggling his toes under the blanket, *Naji* returned, "I'm not sure. But wherever it is, we'll find it."

Rolling to the side, I blew out the lantern saying, "We'll start bright and early." Finally relaxing, I was able to close my eyes.

Minutes later, I heard the sound of glass shattering from outside the window. Sitting up in the bed I asked, "What was that?"

"It was nothing. Probably just a bird on top of the roof, go back to sleep," *Naji* replied. Seconds later, the sound of a woman screaming echoed, jolting me onto my feet.

"Did you hear that? It sounded like somebody shouting," I said.

"Whatever it is, let them handle it. We've gotta get some rest for tomorrow," He replied tiredly. It then became apparent that *Naji's* greed and selfishness was the center of his motives. The short time he'd spent as a smuggler must have influenced these new roguish traits. His resilience had matured into nonchalance and charismatic cunning. Stroking his ego, I returned,

"I thought you said we were like celebrities? Those people look up to you, and the time they need you the most you'd turn your back to them?"

Naji rolled over, then ignited his lantern saying, "I'm sure it's nothing. They're probably just fighting over our autograph or something."

The voice from outside screeched once more, but this time I could make out the words -

"Bandits are attacking the town! Run!"

Quickly turning on the lights, I slipped on my metal glove then began putting on my trousers, when suddenly our bedroom window came crashing to the floor, as a man dressed in all black with a matching mask came swinging in on a rope. Showing only his eyes, he resembled the ninjas I had heard of who inhabit the faraway city of *Tokyio*. Staring us down, the intruder made his move, drawing a shiny sword from his back. Catching us off-guard, he dashed in my direction.

On impulse I dove over my bed, in an attempt to grab my sword and pistol. Tumbling to the floor, I instantly looked up and saw his blade closing the distance toward my face.

Raising my hands in fear, I closed my eyes bracing for impact -

Clang!

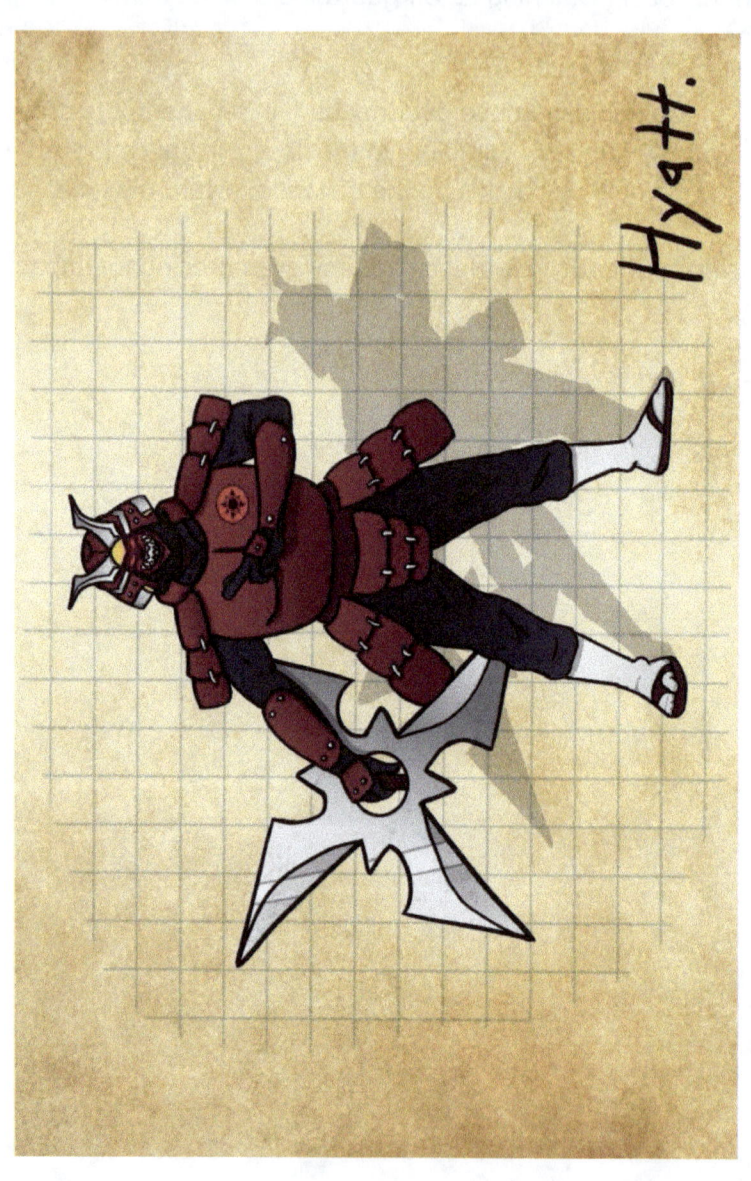

Hyatt.

Chapter 3
(12 Days left.)

I figured death would have been more painful.

I opened my eyes to see a big sheet of metal. "Of course!" I thought. My metal shield glove, how could I have forgotten! Peeking around the shining oval protruding from the back of my left hand, I spotted *Naji* sitting up under the covers with his mouth wide open.

"Do something!" I shouted, snapping him back to our current reality.

"Oh! Right!" He responded. Rolling out of bed, *Naji* reached for the hunting rifle. Then without aiming he immediately fired.

Bang!

Startled by the gun shot, I balled up in a tensed position behind the shield. Seconds later, I felt the pressure from the ninja pushing down against the other side of the metal. Lowering my shield, I then noticed his lifeless body slumped in front of me. A wave of anxiety pulsed through my veins. In all my life, I had never encountered a real pirate before, much less killed a man. A series of thoughts began racing through my head: Was I now going to go to prison, and miss out on the rest of my life? What if there were more guys like him when I got there? I always thought of myself as brave, but nothing my father had taught me could have ever prepared me for this.

"Who the hell was that?!" *Naji* yelled, getting out of bed.

"Oh, now you're worried? I thought you said it was THEIR problem?" I replied.

All of a sudden, two more guys dressed in black came swinging in through the window, one after the other. "Watch out!" I shouted. Drawing my short-sword, I charged our foes. Turning towards the window *Naji* aimed then discharged two rounds in their direction, missing as the the first ninja landed inside, quickly rolling to the right. The bullets sailed into the second intruder, ripping through his left arm, making him stumble back. The next bullet slammed into his chest, pushing him out and over the window pane.

Meeting the remaining intruder, I swung my sword left and then right, intending to maim him. My attack failed, as he managed to duck and dodge my swings. I had practiced these attacks on the dummies in the workshop hundreds of times, but this was the first time my life depended on them. Leaping over my head, the ninja landed with his long sword drawn. Spinning in a circle with my blade extended, I caught him with my shield.
Blow for blow, we exchanged attacks, only to have them parried or deflected. I didn't have time to think- this was the real thing!

Bang - Bang!

Watching the ninja fall to the floor curling over, *Naji* came into view with his rifle's barrel still smoking. "Come on, we've got to warn the mayor," I said panting like a dog. Quickly getting dressed, we dashed downstairs into the lobby.

Entering the foyer we spotted three more ninjas, terrorizing some of the scrambling patrons. Diving to the left, I slid behind the checkout counter, brandishing my four-barreled pistol. *Naji* ran forward, then kicked a coffee table over for protection. Hearing our commotion, the ninjas left the other

47

civilians alone, then turned in our direction while spreading out. Looking at *Naji*, I counted to three and gave the signal. Springing up from my position, I began bursting my pistol, forcing the enemies to duck for cover. Seizing the opportunity, *Naji* leaned around the table in a sniping position.

Hopping over the counter, I crept forward, waiting for their heads to pop up like the pop-up targets on my homemade shooting gallery. Suddenly one of the ninjas arose from behind a couch. With his sword drawn he charged towards me.

Bang!

With a point blank shot, I sent him stumbling backwards onto the floor, as the other two darted from their cover. I couldn't believe I'd actually shot someone, but it was life or death, and I'd practiced for this. Taking aim, *Naji* peppered them with bullets, but missed the targets by inches. Zigzagging through the fire, they quickly closed the gap while flipping and rolling to the sides.
With youthful dexterity and a bit more confidence, I ducked low as the enemy swung at me - barely avoiding a head severing attack. Holstering my pistol, I pulled the sword from behind my waist and thrusted it upward, managing to tear into the ninja's chest, a move I had performed so many times in my training room that it had become a reflex- the blood was new however; it was warm and there was a lot of it.

Finishing the job, *Naji* released another round that jerked the enemy's head to the side, before crumbling to the floor. He was always the better marksman between us, ever since Dad bought us that pellet gun for the holidays. The remaining ninja leaped for *Naji* with an overhead strike, but *Naji* raised his rifle and was able to block the attack. Stepping into the ninja's stomach, *Naji* kicked him back. Swinging his sword from its sheath, *Naji* brought it across the ninja's face, splitting it wide open.

Surveying the room, I looked at *Naji* saying. "We've got to find the mayor!"

Running from the *Moon Lodge* and out into the street, the citizens of *Bloomsfield* were scattering in disarray, as ninja bandits chased them ruthlessly, herding them into a big cage on the back of a horse-drawn cart. Spotting the mayor, we dashed in his direction.

My apprehension faded, and the rhythm of combat began to feel natural. Swinging my sword at the few ninjas approaching, we easily gained their attention. I then slid on my knees in between two of the ninjas, sundering the leg of one, and impaling the abdomen of the other. Hopping to my feet, I continued dashing forward while slashing the back of an unaware enemy. I then spun around, raising my shield to block another incoming attack.

Bang!

Naji fired a round into my opponent's back, rendering him useless. Two more then quickly approached him. Grabbing the barrel of his rifle, *Naji* swung it across the head of a ninja, then tossed his gun to another. Catching it in surprise, the enemy looked confused, as *Naji* sprang towards him with his sword held high above his head. In the blink of an eye, the ninja's hands were rolling by his feet (*Naji* was really good at this; what had he been up to since I'd seen him last?). Shield bashing the foe to my right, I followed up with a crippling strike; downing another adversary while making my advance.

Parrying to his left, *Naji's shoulder* bumped the ninja behind, then sliced a line down the enemy standing before him. Rotating his blade, *Naji* then thrust it under his own armpit, penetrating ninja behind him. Clearing a path, we made our way to the mayor. As a benchwarmer in the youth baseball league, I spent all summer perfecting my swing. If he was here right now, my coach would have been proud, and freaked out.

"Oh thank goodness you're here! I don't know who these people are or what they want, but please, you have to help us!" The mayor trembled while breathing hard.

"We'll do whatever we can!" I replied.

Suddenly a loud voice bellowed, "Not so fast!" Gaining everyone's attention.

Slowly the band of ninjas ceased their attack, clearing a small walkway for a silhouetted figure who crept into view. Under the dark sky, flickering flames cast shadows as the raging fires engulfed nearby buildings. The smoke from the timber caused my eyes to water.

A tall and burly man wearing heavy ninja gear stepped forward, sporting a burgundy chest plate with matching arm guards. He jingled like a bag of coins with each step. "My name is *Hyatt,* 7th division leader of the *Red Ring.* This town and all of its supplies belong to me now," he said with a sadistic sneer.

Watching Mayor *Bloomfield* quiver behind me, I cautiously stepped forward replying. "I'm not sure what it is you want but, I can't let you harm these people."

Pausing for a second, the bandit began to chuckle. "Your bravery is matched by the skill of your blade. Few are able to say they've seen a member of the *Ring* & lived to spread the tale," *Hyatt* explained with an *Asiana* accent.

Mayor *Bloomfield* leaned over my shoulder and shouted, "That's right, you ruffian! These two noblemen here are trained warriors from far away, they'll show you!"

Naji then elbowed him in the chest, whispering, "Shhhh!" causing the Mayor to rub his sternum in pain.

Stepping closer, *Hyatt* said. "Nobleman, from far away? I'm sure you'll fetch a pretty penny at the auction house in *Egyptia.*" He then pointed his large star-shaped knife in our direction. The weapon was about three feet around with tapering metal blades extending like points on a compass. "I challenge you!"

"What"? I replied.

"If you two are formidable warriors, then we must do battle!" He returned.

"C - c - come on, big guy. You don't have to do that!" *Naji* stuttered while inching behind me.
"Enough games, we battle now! If I win, I take you as slaves. If you win, we leave and never return," *Hyatt* shouted. Looking around, I could see the commonfolk peeking out of their windows in terror, while others laid in chains on board the horse-drawn cart. Turning the other direction, I could see *Naji* and Mayor *Bloomfield* cowering behind me. A platoon of ninjas had already encircled our location, ready to strike.

I thought for a second then said, "You got a deal... Which one of us do you want to fight?"

Hyatt chuckled again before saying. "The both of you."

Turning to the mayor, *Naji* swallowed a lump of spit saying, "Just great, now I'M going to die. This is all your fault."

Flinching, the mayor returned, "Oh come on. From all the stories you told us, surely you can beat this creep.

Grabbing *Naji's* shirt, I said. "Then it's time to prove it. Let's go!"

Stepping into the middle of the crowd, we raised our weapons and defense. *Hyatt* joined us in the middle. Twirling his giant star blade, he gave a loud war-cry. Enough to make any man quiver. My first time fighting for my life, and now I have to fight this guy!? I realized I'd have to give it my all and hope for the best. Banging my sword against my shield, I let out a roar of my own, then charged into battle. Raising my blade high, I brought it downward faster than a bolt of lightning.

Bang!

Hyatt's weapon crashed into my shield from the side, feeling like a cannonball had hit the thin piece of steel. Swiftly grabbing my throat with one hand, he raised me off my feet. I couldn't help but notice the silver ring with an onyx stone he wore on his middle finger, bearing the emblem of a crimson sun. Before I knew it, I was thrown aside like dirty laundry, rolling backwards onto the floor. Once I had stopped, my blurry vision of *Naji* spun in a circle.

"Okay. It's your turn," I said, holding my head.

Spinning his scimitar with confidence, *Naji* dashed for *Hyatt*, thrusting for his midsection. Sidestepping his advance, *Hyatt* kneed him in the stomach, then knocked him backwards with the side of his blade. Tumbling to the floor, *Naji* laid out like a starfish.

Helping him onto his feet, I managed to say. "This guy's nothing but a brute... I think I have a plan." Running back into the center of the crowd, I began swinging tactically, as *Naji* soon followed suit.

"Hahaha. Is that all you got?" *Hyatt* chuckled lightly while managing to offset our attacks. Launching his giant *shuriken* through the air, it zoomed on a wide course to return like a boomerang. Barely ducking his blade, I improvised in an attempt to get behind him. *Naji* then seized the opportunity, & stabbed him in the right leg. Growling in pain, *Hyatt* tried sideswiping him with his blade, but rolling underneath his wild swing *Naji* evaded the attack. Seeing my chance, I fell upon his calves, slicing them in one motion with a vital strike.

"Graahr!" He roared. Turning around slowly, he stumbled into a desperate swing that I dodged with ease. Piercing his sword into *Hyatt's* back, *Naji* then yanked it out, tearing a plug of flesh with his blade's hook. It was pretty gross, and that's coming from a guy already covered in ninja blood. *Hyatt* exposed his upper body while reaching for his back, shattering his defense. Leaping up high, I dragged my sword through the air then plunged it into his chest.

"Ahhgk!" He bellowed. Feeling his body suddenly loosen up, I withdrew my sword from the horizontal plates covering his chest then stepped back. Inching forward he stopped in his tracks, leaning over to cough up blood.

"Not bad - *cough cough* - not bad at all. You two are worthy adversaries... We shall meet again," *Hyatt* struggled to say. Turning to the ninjas guarding the captured citizens, he then raised his hand saying, "Release them!"

Unlatching the cage, the ninjas opened the gate, as the prisoners hastily escaped their confinements.

"Are - are we safe now?" The Mayor asked, still shaking in fear.

The remaining ninjas escorted *Hyatt* onto the wagon, surrounding him. They then retreated from the town of *Bloomsfield* on their horses.

"Yeah. You're safe now," I said to the mayor.

"Thank goodness. How can we ever repay you?" He replied.

Lowering my weapons I replied, "It was nothing. I just want some sleep." My head continued to throb.

"Oh please. There must be something?" Mayor *Bloomfield* insisted.

Clearing his throat, *Naji* said. "Well, I'm glad you mentioned that Mayor, I was thinking. Normal rate for noblemen like ourselves would be- "

Giving a disappointed sigh, I shook my head, starting to walk back towards the inn before hearing one of *Naji's* fairy tales again. While walking back to the *Moon Lodge*, I observed the citizens as they began to slowly re-enter the streets, surveying the damages and putting out small fires. Before long I was face down, sinking into my fluffy pillow in our suite. I opened my eyes suddenly remembering that I was still covered in blood; so much for this luxurious bedspread. I'd better clean myself up before going to bed was the last thought that raced through my head before I fell asleep deeply.

The next morning I awoke just short of 12 o clock, scrubbed myself in the tub, and gathered our gear. After a hearty breakfast of savory deer sausages and fluffy scrambled eggs, we were ready to embark on the journey ahead. Pulling the tarp off the *Model - 1*, I refueled the tanks and tested the gauges. The feeling was a breath of fresh air.

Throwing our supplies into the plane's small cargo space, I turned around to thank Mayor *Bloomfield*.

"It's been a pleasure Mr. *Bloomfield*. Thank you for your hospitality."

"The pleasure is all mine, gentlemen. I hope what little supplies we were able to give will help you both on your adventures," the Mayor said, holding the sides of his fur coat.

Naji waved farewell to the gathering crowd, scattered across the open field. He then climbed on board.

"You're always welcome in the town of *Bloomsfield*. Safe travels and I hope you find that *Lost City!*" Mayor *Bloomfield* continued.

Giving a salute, I pulled down my pilot's hat and goggles then pressed the ignition button. As it cranked up, the engine let out a few loud bursts, sputtering before shutting off. So much for a heroic exit. I banged my fist on the hood of the engine until it coughed up white smoke and slowly came to life. I flipped the switches, preparing the plane for takeoff.

As I started to pedal the gears, *Naji* stopped me. Putting his hand on my shoulder he said. "Wait... Do you think I can fly this time?" Looking back at him, I studied the sincerity on his face. "Oh come on, we're a team. Like peanut butter and jelly - cereal and milk," He eagerly continued.

Deciphering his logic, I decided to give him a chance. "All right, fine. But take it easy on the gears. It's still a prototype," I said, climbing out of the seat.

Pushing me aside, *Naji* slid into the cockpit saying. "Yeah yeah, I got it. Trust me, you're in good hands."

As I sat down into the passenger seat, I clenched my hands around the inside of the carriage, thinking, "Yep, We're dead." After a brief crash tutorial of the controls, I gave him the okay. Pulling back on the handle, *Naji* pedaled the gears, inching the *Aero-plane* forward. As the propeller spun, we quickly gained speed, the rubber wheels trampling flowers underneath.

Carefully we ascended into the air.

"Okay, now flip that switch right there and level her out," I informed him while pointing over his left shoulder at the console. Flipping the switch, *Naji* leaned the controls forward, stabilizing the plane. Tilting the wing to the right, we veered into a circle around the town of *Bloomsfield*. Looking up at us from below, the townsfolk waved goodbye.

All of a sudden, blue flowers began blooming across the early morning field, painting the entire pasture sapphire. Captivated by the rare occasion, I thought to myself, "Even though situations may be hard to see through at first... Maybe some things ARE worth fighting for."

Swooping down low, *Naji* brought the plane a dozen feet above their heads before raising up for the last time. "See, piece of cake!" he boasted. We soon climbed through the roof of the clouds above us. Entering an unexplored world of possibilities.

Gliding over the clouds was breathtaking. My imagination ran wild with thoughts of the creatures from old, millenia ago. The ones that probably lived in the sky or the colossal giants who towered over the small world below. But... those tales are just fantasies.

Watch this!" *Naji* yelled. Pulling back on the yoke, the *Model - 1* lifted nose up. Slowly continuing around in a circle, completing an inside loop. Bracing myself into the seat, I looked around once we were upside down, noticing the clouds above us.

"Hahaha, I love this thing! Hang on!" He said, as we leveled out. Barrel rolling to the right, the *Model - 1* rode the wind off of an air thermal, setting us aloft on a warm breeze.

Hours later, we were coasting over cream colored clouds cast with an orange hue. Punching a hole through the clouds, our pilot *Naji* descended a couple hundred feet. We now floated above thick vegetation. Looking over the sides of the plane, I spotted numerous flocks of birds gliding above the dense green canopy. Dropping down to about 200 meters, we mixed in with a family of brightly colored parrots.

"Where are we?" *Naji* asked, the Model-1 spooking the parrots, who squawked away in separate directions. Pulling the map from his pocket, he passed it over his shoulder to me. I unfolded the map, holding it up to charter our destination. Scanning my finger from the tiny dot known as *Bloomsfield*, I followed it across plains of *Highland,* and over rivers branching in many directions. I soon came to a sprawling bundle of trees blotting the map.

"Says here, we should be near the *Amazonian* rainforest!" I said, assuming our location.

"You mean that jungle from the textbooks in school? Here, let me see - you must be reading it wrong," *Naji* replied. Grabbing the map, he positioned it on the instrument dash with both hands. Pausing for a second, he pointed his finger saying, "Hmm, what do you know, it seems there IS a jungle around here. There's also some really tall mountains coming up ahead. Let's try there, maybe we can see the area better."

"Good idea". I responded. As we lowered the treasure map from over the dashboard, I sounded, "Look out!"

We were suddenly heading for a tree.

Quickly pulling the handles, *Naji* jerked the plane to the side, skimming the underbelly against the emergent layer as we tried to evade death. The giant trees of the *Amazonian* cluttered our path, sending us into a panic. Speeding over 100mph, *Naji* steered the plane left and right, trying his best to dodge the trees ahead. Hearing the branches bang against the metal chassis, I reflexively braced for impact as we zipped through the forest canopy.

"What do I do!?"*Naji* shouted.

"Just try to get lower! Take her down easy!" I replied. Putting my foot against the carriage for support, I pushed back into the seat-

Bang!

Losing a small chunk of the right-wing, I turned to see the trail of smoke behind. Slowly dropping in altitude, *Naji* flipped a switch, closing the tail flaps into an upright position, managing to decrease our speed. Whizzing into the understory of the forest, the *Model - 1* tilted side-to-side throughout the trees.

Clang!

Suddenly a blade from the propeller shot from over *Naji's* head and into my direction. Seeing tunnel vision, my body instantly reacted in time, allowing me to duck the fatal projectile.

Losing most of our momentum the Aero-plane dropped into free-fall at a 45° angle, bumping into trees along the way. We soon came to a clearing with a small pond. Holding on to the seat, I anticipated the crash.

The rapidly passing rainforest appeared eerily silent without the noisy propeller turning. Once the engine shut off, we slammed into the vine covered floor with a loud thud, sliding over lumps of sticks and rocks along the way. Sparks kicked up behind us as we felt the whiplash of tossing from side to side within our seats. Listening to the horrible sound of the *Model - 1* crunch and bend against the mossy forest, I gritted my teeth in sorrow.

Slowly grinding to a halt, we crashed into a small boulder, the recoil slamming my head into the seat in front of me. Loosening up, I leaned back into my seat for a few seconds, taking it all in. Feeling the sharp pain along my right shoulder and bruises all over my body, I began to exhale.

Hearing *Naji* groan in the seat before me, he eventually said, "Are you alive back there?" while stumbling to his feet.

Immediately my heart dropped. His usual reckless reputation had preceded him once again. However, I was glad to be alive. "Yeah. I think so," I responded with a moan of my own. Climbing out of the seat I wiggled down to the floor.

Stepping back, I surveyed my newly remodeled prototype laying like a fallen tree made of metal. The left wing was still intact and the propeller still had one of its two blades. Limping towards the engine, I popped the hood, noticing most of the parts were undamaged. A little bent up, but undamaged nonetheless.

"How bad is it?" *Naji* asked, biting his lip.

"Pretty bad. But with the proper tools, I think we could fix it." I replied.

Standing on the moist dirt covered in moss, *Naji* spun around saying. "These trees are humongous. How are we going to find that mountain from down here?"

Looking around at our new dilemma, I decided it was best to forget about the *Model-1* for now. Retrieving the silver compass watch from my pocket, I watched it spin aimlessly before losing interest, and decided on my own direction.

"Well, the map said it was East... Let's try that way," I said pointing my finger. Nodding his head, *Naji* led the way as we both limped in search of higher ground. I thought to myself, "He's never driving again..."

Chapter 4
(11 Days Left)

While trekking the vast regions of the *Amazonian* rainforest, we came across a plethora of plants and wildlife. The sweet dew from the leaves entered my nostrils. The undergrowth was draped with vines, and thick roots covered the ground. Carnivorous insects swarmed overhead, preying on unsuspecting critters. The streams were stained brown as if drawn through a tea bag. Crossing one of the streams' cool waters, some curious catfish trailed us with caution.

Stepping over a boulder, *Naji* asked, "What is this stuff?" as his foot fell into a slime covered ditch.

Watching him brush off the trail of ants now climbing up his leg, I said. "I'm not sure, but be careful. You wouldn't want to get infected out here." Picking up a thick branch, I used it as a walking stick, distributing some of the weight off of my injured left leg. *Naji* was having a hard time maneuvering through the forest. Walking into spiderwebs and swatting 6 inch mosquitoes wasn't either of our idea of fun. Orange frogs eyed us from decaying plants. Coming into a tiny clearing we spotted a tree with a rope ladder dangling at its trunk.

"Check it out," I said curiously.

"Someone must have left this here. I wonder what's at the top?" *Naji* replied.

Limping closer to the tree, I responded, "Go on up and see if you can find that mountain."

Going into his backpack, *Naji* pulled out his pocket telescope then climbed up the roped ladder. He was soon suspended on a wooden platform. While turning around in circles, he looked through the lense.

Bothered by his silence, I asked. "Well? What do you see?"

"Trees, trees and more trees. But I can see a piece of the mountain over there," he replied, pointing back in the direction we had come from. The setting of the sun was now upon us.

"It's starting to get dark," I stated. "Maybe we should set up camp and find some food for the night?"

Closing the telescope, *Naji* agreed. "Yeah, we'll head for the mountain in the morning."

Preparing to descend, he noticed a bow and three arrows propped up against a tree. Raising it high he said, "Look what I found. Seems whoever built this platform had intentions of coming back."

Once he was grounded, I analyzed the weapon. "These are made of wood and tied with tree fibers. Looks primitive."

"Oh yeah, well let's see that caveman climb the tree now," *Naji* added. Pulling the ladder from around the tree, he dropped it down to the floor.

"What are you going to do with that?" I asked.

"Survival of the fittest. I'm taking the rope so that nobody else gets up there but us. Besides, with that limp? I don't think you'll be climbing anytime soon," Naji answered.

Turning to leave, I retorted, "Let's just find some food before it gets too dark," as we then started back the way we came. Following my lead, *Naji* cautiously looked around behind us, then said. "Good idea. I'm starving."

A few hours later, we were lounging around a welcoming campfire beneath the moon light, roasting fried fish on twigs.
Sitting on top of the *Model - 1* engine hood, *Naji* dangled his feet, devouring a small trail ration.

"See? This wasn't so bad. Two amigos, braving the wilds, hunting for treasure. We should make the story into a novel." He said while chewing loudly.

"Yeah, right." I said, laughing lightly beneath the star-filled sky. Pulling a tender piece of catfish filet apart, it slid easily off the bone while I stuffed it into my mouth. With my back against the plane I sat, twisting a fish over the campfire. Looking at the treasure map, I thought for a second.

"What do you think Mayor *Bloomfield* meant when he said the *Lost City* was on a floating island"? I asked.

Licking his fingers, *Naji* slid down the plane. Grabbing the tent from the storage area, he then laid it out, beginning its assembly.

"Not sure. Maybe it's a riddle of some kind. Once we reach that huge mountain it should give us a better idea," he replied. Holding up the map, I arose and gave him a hand with the tent. Seconds later, I paused to hear the rainforest come alive.
Grasshoppers and crickets chirped in the bushes. The low hum from the bugs and insects would have been soothing, if it wasn't for them swarming around our face.

Before long, our bright orange tent was erected, 7 ft tall and 6 ft wide with a curved roof. Rolling out my sleeping bag, I decided to call it a night. Putting dirt over the campfire, we extinguished the flame.

"I'll be back. I gotta take a leak," *Naji* said, while stepping into the bushes. Securing the other supplies back into the *Model - 1* cargo compartment, I made my way back inside the tent, when *Naji* suddenly screamed, "Ahhh!"

Halfway inside the tent, I turned around stepping back outside. Seeing some movement in the shrubs nearby, I said "*Naji*? Is everything all right over there?" as the bushes continued to rustle. I then dashed inside the tent, grabbing the hunting rifle. Inching outside, I snapped the clip into place then pulled the hammer back.
"All right, the joke is over *Naji*... I sure hope that's you over there?"

Aiming the rifle, I shook the bushes with the barrel. A purple *honeycreeper* with yellow feet immediately flew out with its curved bill. Slowly tip toeing over the moist dirt, my feet snapped the twigs underneath. Scanning from right to left, I awaited a sound. A few steps ahead, *Naji* was laying face down beneath some tall plants like a limp noodle.

Cautiously I approached his side, tapping him with my foot... But no response. Kneeling down, I flipped him over to check if he was still breathing. Placing my left hand onto his chest, I could feel it rise and fall.

"Whew. He's alive," I thought, standing upright. Turning around in circles, I looked for anything suspicious, when all of a sudden the bushes up ahead began to rustle once more. Pointing the rifle, I slowly paced forward saying "Come out, come out, wherever you are..." Just feet away from the wrestling plants, I added, "That was your final warning, now

I'm going to blow you into next week!" While reaching my left hand for the bushes -

THWACK!

I suddenly felt something crack me over the head, sending me to the floor. As I rolled over in pain, I stared up into the pitch-black darkness. A shadowy figure hovered above me raising their weapon for one last strike.

Everything went black.

Wiping the cold from my eyes, I woke up with a throbbing headache & rolled onto my back. Sitting up, I immediately scanned the forest floor for *Naji*. He laid beside me on a tuft of grass, wrapped in a net.

"Naji! Naji! Wake up!" I shouted.

Slowly he began to come to his senses, as he squirmed in the net. "Huh? Where - where am I?" He mumbled.

"It looks like you're caught in a spider web! Hold on, I'll get you out," I stated. While trying to stand, I realized I too was entangled in webs. Pulling my arms forward, I tried to break free, then remembered the metal shield on my wrist. Clenching my hand into a fist, I engaged my buckler, its spinning action cutting the web around my forearm and springing me from the trap.

"Hurry up, will ya? I feel like a helpless moth." *Naji* said, while I removed the rest of my bindings.

"We should get going. Whatever spun these webs, can't be too far away," I replied, making my way to *Naji*. Suddenly, he was yanked across the ground and up into a tree.

"What the? Hey, what's goin on!?" He wailed, kicking and screaming. But while reaching my hand for him, I was too short, as he was now dangling 15 feet above me. A giant gray spider then surfaced from the canopy. Slowly reeling him in, the spider's mandibles chattered.

"Heeeelp!" *Naji* screamed.

While jumping fruitlessly, I waved my hands through the air, soon realizing my adopted brother was too far away. Turning to pick up a nearby stone, the leaves on the trees then began withering away, falling to the floor. A mysterious fog began to sweep over the rainforest. Spinning around I faced *Naji*, but found no trace of him nor the spider.

"Huh? They were just here?" I said to myself. Immediately, I heard the sound of laughter behind me. With each second, the voice grew more terrifying. "Who's there, what do you want?" I asked, cautiously creeping through the fog. As the laughter became louder, I soon came to an eerie swamp. In the middle stood a hooded figure, cloaked in darkness. Lifting his palms, the shadows on the floor suddenly began to twist and take shape.

Strange creatures then materialized from the ground, with sharp teeth and glowing red eyes. The lanky monsters hunched over on all fours, like a gorilla. Cackling menacingly, the silhouette pointed in my direction.

"Come, to the *Wicked Forest*. The time is near..." The sinister voice resonated inside my cranium.

The frightening creatures then blitzed for me. While trying to run, I was easily outnumbered and pushed to the floor. Clawing at me with their razor-like talons, I was soon engulfed in pitch black darkness, screaming for a way out...

Blinking my eyes, I slowly regained consciousness. As a swirl of bright colors rotated into a blurry visual, my eyesight soon came into focus.

"*Thomas*? *Thomas*?" I heard nearby.

"*Thomas*? Wake up!" The voice repeated louder.

Turning my head, I spotted *Naji* beside me. He was tied to a wooden log by some ropes binding his entire body. It was then I realized that it had only been a dream...Or more of a nightmare. For the past few weeks, I had been having them regularly but couldn't understand them.

"Finally, you're awake," He stated.

Shaking my head, I tried to move then noticed I was too was bound. "What the hell is going on? Where are we?" I questioned.

"I don't know, but we've gotta get out of here. Those women over there look hungry... And I'm getting the feeling we're the main course." *Naji* said.

Turning my head to the right, I spotted a group of very tall, chiseled women under the moon's light. With beautiful faces, some had brown skin and the others were fair. In a test of might, they would give even the strongest man a run for his coin, hands down. Standing in front of a large bonfire near some straw huts, they conversed in a foreign tongue.

Pointing in our direction, they held spears and bows in their hands. From afar they appeared to be sharpened with coarse stones. The armor they wore was quite revealing, but carefully sewn together.

"Are they going to eat us?" I asked.

"Seems so. But what better way to die, right?" *Naji* replied. When suddenly another group of women came filing out from the bigger hut, walking our way.

"Well I don't know about you, but I don't plan on dying today," I returned.

As they approached, it was hard to ignore their voluptuous bodies sashaying side to side, while their styled hair glided through the wind.

Standing before us, the only woman wearing a colorful feather headdress said, "Why have you come?" with curiosity in her voice.

Out of fear of *Naji* saying something incriminating, I spoke first, "We are travelers in search of a treasure. Our aircraft crashed somewhere in this forest, we mean you no harm."

Not impressed by my answer, the woman I assumed to be their leader responded in her native tongue. "Man always mean harm. He come and destroy rainforest for own again. Cut trees, kill animals. Only think of self ! If we let bandit live, he come back with more, and try raid village again."

One of the athletic vixens standing beside her sporting a mohawk, stepped in front of me saying, "Princess. Let's kill them. Man here to burn village and take supplies. He want make us prisoner," raising her spear, preparing to impale us.

The princess replied, "Not yet."
Respecting her command, the other woman lowered her spirit in anger. The princess then walked around us, examining our clothes and touching our hair.

"You are weak frail men. What treasure you seek?" She asked.

"First of all, we're not bandits. We're just looking for the treasure of the *Lost City*," I replied. Suddenly they all began to chuckle.

The princess teased. "Silly man, that story just fairy tail. City of gold and flowing crystal water no exist."

"Oh yes, they do. I can prove it to you... If, you let us go," *Naji* chimed.

"See? Man want trick *Amazonian* princess. If we free them, they try fight us. We must kill them!" the other woman said while becoming enraged. Lifting her spear once more, she prepared to joust us. When out of the blue, the smallest of the women surrounding us stepped closer with her spear.

"Wait!" She yelled.

"Out of way, sister. Man no good. Only helped make babies," The mohawked woman with the spear responded.

Standing before us, I could tell that our protector was a little younger than the other woman. Maybe even our age. Her springy brunette hair bounced over her shoulders, with each graceful step. Wearing less protective gear than her comrades, most of her body was bare. Her studded leather gauntlets and matching shin guards were possibly curated for maneuverability.

"How we know they not tell truth?" She responded.

The princess then told her. "*Sasha*, stand down." As she came closer, then put a hand upon her smaller sister's shoulder. "One day you learn. *Amazonian* stronger together. No need Man help. You still young, when Sasha older, You see man only help self... All man."

As the princess turned around to leave, she added "*Misha*. Kill them."

The woman with the spiked hair began to smirk, while pushing *Sasha* aside. Inching forward, the brown-skinned bombshell pulled back her spear, ready to strike once again. The situation was taking a turn for the worst, and we were probably miles away from our weapons. Thinking back to the dream of the spider web, I formulated a plan.

Watching *Naji* tremble in fear, I closed my fist, activating my shield. Cascading into its activated form, the metal shredded the ropes binding me in half. In an instant, I dashed to *Naji's* side then swung my shield upward, slicing the ropes.
Surprised by our escape, the *Amazonian* princess stepped back in awe. *Misha* and the other women nearby jumped in front of her cautiously. While crouching low like a tiger showing her teeth, *Misha* growled. "See! Man no good!"

Standing in front of *Naji*, I slowly pushed us back, keeping the shield extended. Hesitantly looking around, *Naji* spotted two spears leaning against a straw hut nearby. He then darted for the weapons as I followed, providing cover.

Moments later, we were surrounded by a deadly dozen *Amazonian* women. Their skin tight ensemble was entrancing to young Edenian men - however, for our circumstance it was a nightmare. Grabbing a spear, I threatened them by waving it through the air twice while *Naji* began to twirl his spear with intimidation.

Misha yelled. "Get them!" Sending the furious pack charging at us, and fast. But from the look on *Sasha's* face, I got the feeling she didn't want to attack us.

"Quick! That way!" *Naji* yelled, as we sprinted opposite the crowd. With a poor lack of judgment I followed *Naji*. Taking us into the bushes, he pushed aside small shrubs and leapt over fallen logs. I tried my best to keep up, limping behind. Through spider webs and over ant hills, we traversed the forest. The vicious women behind us were still hot on our tail.

Running past carnivorous plants and sprouting pineapples, *Naji* suddenly lost his footing and began to stumble. Too close behind him to slow down, I bumped into him, sending us both rolling down a muddy slope. As we tumbled downhill, our pursuers soon followed suit, athletically sliding down on their feet.

Landing into a soft patch of grass, I slowly rose to my feet. While I helped *Naji* stand up, the barbarians once again surrounded us with spears and pointed arrows. As they crept closer, *Misha* was still leading the forefront.

"It's been nice knowing ya, man". *Naji* whimpered, readying his spear.

"Likewise". I replied, bracing my shield for impact, when all of a sudden, a frightening roar bellowed nearby.

The large plants around us began to bend, as a wide silhouette slowly approached. The dense vegetation and lowlight reduced my visibility. Startling the *Amazonian* women, they instantly began scurrying back towards the slope.

In confusion, I looked around us. "Whatever is beneath those plants sure has been spooked. Be careful." Inching backwards, we stood defensively. And while surveying the bushes rustle once more, they eventually came to halt. Then suddenly, a creature sprang from the bushes, landing before us.

"Grahr!" It roared.

A giant of a beast, it's hide was sickly yellow with fangs bursting from his mouth. About 6 feet in height, it's jade colored eyes pierced like daggers. Stalking around us in a circle, it showed its razor sharp teeth while growling menacingly.

"What is that!?" *Naji* asked.

"It looks like a jaguar, but... I've never seen one so big." I responded.

Attempting to scare the overgrown cat away, *Naji* jousted the air with his spear, saying. "What are they feeding these things in the *Amazon?*"

The jaguar crept lower with each step, then pounced through the air. Raising my shield in time, it slammed against the middle, forcing me back.
Watching it bite and claw furiously around the edge of the shield, I gave a couple thrusts from my spear missing each time.
Jumping in, *Naji* swung his spear side to side, managing to scratch the jaguar, which only appeared to fuel its rage.

Leaping off my shield, the jaguar dove into *Naji*, tackling him to the floor. As they rolled around, the jaguar soon pinned him to the floor, trying to bite him. *Naji* kept the creature's mouth from mauling his face by holding the spear sideways. Clamping down on the spear, the beasts massive jaws quickly split it into two halves. As it prepared to devour his face, I desperately heaved my spear impaling the jaguar's side, causing it to roar in pain.

Falling to the floor, the jaguar turned on its side, then broke my spear with its razor sharp claws, leaving the other piece lodged deep inside. *Naji* wiggled back onto his feet, spinning the spear pieces in his hand.

"I think he's mad," *Naji* said, breathing heavily. Viewing the animal, the hairs on his back stood up in a sharp line trailing down its back. The cold stare in its eyes grew frigid with each breath. The beast then roared once more.

Charging full speed, the monster leapt at us with fervor. In our defense, I stepped forward to meet the attack. Swinging my shield, I collided with the behemoth. While I wrestled it from the other side of my shield, *Naji* struck from the side, plunging the broken spear into the jaguar's spine. Clawing at *Naji*, the jaguar instantly crumbled to the floor, squirming in agony.

Picking up a large rock nearby, *Naji* sprang for the final blow, howling his warcry:

"Raaah!"

I stepped in front of him before he could land the killing blow-

"Wait!" I contested. Watching the jaguar wince in pain, it continued thrashing about on the floor. Empathetically, I continued. "He's had enough...It's over."

Lowering the rock in his grasp, *Naji* retorted, "Had enough!? That thing just tried to eat us alive! Here, lay down, I think you're catching jungle fever."

Although trembling, I walked over to the creature and knelt beside it, cautiously rubbing it's fuzzy coat. Gently holding its head, I reassured it that I meant no harm.

"What are you doing?! It's going to kill you!" *Naji* shouted.

Staring death in its green eyes, they glistened under the night sky. Soothing the beast, I gave a quick tug - yanking the splintered wood from its body.
Panting lightly, the animal suddenly loosened up and began to breathe easy. Releasing him, the creature slowly rose to his feet, giving me a vigilant gaze as we peered into each other's souls. He then limped away back into the bushes.

Walking over to help me up, *Naji* said, "It's not over yet, look. The *Amazonians* are coming back."

The plants rustled behind us, as the 7ft warrior vixens emerged with amazement upon their faces. Coming closer, the chocolate-covered *Misha* asked. "How small man run beast away? Beast killed many *Amazonian*. Eat them like food...You do magic?"

"No magic. Just compassion." I said, lowering my guard.

"That impressive. Where traveler man come from?" The *Amazonian* princess said, stepping forward.

"A city high up on the hills, called *Edenia*. We're not here to harm the *Amazonian* women, we're just trying to reach those tall mountains nearby," I responded, while pointing in the distance. "The *Mountain of Giants*? We've never seen man fight like *Amazonian*. You skilled warriors. Come, stay tonight," the princess returned.

Instantly, *Misha* cried, "But princess? Man can't come *Amazonian* tree house!? It's sacred, and not have much food?"

Standing beside the princess, the slightly smaller five foot tall *Sasha* said, "You seen traveler man scare beast? They good warrior. Princess has spoken," staring her down, defiantly.

The princess clapped her hands, saying, "Enough! We leave now. Soon, more beast come." Turning towards us she stepped closer, finishing, "Join us."

Looking at *Naji's* face, his fear subsided. "You don't have to tell me twice," he returned, while drooling with eyes wide. Nodding my head in confirmation, the *Amazonians* guided us back up the slope, then deep into the forest.

About 40 minutes later, we pulled up to a lake illuminated by torches lining the bank. Even in the stark blackness of night the crystal water was clearly visible, appearing as glass glistening on a smooth floor. The *archerfish* & *toucans* in the lateral zone were quite observant, eyeing us as we passed. Stepping through bushes and brushing some plants aside, we finally reached our destination. Surveying the *Amazonian* compound, I was captivated.

An arboreal village was suspended in the canopy. Hanging from ropes and wooden platforms, many straw huts sat high atop the gargantuan *Kapok* trees, at least 300 feet in height. Woman toiled about like an ant colony. Some carried baskets of goods, while others were crafting wares or sparring in heated competition.

"Welcome to *Amazonia*. Home of warrior women. No man welcome. But you first exception," the princess said, as we came to the base of a giant tree.

Standing in front of a platform, we followed the princess onboard. Two women on the side pulled the ropes to a pulley system, raising us up towards the village. Watching the people shrink down below, we ascended to the treetops. *Naji* & I hung over the roped railing, stupefied. Moments later, we were stepping off the elevator and into an enormous treehouse. As the princess led the way, we followed her over wooden bridges and through open huts.

The burning candles and incense spread a delightful fragrance throughout the village, and as we warranted onlookers with each step, the natives gasped in awe at our tour of *Amazonia's* confines. Coming to a small hut with vine-braided hammocks and animal fur rugs, the princess said, "You sleep here tonight. No worry, women not hurt you. Some just no see man before."

"Thank you *Amazonian* princess," I replied.

Looking around hesitantly, we entered the hut. It was clear we were the main attraction...

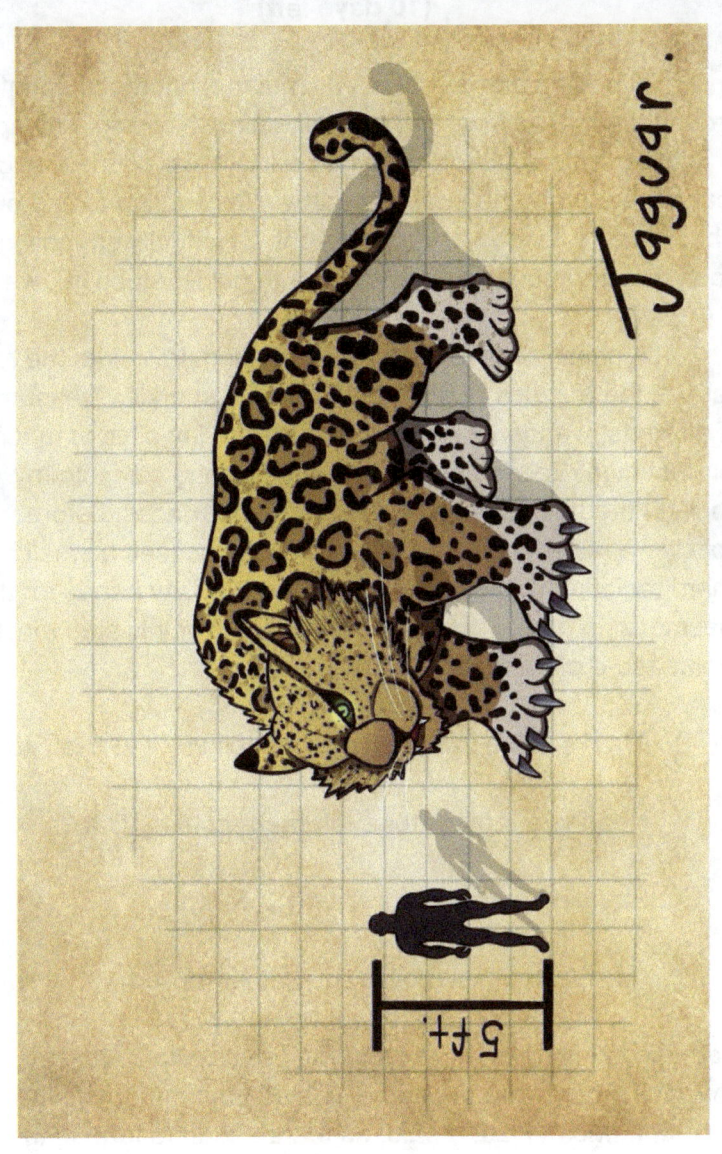

Jaguar.

5 ft.

Chapter 5
(10 days left)

Standing alone in the *Amazonian* rainforest, I spun around, finding darkness in each direction. Noticing a glimpse of light up ahead, I decided to follow it. All of a sudden, a loud roar echoed from the bushes nearby. Not wanting to find out what it was, I flashed toward the light. Eventually stumbling upon the entrance to a room filled with gold, I stood in awe.

A shining light from above beaming down into the room caused the bundles of gold to glisten and sparkle. Treasures of all kinds; weapons, jewelry, artifacts, all lay piled in mounds ten feet high. Eagerly walking around stuffing coin into my pocket I tried on a few jewel encrusted necklaces, before noticing a raised altar. As I approached, I noticed a small blue shard radiating with exuberance. Extending my hands for the mesmerizing gem, I thought to myself, "All of this stuff must be the treasure of the *Lost City*? This is unreal."

Then a voice from behind me replied, "It IS real, son."

Hearing a familiar tone, I turned around. "Dad?"

Standing before me were my 2 parents.

"My how you've grown," my father replied with a smile.

Confused at first, I then ran into their arms with a warm embrace. They wore the same clothes from the day of the accident. "Mom! Dad!" I said, as tears began to form in the corners of my eyes.

"*Thomas*, we're so proud of you," Mother said.

Wiping my eyes, I rambled. "I have so much to tell you! I got the *Model-0* to work. It just needed a few adjustments to

the engine. I even added a steam converter & repositioned the
- "

When suddenly my father knelt down in front of me,
grabbing my shoulders. "We love you, son." Staring into his
eyes, I felt a wave of deja vu. The ground then began to quake
and tremble. Chunks of stone started to burst from beneath
my feet, enclosing us within a walled room. Losing my footing,
I stumbled backwards out of my parents grasp. Reaching for
my father's hand, the distance between us grew, as it felt like I
was being pulled back. While the floor continued to shake, I
helplessly watched the stalagmites collide over our heads,
sealing us inside a cave.

Turning back towards my parents, they were no longer
there. Heaps of rubble were now plunging down from the
ceiling, smashing into the golden treasures, scattering them
everywhere like a puddle. While zigzagging through the rocks,
I desperately tried to avoid getting crushed, but the violent
tremors pushed me to the floor. A large boulder then crash
landed on my legs, pinning me to the floor. Watching the room
collapse, I thought. "How is this happening? Wasn't I just
sleeping in a straw hut?"
While I struggled to break free, a soft voice then said.
"Hungry?"

Looking around, I noticed *Sasha* standing behind my head.

"Oh thank god, you're here! I need your help, the place
is collapsing!" I shouted.

Sasha simply replied once more: "Hungry?"

With confusion on my face, I stared at her as the
situation became clear. Blinking my eyes, the cave suddenly
vanished like a mirage. I awoke in a sweat...

"Traveler man, hungry?" The gentle voice repeated. Jolting from my strange dream, I was met by a pair of dazzling green eyes.

The tiny scar resting above her left eye complimented her tan complexion. It WAS *Sasha*. Holding her hand out, she awaited my response.

"Huh - oh, yeah. Sure."

Grabbing my hand with a warming smile, she yanked me out from the hammock.

"Come. *Amazonian* at table," she informed me.

Feeling well rested, my body was no longer sore. A light rain showered the forest as we navigated the bridges and walkways of the tree house. It felt like a scene from a book I'd once read at the orphanage called '*Peter Pan and the Lost Boys*', only with beautiful women instead of bedwetting toddlers.

Gathering my thoughts, I reminded myself where I was. Wiping the sleep from my eyes, we came to a long table filled with delicacies and sweet aromas filling the air. The *Amazonian* women were all gathered around, feasting on roasted fish and fresh exotic fruits, apples, bananas, oranges, loaves of fresh bread, fowl, salmon. The cornucopia wasn't exactly fine-dining, but there was enough to go around.

Naji flagged me down from the opposite end of the table. Wolfing a loaf of bread down his throat, I could tell he was enjoying himself. Coming over he said, "It's about time you woke up. The food here is great!"

Sasha pulled me along, stating, "Come. We sit there. Next to princess."

Following her request, I sat down with my legs crossed upon one of the hand stitched pillows decorated all around the table. Grabbing an orange I began to peel it. The princess sat on the other side of the table, plucking grapes from a bundle laid before her. *Naji* soon joined beside me.

Noticing our appearance, she said in her native tongue, "Good, our guest awake. We not have many foods, but little we do have your welcome to it... Sleep nice?"

Breaking a piece of the orange, I placed it into my mouth. "Oh yes, we slept well. Thank you for letting us stay."

"Again, tell me? Why man come to *Amazonian* rainforest?" she continued.

With a mouthful of bananas, *Naji* explained, "Well princess, like we told you before, we're very experienced adventurers in search of treasure. Our flying machine crashed in the forest, on the way to the tall mountains not too far from here."

Sitting next to the princess was her right hand in command, *Misha*. Spitting out the juice from her wooden goblet, she replied. "Flying ma-chine? See, I told you traveler man do magic."

"Ma-chine? Where it now?" The princess curiously asked.

Chewing another piece of orange, I returned. "Somewhere in a small clearing. Not far from where you found us."

"What man want at mountain? Go to slay Giants?" She continued.

Chewing loudly, *Naji* added. "We were hoping to find the directions on a treasure map. And besides, there's no such thing as Giants princess. That's just a tall tale."

"Giant real. He kill many man. Play them like toy. This treasure you seek, how man know It real, and not lies?" the princess replied.

"Well, princess... truthfully? We don't. But we're going to find out." I responded.

"Why man fight for treasure? Want fame? Power?" She snorted.

"No..." I replied hesitantly. Looking around the table, I noticed the princess and *Misha* were curiously tuned into the discussion, as they leaned over the table. Breaking off small pieces of cheese into his mouth, *Naji* anticipated my response. Sitting beside me *Sasha* hadn't touched a morsel of food since we began. The intrigued expression on her face told me that she was a dreamer, much different from her *Amazonian* sisters.

"An evil man wants to take everything my family has worked so hard to achieve... I'm fighting for our legacy," I continued.

Showing sudden concern, the wrinkles on her face smoothed out. "*Amazonian* also fight for home," said the princess.

Misha then lowered her defense, nodding her head with understanding. "Come. We help man find ma-chine," she stated, rising from her seat.

"Really? That's great! I'll go with you." *Naji* replied. Standing on his feet, he turned to me. "The sooner we fix the plane, the sooner we can find the treasure."

"Good idea," I replied.

Nodding her head, the princess added, "Be safe."

Misha nodded in respect to her princess and replied, "Yes, princess," Before departing from the table. *Naji* and a couple of the warriors trailed behind her.

The princess rose from her cushioned pillow as well, stating. "I too must go now. Much things to do." Wearing a smile, she continued. "*Sasha*? Tend to guest."

As she then waved farewell, swinging her iconic royal figure.

We watched as the princess disappeared through a tiger fur curtain, into a large hut. After an awkward silence, I decided to break the ice. "So? Where are all the men?"

Studying me briefly, *Sasha* replied. "We kill them. *Amazonian* warrior no need man. They only for mating."

"So, where do you find these...mates?" I asked quite surprised by her blunt response.

"Find travelers who come to rain forest. Take them for breeding, then kill them. Sometimes we give to beast, leave as food," *Sasha* answered proudly.

Having little understanding of the *Amazonian* history, I questioned, "How did all of you end up here? Was this where you were born?"

"Some *Amazonian* born here, at tree house. Others come from outside forest. Meet warrior princess and stay," *Sasha* explained.

"How about you?" I answered.

Sasha thought for a second, while looking at the hardy feast laid out before us. Then picking up an apple, she started, "I come when young, small child. Family pass through forest, try escape bandits. We stay three days, camp for night. Until... One day strange man come, ask for food. Family let man stay camp. And in morning man leave, try steal food. Family try stop man. Man kill both *Sasha* parents, and leave child. Then *Amazonian* warriors come, kill strange man and take child here to treehouse. Raise *Sasha* into strong *Amazonian* warrior."

As she put the uneaten apple back on the table, I said to her, "I'm sorry you had to go through that. But not ALL men are like that."

"Ha!" She huffed, "Man greedy, only want destroy. Take things for self," she said, while standing on her feet.

"That's not true. Then why did the princess bring us here?" I concurred, rising along side her.
My suddenly standing caused *Sasha* to size me up, she then said. "Not sure. Maybe *Amazonian* hope traveler man different?"

Pausing for a second, we gazed into each other's eyes. I could see a light buried deep inside of her, waiting to burst forth. In spite of the violent experiences she'd grown up with in the jungle, she was still so new to life, & her innocent curiosity was ready to explode. Contrary to everything she may have learned here with the *Amazonians*, I could tell she was yearning for adventure. Daring to go against the grain, she was a seeker of truth.

"Well *Sasha*...Maybe I am," I returned.

"If that true, *Amazonian* find out. Now, time for chores," She said.

"Chores?" I repeated in confusion.

"Need help build hut and gather food. Come." She replied. Starting for the other direction, *Sasha* waited for me to follow. After grabbing another orange from the table, I was escorted through the village.

Exploring the treehouse with *Sasha* was quite an experience. It gave me a better understanding of the *Amazonians* and their culture. Watching the sisters weave palm fibers into baskets and helping the carpenters cut wood for the new platforms was sort of therapeutic.
Sasha showed me the steps toward making an efficient weapon out of the natural resources around. Whittling away tree bark for a spear & sharpening stone arrowheads was no easy task. They were real survivalists.
The finesse these warrior women displayed during their exercise was phenomenal. Combat came easy for them, mostly due to their strong stature. Even young *Sasha* had a sense of strength & fortitude.

Approaching a rest area, I plopped down into a cushioned seat, finely crafted with oakwood. Melting into the chair, I took a deep breath.

"Ugh, I'm so drained. I'm sore in places I never knew I had," I said as the fatigue set in.

"Traveler man scare beast, but can't keep up labor? Hehehe, you funny," *Sasha* replied.

Watching the cute dimples form in her cheeks as she laughed put a goofy smile on my face.

"Hey *Thomas*! Look what we found!" A voice called from below.

Confused, I stared at *Sasha*. We both moved toward the railing of the wooden platform, encircling the giant tree. Looking over the balcony, I spotted *Naji* waving with excitement.

"The *Model - 1*?!" I exclaimed.

"That's right! *Misha* and I found all of the pieces, even the broken wing! Now we can fix this thing and get out of here! We're on our way up!" *Naji* responded.

I turned to *Sasha* after his statement and we fixed eyes. I could tell the news of suddenly departing made her a little uneasy.

"That good. Now traveler man can find treasure," she said, forcing a smile.

Turning to leave, I followed *Sasha* as we soon made our way to the pulley system.
Naji and *Misha* were standing alongside the other warriors on the platform. The *Model - 1* laid in pieces behind them, beside the rest of our gear.

"You wouldn't believe the time we had. We battled giant wasps, crossed a pit of snakes- oh, we even swam with alligators. This rainforest is amazing!" *Naji* blurted.

"We're glad you all made it back. *Misha*, thank you and your sisters for all your help. Traveling with *Naji* can be a real... task, if you know what I mean." I stated.

"No problem. Traveler man help *Amazonian*. Make good decoy when he run like girl," *Misha* returned.

Moving in closer, I filed through the wreckage with my hands, assessing the damage done to the plane and possible ideas for repair.

"All right, let's get this somewhere with a little more room to work on. *Misha*, do you mind giving us a hand?" I asked.

"*Misha* help. Come," she replied, walking to the heavy scrap of metal. Seconds later, she and the other women each hoisted the 900 lb aircraft, effortlessly toting the pieces to another location.

"I'm starving, let's get some grub." *Naji* said, following two nearby villagers carrying a basket of food.

Sasha replied. "Sound like plan. Come, we eat." Heading to the large table, we decided to take a break.

As night fell, gleaming stars hung over the rainforest. Moonlight shining through the leafy branches above the tree house, illuminated the pathways. Neon colored lightning bugs and fluorescent butterflies fluttered around the compound. A cool breeze shook the wind chimes, decorating the huts. Playing a serene melody that was actually soothing. As *Naji* and I prepared to sleep, my mind raced.

After staring off into the distance and thinking to myself for a while, I informed *Naji,* "The longer we stay here, the closer we're getting to the Zep-Tec foreclosure deadline. It's already going on 4 days."

Naji sleepily replied, "Don't worry, we'll find the treasure. And when we do, we're going to make sure *Deacon Blues* gets what he deserves," as he squirmed into his sleeping quarters.

"I hope you're right." I returned, climbing into my hammock. While laying down thinking to myself, I stared at the straw roof, growing weary. As my eyelids grew heavy, I turned on my side facing the wall. Moments later, I blinked myself into a deep slumber.

That next morning, I awoke to the sound of chirping birds. Rising with ambition and a drive to get the *Model - 1* back in the air, I swung my legs out of the hammock, then onto the floor. Shaking *Naji* from his sleep, I pulled him to his feet.

"Rise and shine. We've got work to do," I said.

With little fuss, he was up and ready to lend me a hand. Grabbing a couple fruits and a loaf of bread along the way, we made our way to an empty platform suspended on the side of a tree. The Aero-plane sat in shambles. With no time to waste, we sprang into action. Pulling fuses off parts from under the engine cover, I manually rotated the gears, while *Naji* reattached rods that had slipped off the piston.

"Hand me that wrench?" I requested.

"This big one?" *Naji* responded.

"No, crazy. The 12 millimeter," I retorted.

As he tossed me the wrench, I caught it behind my back with my left hand, then spun it around before fixing it into position to tighten some lug nuts.

"Impressive," he said, clapping his hands.

Lifting the wing, *Naji* held it still for me to screw the flaps back into place. Hammering new nails into old rivets and tirelessly tightening the wrench, we were making the most of our limited supply of resources. We flushed new water through the converter and priming the gauges. The *Model - 1* started to resemble its original design.

Making minor adjustments to the hydraulic converter, I reattached the splash shield under the engine. Taking a step back, *Naji* continued fastening exterior screws, while I viewed the mangled propeller.

"Hmmm, what are we going to do with this?" I questioned.

Naji then stood up to check the front of the plane, saying, "Don't know. That thing looks too bent to repair without the proper tools... Any ideas?"

"I have a plan." A gentle voice said from behind. *Sasha* then crept into view holding a large piece of bark and the same stone knife we had used from earlier, to carve weapons. Coming closer, she looked me in the eye saying. "Sasha help. Trust me."

Giving her a smile I nodded my head, accepting her assistance, "Okay *Sasha*. Show us what you've got."

Placing the mangled propeller down on the large hunk of bark in her hands, she accurately measured the dimensions of the blade. Then she began to cut and whittle away the bark

90

until the desired shape took form. About twenty minutes later, *Sasha* produced an exact wooden replica of the *Model-1's* missing propeller blade.

Holding it in my hand, I tried bending it to check its durability for any defects, but only found it to be sturdy, and a great replacement for the original.

"Wow! *Sasha*, this is amazing!" I exclaimed.

"No trouble. Man need ma-chine to find treasure. *Sasha* want help." She returned, with a genuine smile.

Hearing the sincerity in her voice, I gave her a warm hug, saying. "Thank you."

Standing before the plane, I held the wooden propeller blade up to the rotary, and was surprised by its perfect fit. Then using my right hand, I tightened the screws in the holes *Sasha* cut for the blade. Minutes later, the propeller was attached. The newly-refurbished *Model - 1* was a triumph to the *Amazonian* environment and our mechanical genius.

"Well, what are you waiting for? Crank it up." *Naji* said with excitement.

Nodding my head, I climbed into the cockpit then took a deep breath before pressing the ignition button. When someone suddenly shouted. "*Sasha!*"

Turning my head, the princess slowly revealed herself alongside *Misha* and two other women. "There you are. Sisters look everywhere for you," The princess admonished.

"*Sasha* watch traveler man. Help fix ma-chine, look!" *Sasha* said excitedly, while pointing to the *Model - 1*.

Simultaneously, the engine began sputtering and coughing up white smoke. The clanging from under the hood frightened the women. Taking defensive steps back, they raised their spears. *Sasha* stood captivated by the experience with her mouth hanging low.

Pop - Pop - BOOM! The engine choked.

Moments later, the propeller kicked into its normal rotation, producing a familiar hum. Checking the gauges on the dashboard, all major parts were evenly distributing pressure throughout the pipes. She was alive, the *Model-1* was back in action.

"It works! We did it!" I shouted, hopping out of the cockpit down to the floor.

Running to congratulate me, *Naji* and I shook hands. "Great job *Thomas*, you the man! We'll be back on track in no time," he said.

Lowering their guard, the *Amazonians* came closer. "This ma-chine? *Amazonian* no see nothing like before," said the princess.

"That's right princess. First of its kind," I responded with a proud swagger in my tone.

The princess replied, "Guess this calls for a celebration. Come. We feast." She then clapped her hands twice before turning to leave, *Misha* and the other 2 warriors immediately trailing behind her.

Pulling out the treasure map, *Naji* pointed his finger to the big X on the parchment. He began explaining his idea for a new course and directions, calculating a better route to make up for lost time. Still ecstatic over the Aero-plane's recovery, I agreed to his new terms, then started gathering our spare tools before dinner.

Then all of a sudden, *Sasha* shouted, "Wait!"

With all of our attention turned towards *Sasha*, we stopped in our tracks. Taking a few steps closer, the princess approached her and asked, "What wrong? Sister no hungry?"

Staring into the *Amazonian* princess's eyes, Sasha replied, "I want to explore, want adventure."

Raising her eyebrow, the confused princess returned. "What sister mean?"

Sasha took a deep breath and let it out, "*Sasha* wants to go with traveler man…"

Sasha.

Chapter 6
(9 days left)

The expression on the princess's face explained her confusion. Stepping forward, *Misha* replied. "What?"

"*Sasha* want go with traveler man." *Sasha* replied.

"Why sister want leave home? No like *Amazonia*?" The princess asked with a look of concern.

Sasha responded. "*Sasha* LOVE Amazonia! Love princess and sisters! But...*Sasha* want more."

"More, what?" The princess continued.

"More to see! More to do! Want meet new people, and want see world! *Sasha* want find dream." She answered.

Surprised by her sudden revelation, the princess briefly looked *Sasha* in the eye. Then with concern all over her face, she gently grabbed *Sasha* by the shoulders. "*Sasha* really mean that?"

Sasha carefully nodded her head, confirming her response. The princess then faced me, saying, "Traveler man want *Sasha* go with?"

Seeing the sincerity in her gaze, I could tell that it was a heartfelt question. I looked at *Naji* and he shrugged his shoulders and said. "Don't don't look at me, you're the Captain, Slick. Besides...We could always use another hand."

Turning towards the princess, I glanced over at *Sasha,* saying, "Who am I to stop someone from chasing their dream? We would love to have *Sasha* onboard."

Listening with caution, *Sasha's* face slowly broke into a heart-warming smile. Turning back to *Sasha*, the princess then placed both her hands upon *Sasha's* cheeks.

The Princess declared regally, "Then it settled...*Sasha* may find this dream. But, must Never forget *Amazonia*."

"Oh thank you princess!" *Sasha* replied ecstatically, as they then shared a hug.

Leaning his arm on my left shoulder, *Naji* teased, "Aww, that's sweet... She's sitting up front with you right?"

"Now, back to feast! Tonight, we celebrate!" The princess continued, while clapping her hands once more.

As my stomach growled, I fell into the conga line heading for the dining area. The other villagers soon joined in.

Sitting before the long log table, I was in the company of new friends. The savory smell of fried fish was mouth-watering, and the delectable banana bread was orgasmic. Sipping from my finely carved goblet filled with jungle juice, I was actually able to forget about the world for a few minutes and loosen up. *Naji* was doing a silly jig on top of the table, spilling his cup from side to side. *Sasha* ate from a roasted fowl laid before us, while cheering him on. *Misha* and a few other women were holding an intense debate about war strategies. All while the princess's outstretched almond colored hand picked from a bundle of succulent fruits sprawled across the table.

Taking another sip of my drink, it was pleasing to see all the sisters enjoying themselves, especially considering the fact that only yesterday we were about to become shish kabob.

Standing onto her feet, the Amazonian princess raised her cup: "Attention!"

We fell silent; she then continued in her native accent, "This night for merry. This night for fun. This night *Amazonia* honor guests. Traveler man show us some man not bad. Not ALL...But some...Tonight *Amazonians* lose sister."

As she then turned to look at *Sasha*, who now held a remorseful frown on her face. The princess then continued. "But, gain Warrior." Opening her arms wide with a smile.

"For *Amazonia*!" She rallied.

Seconds later, the sisters began to chant native war cries, while the other villagers started banging rhythms on bongos. As I looked around, it wasn't hard to tell that this was a joyous occasion. Their cheers resonated all throughout the rainforest.

Turning to leave, the princess bid her farewells. Jumping down from the table, *Naji* exclaimed, "These people really know how to party!" while grabbing a handful of cashews.
Standing up, I walked over to the roped railing, chewing on the apple in my hand. While staring up into the constellation, it was then I realized that life outside *Edenia's* walls wasn't so different from the inside after all. Despite the fact the *Amazonian* society had little in modern conveniences, they remained joyful and easily found ways to have fun. I then thought to myself, "Maybe Pangea's inhabitants ARE more alike than we thought."

Anticipating our departure, a soft voice said from behind. "Stars beautiful." Hearing her tribal accessories jingle, I felt *Sasha* pull up alongside me.

Biting into my apple, I stared ahead saying. "Yeah. Makes you wonder, doesn't it?.. I've got to ask. What made you decide to leave your home? Your family?"

Pointing to the stars she replied. "Up there... When small child, family watch stars with *Sasha*... *Amazonians* no worry over sky. But *Sasha* know there more to see."

Overhearing the conversation, *Naji* squeezed in between us saying, "Good, because we're going to see plenty. Now, I've been thinking-" Digging into his pocket he retrieved the treasure map. Unfolding it with one hand, while using the other to eat a banana.

He continued - "When we get to that mountain, it should point us in the right direction of any floating islands. That's got to lead us to the *Lost City*."

"*Amazonian* help find treasure. Know how get to Mountain." *Sasha* replied.

Naji then shook her hand, returning. "That's great! Welcome to the team!" Facing me, he continued. "Maybe SHE can fly this time, my arms a little banged up from before?"

Forcing a smile, I told *Naji*. "Heh heh, I think I'll do the flying from now on. Now, let's get some shuteye guys. We leave early in the morning."

"Yeah, good idea. We've got a big day ahead." He responded, then turned to leave.

I then said to *Sasha,* "We'll see you in the morning." She nodded her head before vacating. *Naji* and I made our way back to the hut, as the others continued their celebration. Walking through the village, I took one last look at the splendor of the compound. Hidden deep in the rainforest, it was definitely an experience I could never forget.

—-----------------------

Early the next morning, I awoke rejuvenated. No longer feeling the minor bruises from *Naji's* crash landing, I was pumped up and ready to go. I woke up *Naji and* we quickly handled our morning routines, then made our way to the platform storing the *Model-1.*

Crossing over bridges and passing through open huts gave me an admirable feeling for the warrior women. They began cheering us along the way. It pumped me up to know that the *Amazonians* accepted us as equals, despite the hatred for outsiders.

Coming to the platform I stood before the plane, then climbed into the cockpit, pressing the ignition button. Listening to the engine sputter as it cranked up, I checked gauges to ensure the *steamline* was in order. Spewing steam from under the engine cover, the propeller slowly increased to its assigned speed.

Lookin at *Naji,* I raised my thumb saying, "All systems are a go!" over the loud hum from the motor.
"Great!" A voice said from the side of the plane. Turning my head, it was none other than *Sasha,* sporting a leather backpack.

"Good, you're here!" I said.

"Yeah! Ma-chine loud, wake whole village!" *Sasha* replied.

"Well you're just in time, come on! *Naji*, unlatch the hook holding the wheels!" I commanded. Give me a salute, he ran into the underbelly of the plane, then detached the hook preventing the plane from moving.

In no time we attracted a large crowd, including *Misha* & the princess themselves. While *Naji* climbed into the back seat, *Sasha* paused for a moment, looking at her sisters. The princess took a step forward then bowed low. Seconds later, all the *Amazonian* women were bowing, showing *Sasha* their respect.

"What are you waiting for, come on!?" *Naji* asked, regaining *Sasha's* attention. She waved goodbye, then climbed into the passenger seat with Naji.

"It's showtime!" I stated. Putting on my pilot's helmet and goggles, I began pedaling the gears.

Backing away from the plane, the *Amazonians* watched in awe. Two of the women untied a section of the rope railing, wide enough for the plane to pass through. Carefully steering across a few platforms, I eased the aero-plane to a stop on the pulley system elevator platform, which lowered us down to the forest floor. Seeing a clear path with enough space, I flipped the switch, releasing a burst of steam into the manifold. Mashing the gears with all my might, the *Model - 1* accelerated and rapidly shot away from the tree house, down the crystal river bank ahead. Pulling back on the controls, we began to rise in altitude, coughing up a trail of smoke behind.

Winding above the river as it snaked throughout the forest, we climbed into the sky.

"This amazing!" *Sasha* explained.

As I swooped down low for momentum, *Naji* said, "Oh you ain't seen nothing yet!"

Zooming over the treehouse, we could make out the ant-sized people below through the canopy, as they cheered ecstatically. A beautiful flock of rainbow-colored parrots escorted us above the *Amazonian* rainforest. The early morning sun rays twinkled in my eyes, as we darted into the orange clouds.

Looking down at my spinning compass, I said, "Are you sure it said East?"

Struggling with the treasure map as it blew in the wind, *Naji* replied, "Of course I'm sure! That's what the map says."

"We should have seen it by now!" I rebutted, while battling the ear numbing hum from the plane.

Squirming around in the seat, *Sasha* said. "Ow! You're on foot!..Ma-chine fly for hours, how much longer?"

Naji squirmed back and replied, "I'm not sure, but next time, you're riding up front!"

Moments later we descended thought bulbous clouds, stumbling upon a mountain range. I curved the *Model-1* towards their direction. "Look! Up ahead! I told you we were close!" *Naji* shouted.

Soaring above the snow filled peaks, I lowered the plane for a closer look. As we raised in altitude, I could feel the cold air nip at my face, while I surveyed the area. A valley of jagged rocks lay sprawled over the terrain, all fifty shades of gray.

"Where should I take her down?" I asked.

Reading the map, *Naji* returned, "Umm, find the tallest one you can find. It should give us a better view."

While taking the Aero-plane into a circle, *Sasha* shouted. "There! That one!" As she pointed to a small patch of clouds. Seconds later they began to part, revealing an enormous mountain. Coming closer, I noticed a safe clearing long enough for us to land.

"That *Mountain of Giants.* Sisters say mountain many thousand years old. Must be careful." *Sasha* warned us.

"Oh come on, do you really believe that? What's next, a man-eating tooth fairy?" *Naji* teased.

Positioning the plane for landing, I gritted through my teeth, "I hope you're right."

Moving the controls forward, the plane dropped in elevation, while creeping onto the mountain ledge. Feeling the vibration from below as we rolled over the bumpy gravel, I maneuvered the plane away from the large chunks of rocks, cluttering the ground. Coming to a stop, we spotted the mouth of a cave nearby. Killing the engine I stood up in my seat, lifting the goggles above my forehead.

Instantly a freezing gust of wind swept over my body, giving me the chills. Holding my arms, I began to shiver saying, "Well. Here we are."

Naji & Sasha had trouble exiting the seat, as they tried squeezing out simultaneously. "You're a lot heavier than you look," *Naji* stated, climbing down to the floor.

"It f-fre-freezing here," *Sasha* mumbled through her chattering teeth.

Stretching his arms, Naji scanned our surroundings. "The mountain comes to a peak up ahead. Let's start there," he said. Agreeing with his decision, we left the *Model-1* and advanced up the icy mountain on foot.

Marching over the rugged terrain proved difficult. The rocky path was inclined & the cold air ensued frostbite. After twenty minutes of hiking, we came to a winding stairway carved into the top of the mountain. Coming closer, I touched the bottom step with my foot, testing its durability.

"It seems pretty sturdy. I wonder who built this here?" I said.

Using her six foot long wooden spear as a walking stick, *Sasha* replied, "Maybe giant build, to get better view of mountain?" As she trembled fiercely from the harsh gale.

"Whoever it was, remind me to thank them later. Come on." *Naji* returned, rubbing his arms to warm himself up.

We then started up the stairway. Step after step, the air grew frigid. Due to the high elevation the air grew thin, making it harder to breathe. The ice covering the steps made it slippery and dangerous for us to scale the uneven rocks. In due time we managed to safely ascend the mountain, reaching its zenith. With only a little room to stand on, I turned in a circle, astonished by the breathtaking view.

"Can you believe this? I've never seen anything like it." I said.

Walking onto the edge *Naji* shouted. "Hey, check this out. I'm the king of the world!" While opening his arms wide, as his voice echoed into the void.

"*Sasha* never knew world so tall." She said, entranced by the landscape.

Pulling the small telescope from the strap on *Naji's* belt, I raised it high, gazing through the lens. While squinting my left eye, I scanned side to side, but I could only see a thick layer of morning fog. The low lying clouds were foreshadowed by speckles of falling snow.
Turning my telescope the other way, *Sasha's* head was enlarged and framed by the lens. As she stared off into the distance, I couldn't help but notice the beautiful coiled hair bouncing off her neck. Her smooth skin, the color of honey, was free from blemishes. She then turned in my direction wearing a smile.

"What do you see? Hellooo?" *Naji* said, trying to gain my attention.
Spinning to my side, I was startled by giant blinking eyes engulfing the lens.

"Ahh - the giant!" I yelled, frightened.

Immediately I lowered the telescope, revealing a bald *Naji* standing inches away from my face. Like a kid in a candy store, he grinned from ear to ear.
"So? What did you find?" he asked once more.

Handing him the telescope, I answered, "I'm not sure, it's a little foggy. Here, you try."

Grabbing the telescope, he put it to his eye. Slowly looking from left to right. "Hmm. It is hard to tell with all this fog in the air... Maybe we should try again In an hour or so, when the sun clears it up? Besides, I'm starving anyway," *Naji* said, lowering the telescope.

"I saw the mouth of a cave near the plane. We should set up camp there for a while." I replied.

Heading towards the steps, *Sasha* added. "Good. Let's go before freeze to death." We then traveled back down the icy slope, descending the mountain peak.

Upon reaching the *Model-1*, we began to unload some of the cargo, taking it to the small cave entrance nearby. About fifteen feet wide and twenty feet tall, the inside overlooked the mountain's high pass. Filling the copper pot with snow we lit a fire, bringing some water to a slow boil. *Naji* dropped in a few potatoes, carrots, and handfuls of wild rice he had saved from our dinner with the *Amazonian* sisters.

He was always an excellent chef, and probably the main reason we stayed alive after our parents passed away. *Deacon Blues* never fed us often. "Now, it's not much to work with, but I think I can whip us up something nice," He explained.

Feeling the cold breeze blow throughout the cave, we wrapped ourselves in green fireproof blankets from our sleeping bags.
Huddled around the campfire I looked at my compass watch, realizing it was approaching midday.

Pulling our weapons from the bags, *Naji* tossed me my sword and four-barreled pistol, while fastening his silver sword around his waist. "*Sasha, you're* going to need a weapon. Here, have these flares," He said, reloading his rifle.

Grabbing the small box, she questioned. "Flares? What's that?" Pulling one out the box to examine it, she eyed it cautiously, then bit the end -

Pop!

-the flare sounded as it ignited. Startled, *Sasha* fell backwards off the small rock she sat upon. While sitting up, she shouted with a smile. "Ooo, Magic Stick! *Sasha* like," causing Naji to snicker.

Reloading my pistol, I holstered it onto my side then grabbed my sword. "The food should be almost done," I said.

Rubbing his hands together, *Naji* asked, "Great! Hey, where are the plates?" while looking around.

Standing up, I returned. "They should be in the other bag. I'll go get them." Wrapping the blanket tight around my shoulders, I walked to the front of the cave then out into the growing blizzard. As I passed through small rock formations, the ground beneath me suddenly began to shake.

"What the hell was that?" I thought to myself. Continuing towards the aero-plane, I peeked around the large boulder. Then was taken by surprise, as my mouth hung low and eyes widened.

"Hey *Craig*. What do you think this is?" A squeaky voice said.

"I don't know *Barry*. Maybe it's some kind of bird or something," a deeper voice responded.

Two enormous olive skinned men stood before me, on the opposite side of the rocks. About fifteen feet tall, they were draped in animal fur, both with black unkempt hair and horrendous teeth. Chewed bones dangled from around their necks and waists. Their padded leather armor looked a little heavier than quilted cloth, providing only basic protection.

"Giants?!" I whispered to myself.

The taller giant with the squeaky voice grabbed a hold of the *Model - 1*, putting the left-wing into its mouth. "Blah - this don't taste like no bird." He said.

So the smaller deep-voiced giant replied, "That's cuz you've gotta cook it first, ya dummy," while pulling on the other side of the *Model - 1*. Shaking it from side to side, he then lifted the entire plane up to his ear. Suddenly the cargo compartment popped open, spilling out the rest of our gear.

"Huh? I think it was pregnant," The giant said in a deep voice.

"Great. Now I can make my famous egg salad. How much do you think we'll need *Craig*?" said the larger squeaky-voiced giant.

"Just grab them all *Barry*. We'll save the rest for later," *Craig* responded in a deep baritone.

Slowly stepping back, I whispered to myself, "This isn't good, I've got to warn the others," when suddenly I accidentally kicked a rock supporting the boulder I hid behind, causing it to tumble down. Left with little room to hide, I instantly crouched low, then scurried behind what was left of my cover.

"What was that?" Said *Barry*, in a heavy *Britainus* accent.

Still examining the plane, *Craig* replied, "I don't know, go check it out."

Feeling the tremors beneath me, the giant slowly approached. Hovering over my head, I could see the humongous shadow that his massive frame cast. My heart fluttered like a hummingbird, so I held stiff like a statue.

"Hmph. Must have been a seagull or something," *Barry* said, while slowly returning to the plane.

Craig replied, "Seagulls live by the water, ya dummy. It must have been a pelican. Now, come and grab these eggs. I'm hungry." As he continued to rattle the plane.

Releasing a breath of air, I cautiously rose to my feet, preparing to leave. Suddenly, a voice shouted from behind.

"Hey *Thomas*! What's the holdup, we're starving over here!" Choosing the worst time, it could only have been -

"*Naji*." I sighed with disappointment.

Simultaneously, the giants faced *Naji*.

Craig spoke first, "Is...Is that a human?" He lurched forward.

Rubbing his hands, *Barry* hopped up and down saying. "Mmm, suppertime. He'll go good in a stew." The floor shook as they approached and I sprang from behind the rocks shouting,

"Ruuun!"

In shock, *Naji* hesitated to move as I dashed beyond him. Then drawing my pistol, I fired two rounds at the giants.

108

Unfortunately causing no damage, the bullets pinched their tough skin like a bee sting. Pulling *Naji* along, we sprinted for the cave, leaping over the jagged terrain along the way. While running, *Naji* asked, "Is that what I think it is!?"

"Oh that thing, it's just a man eating tooth fairy! Maybe you should introduce yourself!" I shouted, exasperated.

"*Sasha*! *Sasha* grab the gear!" *Naji* yelled, as we closed in on the cave.

Walking to the entrance, *Sasha's* jaw dropped in terror as she mumbled,

"Gi - gi - giants!"

Spinning around with the plane, *Craig* launched the *Model - 1* over our heads and into the cave. Ducking just in time, *Sasha* dodged the metal projectile as it crashed into pieces. Our dinner flew out of her hands and onto the cold cave floor.
"Come on!" I shouted, as we darted past the cave. With no time to mourn the loss of my invention, I focused on escaping our ogreish pursuers. Feeling the ground tremble up ahead, I could tell this wasn't going to end well...

Giant.

5 ft.

110

Chapter 7
(8 days left.)

Scurrying away from the Giants proved difficult, as we dashed from the cave in terror.

"What are we going to do!?" *Naji* yelled.

"We've got to get somewhere safe. Just keep running!" I responded.

Craig was hot on our tail as *Barry* straggled behind. With each step they shook the ground loose. In a full-on sprint, the giants pursued us with an insatiable hunger. *Craig's* voice carried, "Don't let them get away!"

Stumbling over the obscure rock cluttering our path, I could feel vibrations from up ahead. When all of a sudden, another giant approached from around some large boulders, carrying a dead animal behind his neck and shoulders.

"Hey guys, look what I found. It's a goat," He said.

Coming to a screeching halt in front of him, we were struck with fear. The plain look on his face wrinkled in confusion as he stated. "Wait a minute... Are those humans?"

"Grab em you twit!" *Craig* snapped.

Flinging the goat carcass aside, the giant then reached for us with both arms wide.

Bang!

Naji's rifle blared as it lodged a bullet well into the Giants left eye. Screaming in pain, he covered his face while stepping backwards. "Agh! My eye!"

Sprinting under his legs, I shouted. "Let's go, come on!"

Hearing the loud footsteps behind us, they came to a pause as *Craig* admonished.

"Great job *Jim*! You missed 'em!"

"Yeah, great job." *Barry* mimicked.

Giving chase once more, *Craig* shouted. "I'm going to smash 'em to pieces! Then use them for toothpicks!"

While heading down the mountain, we came to a slope. Over the years, the weather must have corroded the peak, carving crevices into the sides of the mountain. Almost resembling a maze.

Thinking quickly we ran inside, traversing the jagged interior. While zigzagging through the rocks, the giants loomed overhead, grabbing boulders to heave in our direction. Slipping in-between the cracks of the maze, we dodged the soaring rocks, as they smashed into pieces just inches away.

My heart pounded uncontrollably. The debris managed to slow our stride, allowing the Giants to close the distance. Turning corners, we hurdled over uneven rocks as the walls inside began to narrow.

"Space grow thin. We get trapped." *Sasha* stated, as moments later we came to a dead end.

"Now what?" *Naji* panted.

Feeling the floor quake once more, the maze walls began toppling down around us. As the Giants scanned the maze, tall lanky *Barry* squealed, "Look! There they are!"

Pushing my back against the wall, I desperately searched for another way out. *Sasha* tried pushing some of the rocks, while *Naji* trembled like a leaf in the wind. Realizing our fate, I shielded my face and accepted what was to come. Stomping closer, *Craig* reached down with an open hand-

Suddenly, the tremors from his large feet stomping had the entire granite maze shaking. His gigantic palm dangled ten feet from my face, as the walls wobbled once again. A small crack in the wall opened beside me.

Seizing the opportunity, I barked. "Quick! Through here!" Without hesitation, *Sasha* and *Naji* slipped through the opening. Immediately behind them, I squeezed into the space, but soon felt giant fingers wiggling at my feet.

"I've almost got 'em! Get over here and help you idiots!" *Craig* blurted.

With most of my body inside the hole, the giant was able to pry my right leg towards him.

"Guys, I'm stuck," I said in a panic, while trying to squirm free.

Sasha and *Naji* rushed to my side pulling my arm, but our strength combined wasn't enough. So drawing my sword, I raised it high then plunged the blade deep into the Giant's finger.

"Yeoow!" *Craig* screamed, yanking his hand from the hole.

"What? What is it?" *Barry* asked.

"The little bugger bit me!" *Craig* responded with anger.

Sheathing my sword, we hightailed it through the tiny space in the wall. A faint chalky smell hung in the air. The small cave began to rumble, as the giants tried breaking their way inside. Rocks steadily rained down from the dry ceiling, pelting us on the head. We desperately continued sidestepping throughout the passageway. Finally we caught sight of a light up ahead, but the space inside became tighter, forcing us to crawl awkwardly.

Suddenly, the rocks overhead began pouring down, after feeling a loud rumble from outside. "Cave falling! We not make it!" *Sasha* yelled.

Inching towards the exit, the dim light grew brighter. It was clear there was no turning back now. As the tunnel collapsed and caved-in behind us, I nudged *Sasha* and *Naji* forward.

Standing before the exit, *Naji* stuttered. "W-wa-wait!" but he was too late.

While trying not to get crushed in the narrow tunnel, I pushed *Sasha* out into the light. Like dominoes, she bumped into *Naji*, and *Naji* bumped into me, sending all three of us into a 4-second free fall down the coarse side of a mountain.

Screaming horrendously we continued to roll over, trying our best to avoid slamming into the many jagged rocks protruding from the ground. Bouncing from side to side, I resembled a snowball rolling over gravel. Being tossed onto my back, I slid over a hump spinning me onto my left side. After fumbling around I finally regained control and stabilized myself, skidding over a light layer of scree.

Looking down the hill, we eventually rolled onto a sparse field of daisies, lining the base of the mountain. Slowing us down to a complete stop. Taking a few seconds to breathe, I struggled to my feet while stretching my back and shoulders.

"That went well. Are you two okay?" I asked, rubbing my arm.

"Oh yeah, peachy. But next time, I'll take the stairs," *Naji* said, holding his neck.

"*Amazonian* good. Where giants?" *Sasha* replied, dusting off her clothes.

Looking around, I answered, "I guess we left them at the top."

"So what do now? Traveler man ma-chine dead." She asked.

"Yeah, How are we going to get back up there to fix the *Model - 1*?" *Naji* joined in.

Staring them in the eye, I thought for a second answering. "We're not... We're moving on."

"What, did you bump your head? We only have eight days before *Deacon Blues* seizes Dad's workshop AND maybe Zep-Tec. How do you plan on finding a floating island, on foot?" *Naji* ragged.
Allowing his words to sink in, I shielded the sun rays from my eyes. Starting down the bottom half of the mountain, I used my sense of navigation to determine our direction.

"Hey, where are you going?" *Naji* asked.

Instantly, I responded. "East. That's what the map says. Then that's where we'll find this floating island... Are you coming?"

Falling in line, *Sasha* used her spear as a walking stick. "You coming?" She teased *Naji*.

With a drawn out sigh, *Naji* shook his head to the side before catching up.

"Hey! Wait for me!"

Coming down the mountain, we crept past the small patch of flowers, constantly looking back in fear of the giants. Despite our unfortunate circumstance, we were enraptured by the magnificence of the landscape. The cascade of mountains were foreshadowed by beige rolling hills. In a way, the whole scene resembled the backdrop of a painting. A little past midday, the sky began to part, taking the clouds opposite our direction.

Upon reaching the base of the mountain, I noticed the temperature spike upwards. Beads of sweat built on my forehead, as the light layer of grass beneath our feet transitioned to dirt. Reading the map, *Naji* explained, "It says here there is a desert nearby, called the Saharia. Way on the other side, there's a village by a river... If we could get there, we might be able to find some help."

While he was folding the map, I replied. "Then that's where I'm heading. We're going to need some supplies."

Walking with her spear, *Sasha* was using a stone to sharpen the tip. "Sisters once tell *Sasha* story about desert." She said.

"What kind of story?" I curiously asked.

"Long ago, desert filled with animals - trees - fruits. But desert people got greedy. Kill off animals, then start enslave other travelers. Till one day big flood come. Wash away desert. Now no more trees - animals." She continued.

"So? The desert people died too?" *Naji* asked.

Sasha responded, "Sisters say some live, leave to other villages. The rest stay and die, lost forever."

Looking at the dry wasteland around us, I returned, "I guess that explains why there's nothing out here."

"Maybe, but it doesn't explain this heat. I'm burning up," *Naji* added.

"Let's keep pushing. We're bound to find some shelter," I reassured for motivation. Picking up our stride, we marched east. The sea of endless dunes were visible for miles.

Hours later, the sun began to set & the air became cool, as we walked beneath the reddish - lavender swirl in the sky. We paused for a second, to look around in a circle.

"I'm beat. What do you see?" *Naji* said while sitting down, exhausted.

Extending the small telescope, I replied with disappointment, "Just sand everywhere. Not even a cloud in the sky."

"Good, *Amazonian* rest here. Hard find cool breeze," *Sasha* stated while flopping onto her back.

Yeah, I guess you're right. I said, easing myself onto the sand. Without our supplies I knew our voyage wasn't going to be easy.

"Do we even have anything to start a fire?" *Naji* asked. Checking our inventory, I dug into my pockets and pulled out some lint, before shrugging my shoulders. Rummaging her animal hide top, *Sasha* shook her head to the side.

"Great. Everything was on the plane," *Naji* continued.

"Looks like all we've got are these weapons," I relayed with a long face.

Sharpening the final side on her stick, *Sasha* raised her newly fashioned spear.
Her ability to adapt to any environment was fascinating; she was a real survivalist. "We warriors. What else we need?" She questioned.

Seeing the confidence in her jade colored eyes, I turned to *Naji* with a smile saying,

"She's right, we've been through worse than this. Ninja assassins trying to kill us in our sleep - A huge jaguar trying to rip us a new one -"

"- oh, don't forget my favorite: giants almost flattening us like a pancake," *Naji* interrupted nonchalantly.

"-That's right, so we can take anything life throws at us. Bring it on!" I concluded.

Watching the sky turn black, a cluster of stars became visible. *Naji* laid down with his hands behind his head, closing his eyes and saying, "When we find that treasure, I'm going to buy the fastest ship anyone's ever seen."

Moments later *Sasha* curled up into a ball, shivering as the temperature dropped drastically. Scooting over beside her, I removed my waistcoat, then laid it over her body. Leaning back onto the cold sand, I gazed up at the stars then rolled onto my side, my back against hers.

Waking up refreshed, the morning rays shone upon me, warming my body. Stretching into a deep yawn, I could see *Sasha* nearby, eating from a basket of food. "Hey, where did you get those?" I asked, while sitting up right.

While chewing ravenously, she replied. "On cart over there."

Turning my head, *Naji* was stuffing his face alongside two gentlemen wearing desert clothes. The men stood near a mule driven cart with an assortment of foods bundled on the rear.
They then waved in our direction. Coming closer, *Sasha* knelt down beside me, extending a shiny green grape between her fingers. She gently placed it upon my lips.

Confused by the gesture, I gazed into her eyes, as she giggled joyfully. Placing her hands on my cheeks, she slowly leaned closer, fixing her mouth for a kiss.
Feeling my instincts propel me forward, I steadily moved into her embrace. Closing my eyes as we shared a passionate kiss.

Suddenly, I heard a crowd of laughter. Opening my eyes, I jerked my head from left to right. Five men dressed as desert traders surrounded me, each armed to the teeth with

119

swords, javelins and firearms. Looking behind them, I could see *Sasha* and *Naji*, standing near a mule driven cart. They were tied to a long chain with about a dozen others.

Bark! Bark!

Turning my head, I realized there were three black dogs surrounding me. One of the mutts stood in between my legs, licking my face. Making out with *Sasha* had been a dream. One of the traders sported a large red feather on his turban. Poking me with the blunt side of his spear, he spoke "All right, that's enough romance. The way you kissed that dog, I'd swear you've done this before."

Everyone burst into laughter. "Now get up and fall in line," The trader ordered.
I was then dragged to my feet and escorted towards the cart, by two other traders. Within seconds, they fashioned manacles over my wrist, binding me to their chain of captives. *Sasha* being the only female was in the front, followed by *Naji*. I was third in line, before a man with fresh wounds on his back beneath his shoulder length jet black hair. His torn clothes showed signs of long travel, and his pupils were solid white. It was easy to tell he was blind.

"Morning sunshine, sleep well?" *Naji* teased.

"What the hell is this? Who are these guys?" I asked curiously.
"Desert people," *Sasha* answered.

Inspecting my shackles, I replied, "But, I thought your sisters said the flood wiped them all out?"

"Sisters say some lived. Others leave to more villages," She answered.

Trying to break free I pulled on the chains, but found the cast iron too durable. Looking at my left hand, I realized my metal glove was missing.

"It's no use, kid. They've already stripped you of your weapons. They're all laying over there, in that cart," The man behind me said, with an easygoing tone. Suddenly, the trader with the red feather approached us.

"I thought I told you no talking in line, eyes front!" he yelled.

Crack!

A whip echoed as he struck the blind man across the back. Wincing in pain, the blind man responded with a laugh. "Oh I'm sorry? What was that? I'm a little hard of hearing?"

Furious from the defiance, the trader growled in anger, then lashed him three more times, before finally bringing him to his knees. Yanking him onto his feet the trader barked, "Now move!" And the caravan mobilized.

Watching the blind man wander aimlessly with his hands in front of him, I figured his time in bondage had made him suicidal. Were these traders really that bad? What were their motives?
Sasha, *Naji* and I then trudged through the sand, alongside the other captives. The mule driven cart was loaded with a bundle of stolen loot, beneath a patterned rug. The five traders rode camels on each side of us, as their mangy dogs followed. We were officially abducted, and roaming the scolding desert without direction.

For hours we walked tirelessly over a sea of sand, in silence. The gentle breeze forming zigzag patterns on the dunes was my only amusement. Nearby, a golden brown bird with zebra striped wings chewed crickets in its mouth. Raising the fan-shaped crest above his head, it began making a hooping call. If we stopped marching we were lashed, If we were caught talking we were lashed; so far it wasn't fun. The traders trailed alongside us drinking from water skins, while their flea infested dogs scanned the area.

As night began to fall the raging heat subsided, and a cool breeze rolled in. The bare sky was soon illuminated by hundreds of stars, blinking like polished diamonds. One of the traders said to the man with the feather turban, "*Baseer*? We've covered a great distance today, and the slaves are slowing down. Should we set up camp for the night?"

It then became clear that the man named *Baseer* was their leader. He thought for a second, replying,

"We need this coin to feed our village. The people of *Masai* are starving. The sooner we sell them, the sooner we get paid. But... I suppose so. We'll pick up at sunrise."

Whistling loudly, the other desert men came to a halt. The three canines then returned from up ahead.

"Set up here! Feed the prisoners!"

Feeling a tug on the chain, the captives behind me fell to the floor exhausted.

Falling onto the sand, *Naji* lamented. "Ugh - my legs. This is torture."

"*Amazonian* no want be slave. What we do traveler man? When fight?" *Sasha* said, massaging her feet through the sandals.

"Not yet. We need to get to those weapons." I replied.

Hearing our discussion, the blind man from behind said. "Well, good luck. We've already tried."

Turning around I asked. "Well? What happened?"

The blind man began to explain. "A few of my men and I were captured three days ago. We stopped to refuel a ship at a small nearby village. That's when those raiders stormed us. Once night fell, they came to loot our cargo. They managed to snatch a few of us, but the others got away. The next day we attacked them and killed one of their dogs. We almost got our hands on the weapons - but they were on to us... They killed my men, as a warning to the others."

Looking at *Sasha* and *Naji*, I held my shackles saying. "There's got to be another way."

"Oh there is." The blind man returned. "My men will come back to get me. That's when you'll have your chance to escape." Extending his hand in the wrong direction, he then added. "The name's *Spectre*."

I stared at the blind man's thin eyes. Based on his facial features, I concluded he was in his mid-thirties. He was moderately muscular and bore the tattoo of a dragon, running from his upper right arm into his chest. Wearing only a pair of tattered black pants, the scars all over his pale body matched the story.

While turning his hand the right way, I shook his hand. Introducing myself, "I'm *Thomas*. This is *Naji*, and that's *Sasha*."

Leaning forward, *Naji* waved his hands in front of *Spectre's* face. "So, are you like... really blind?"

Turning towards *Naji's* voice, he returned with a smile, "As a bat. Doctors say it's some kind of medical condition."

Moments later, one of the traders came over and began handing out rolls of stale bread and water. Walking down the chain, he then returned to the other traders who were kindling a fire. Shoving the entire loaf into my mouth, I didn't stop, not even to chew. Turning the small cup upside down, I guzzled the water in one gulp. Looking around, I could tell the other captives shared my pangs of hunger.

Naji was picking bread crumbs from the sand, as *Sasha* held her empty cup up to her eye, tapping the bottom. "Where rest of water?" She said.

Watching the traders lounge around the cozy fire and eating REAL food was hard to bear. They were sorting through the inventory on the cart, while the dogs played amongst the camels. *Baseer* drew my four barreled pistol from a sack and examined it closely.
Grinding my teeth, I chose to keep my cool.

"So? Where are we going anyway?" *Naji* asked.

Picking food from his teeth, *Spectre* answered, "To a town on the other side of the desert, called *Egyptia*."

"What for?" *Sasha* replied.

Spectre paused for a second, before continuing, "To be sold to the highest bidder…"

Baseer.

Chapter 8
(7 days left.)

"To the highest bidder?! You mean, as in SLAVES!?" I blurted.

"That's right kid, the whole nine yards," *Spectre* confirmed.

"We're already captured, why march us all the way across the desert? How do you know all of this?" *Naji* asked curiously.

Following the sound of his voice, *Spectre* explained, "Every sky pirate knows about the auction house at *Egyptia*... Where did you guys say you were from again?"

"We're from *Edenia,* and *Sasha's* a warrior from the *Amazonian* rainforest." I said.
"Figures. You three dress funny." *Spectre* replied.

"What's wrong with my suit?" I rebutted.

"It must be nice, living around the Grand *Piku* tree. With all those rivers and streams nearby, I'm sure there's plenty to eat... We don't have that luxury in the city of *Tokyio*," he said.

Feeling a wave of sympathy, I asked, "Why's that?"

"Legend has it that after all of the *Piku* trees went extinct, the wells & lakes started drying up all over *Pangea*. Then no sooner had the *Dark One* vanished, the *Wicked Forest* appeared," *Spectre* continued.

Instantly, my mind jogged back to the weird dream I had just days before. It was like a blur, but still I could hear the evil laughter echoing through my head.

I repeated, "The *Wicked Forest?*"

Spectre continued, "No one ever steps foot in there; they say it's haunted. Rumor has it, The *Dark One* has been hiding there all these years. Waiting for his chance to come back and claim his throne."

"Sounds spooky." *Sasha* replied.

Baseer strolled over then stood before us. Quickly we silenced our conversation. Darting his eyes from left to right, he viewed the slaves.

"Dinner is over! All of you get some rest! You have a lot of walking to do tomorrow," he said, with intimidation.

Turning to leave, he stared at me with speculation. The other captives then lightly mumbled amongst themselves while laying down on the sand. Seeing *Spectre* roll over and curl up, I too fell back, closing my eyes and burying my feet into the sand. It boiled my blood to see the traders carelessly relax around the campfire.

The next morning, a heatwave rolled in. We awoke to insults from the desert men and obnoxious barking from the dogs. Rushing to our feet, we were whipped in the direction of *Egyptia*. For hours, we roamed under the broiling sun, trekking the scorched sand. Horned lizards with thorn like scales buried their flat bodies under the terrain, foreshadowed by juicy cacti armored in needles. Savoring every swallow of spit, my clothes plastered to my skin like wallpaper.

127

"Water.. Water," One of the captives coughed, soon falling to the sand.

Hovering above him on a camel, one of the traders snapped his whip.

Whack! Whack!

"On your feet!" The trader roared. After standing up, the man stumbled back and forth from dehydration. Then collapsing once more, he moaned,

"Ugh..Water."

Snapping his finger, the trader signaled the dogs to attack the slave. Like hearing 'supper time', the animals flung themselves upon him, viciously biting and clawing his flesh. The man began to scream in terror, desperately begging for mercy.

Instantly I became enraged, saying, "This is crazy. We can't just sit here and let them do that."

"You're right. We have to do something." *Naji* added.

As we prepared to intervene, *Spectre* grabbed my arm.

"What are you doing?" I questioned.

Spectre replied with a smile. "Allow me." Scratching my head, I thought to myself. "What can a blind man possibly do to help?"

Walking over to the injured slave, *Spectre* took a defensive stance then gave a frightening roar, cautiously making the dogs back up. Out of spite, the trader drew back for another crack of his bullwhip, then sent it sailing through the air.

To all of our surprise, the blind man's hand moved in a flash, catching the whip barehanded just inches away from the wounded slave.

"What do you think you're doing? Fall back in line!" The trader yelled.

Tightening the whip around his hand, *Spectre* pulled it close to him, ripping the trader from his camel mount, face first onto the sand.

"Now come on, there's no need for that kind of behavior," *Spectre* teased.

Furiously the trader jumped to his feet, then grabbed a sharpened javelin from his camel's load, twirling it effortlessly.

"You think you're bad huh? Well I'll show you." The trader said, as he blitzed with the spear pointed.

Sidestepping his lunge, *Spectre* kneed the man in the ribs, then used a palm strike to the side of his face. Knocking him down onto the floor. Spinning to his feet, the trader jumped up once more.

Circling each other briefly, the trader charged again with a powerful thrust. Catching the spear head on, *Spectre* raised it high, then delivered a swift kick to his attacker's midsection, causing the desert man to curl forward in pain. *Spectre* then stepped closer, tossing his opponent to the ground with a judo hip toss.

I was astonished by his performance. The finesse he displayed was something I would have never imagined from someone who was, you know, blind.

"That's enough!" Baseer shouted. Calling the caravan to a halt, he trotted over on his red camel. "You dare make a mockery of my men and oppose my authority?" *Baseer* questioned.

"What. He started it." *Spectre* returned, following *Baseers* voice.

In no time, the other three traders surrounded him, as the one near his feet arose with anger on his face.

"You know the punishment. Make it easy on yourself.. Now assume the position," said *Baseer*. Showing another smile, *Spectre* then fell to his knees. The other three traitors took steps back, as *Baseer* raised his hand.

"Ready?" *Baseer* asked.

The defeated trader then wiggled his whip like a snake, nodding his head. Wanting to help *Spectre*, I dashed forward. When suddenly a familiar sound bellowed nearby.

Bang!

As it lifted up the sand before my feet. *Naji* held me back, pointing to one of the men on the camels. The desert man was aiming my four-barreled pistol in our direction. Shaking his head, he said. "Don't try it." I growled back menacingly.

Dropping his hand, *Baseer* gave the order. "Begin."

The defeated trader then struck *Spectre* repeatedly with his whip.

Thwack! - Whack! - Wap!

The thunderous cracks carried through the air, while he was lashed over 20 times. The skin on his back began to peel, as blood seeped like a fountain.

"That's enough...Get him back in line! *Baseer* stated.

Steering his riding beast, he headed back to the front of the caravan. Picking *Spectre* up, the trader shoved him back in line then returned to his camel.

"Are you going to make it?" I asked, surveying his wounds.

Spitting out blood, he grinned replying, "I'll be fine, kid. A samurai's spirit isn't easily broken."

"Where did you learn to move like that?" I questioned.

Spectre answered, "It's like they say. When you lose one of your senses, the others become sharper."

"Move!" *Baseer* commanded. Moments later, we were wandering the *Saharian* desert once more. For hours we covered mile after endless mile, as if *Spectre's* rebellion had never occurred. The intense dehydration led me to fear a sudden heat stroke. My feet eventually began to swell; I just hoped *Spectre* wasn't bluffing about help coming.

Once night crept in, we came to a lone palm tree. It had to be the only one around for miles.

"We must be getting close." I overheard *Baseer* say.

The slave-traders then made their decision to stop for the night. Under the shade of trees, they laid their gear. The camels sat on the opposite side of the fire alongside the dogs; not far away was their cart of goodies.

Shortly after, the traders gave us our daily provisions. While I devoured my appetizer, *Spectre* began to pour his cup of water over the wounds on his back. Wincing in pain, he asked,

"So... Where are you kids heading anyway?"

While licking the crumbs from his fingers, *Naji* replied, "We're searching for the *Lost City of Old*."

"Heh heh heh. Isn't that a bedtime story? You know, like the boogeyman?" *Spectre* teased.

"No, it real. Traveler man have map," *Sasha* retorted.

Intrigued, *Spectre* swallowed the remainder of his water saying, "Hmm. Go on?"

I then explained, "*Naji* here came across a treasure map while on an expedition with some smugglers who work for *The Baron*. He brought it to me, then -"

Spectre suddenly interrupted, "Wait a second. Did you just say *The Baron*? As in, *The Baron of the Sky*? 'Yeah? What about it?" *Naji* replied.

Spectre then propped himself onto his right elbow. "Well. He goes by the name *Lockjaw*, on account of the steel plate on his lower jaw. He wasn't such a bad guy... Well, until the power got to his head."

"Did something happen between you two?" I asked.

Glancing at the traders, *Spectre* continued, "You know what they say: 'There's no honor among thieves'. But double crossing your own men? ...That's just low."

"Yeah, I know the feeling," N*aji* added, still salty that the crew manning the *Centennial Eagle* left without him.

Spectre continued, "Well, it all started as a righteous cause. We were going to rally all the pirates together under one banner, just a group of rebels fighting to feed the people. But as the years went by, the greed set in... Soon we were smuggling spice, trafficking humans, eventually raiding the small villages we once vowed to protect. It was around that time when my guilt set in... By then, *Lockjaw* had become a tyrant, calling himself '*The Baron of the Sky*'. That's when my crew and I took his emergency vessel, *The Silver Bullet,* and went solo. She's the fastest zeppelin in the sky.

"Wait, so you stole a pirate ship? From a pirate?" I inquired.

"We didn't steal it. It was more like... We commandeered it, permanently," *Spectre* replied, following the sound of my voice.

Seconds later, *Baseer* walked over saying, "All right, pipe down and get some sleep. We wouldn't want another ACCIDENT, like this morning, now would we?" He chuckled. Turning to leave, his dogs growled, showing their fangs in our direction.

Watching him return to the campfire, I fell back onto the sand. The other captives were sound asleep, drained from days of weary travel. Overshadowed by leaves from the palm tree dancing in the wind, the lustrous stars above soothed me into a slumber.

Morning came all too quickly. My stomach grumbled and feet throbbed, as we continued day three of our *Saharian* expedition. Small sand storms chafed my skin during the journey, and now vultures were circling overhead signaling our demise. I thought to myself; "Hell, At this point, I'd rather be eaten alive than sold into slavery."

Stepping over a pair of dueling scorpions, I was startled by a shouting voice. "There it is! I can see it."

Turning my head, I followed the noise to one of the traders up ahead. Sitting on his camel, *Baseer* stared through his telescope.

"Ahh, the city of *Egyptia*. At last." He stated.

Waving his hand to the slave-traders behind, he shouted, "All right, let's get a move on! I want to be there before sunset!"

Obliging his command, the slave-trader in the back began slinging his whip, "Move- Move!" he demanded.

Forced to pick up the pace, we covered a vast distance. Between the insults and severe heat, I was actually anxious to reach our destination. As we approached the city, I could swear it was a mirage. The outskirts were lined with palm trees, and small children out front ran throughout the stables, chasing a ball.

"This is it," *Spectre* mumbled, as we entered through a gate under the city's fifteen foot reddish clay walls.

Coming through the gates, we were inspected thoroughly before entering the city. City guards carrying crossbows and kukri knives patrolled atop the clay brick crenellations. Following our captors, they led us into the dry dust-covered streets. Carts filled with fruits and vegetables cluttered the walkway, and traders selling fine oils and perfumes sweetened in the marketplace. The stands were packed with all kinds of foreign goods. Merchants hollered robustly as we squeezed through a massive crowd.

"Golden birds! Singing frogs! I've got it all! - Hey, you over there! I can tell you're a man with good taste, I've got a special for you. Look, two headed snakes!" A man haggled at *Baseer*.

"Thank you my friend, but I'm jus here to sell these slaves," *Baseer* simply replied.

Nodding his head, the man then returned to broadcasting his wares elsewhere.

We soon came to a large palace, with a dome on top glistening like solid gold. *The Mediterrissian Sea* could be seen from behind the building, as passing boats dotted the horizon. Dismounting his camel, *Baseer* greeted the palace guards.

"We're here for the auction." *Baseer* said.
One of the guards leaned over then eyed the caravan. After a brief pause, he responded. "Right this way."

Waving behind, *Baseer* signaled for his men to advance. Cracking their whips at our feet, the traders moved our convoy along like cattle. Walking through a golden gate and into a lush courtyard, we entered the main building.

An open walkway with many doors lined our path. The pearl dome above our heads could contain a small ship. There were fire jugglers twirling flaming staffs and exotic dancers winding their waists, all for crowds of spiffy noblemen. Clad in their red coats and yellow sash, the palace guards sported huge scimitars on their hips.

"Right out back. They've already begun." Said the guard, pointing to the walkway exit.

Stepping out from the lavish palace interior, the backyard converted into a port. I could taste the sea salt in the air. Sailboats and trader ships were docked nearby, as a rambunctious crowd loaded cargo back and forth. A few hot air balloons were stationed on the sides, as a couple of others drifted above.

Pulling our chains, the slave traders pushed us into the heart of the crowd. A pair of tan colored women stood before us, with a strip of white highlights in their hair. Pacing back and forth on a small wooden platform, a decorated salesman in front of them pointed to the audience:

"Do I have sixty? Fifty? Fifty gold coins - how about a-hundred? One hundred? One-hundred for this beautiful set of *Cheroki* twins - how about one-thirty? ONE-THIRTY! Going once - Going twice - SOLD to the gentleman with the purple robe!" The salesman rambled in haste.

The palace guards behind them quickly ushered the girls off stage, and into the hands of the new owner. Kicking and screaming the two girls put up a fight, as another group was then rushed on stage behind them. Turning my head, I saw *Baseer* making arrangements with some of the salesmen at the platform. A sense of worry washed over me.

"I think we're going to be next," I said, bumping *Naji's* arm.

Having trouble swallowing his saliva, he replied, "I sure hope that was a bad joke, because if not? We're running out of time."

The roar from the audience intensified my worries. The other slaves were lined up around us, shaking in fear. Some thrashed about in anger trying to escape. Then starting once more, the announcer rose his hand, showcasing the next batch.

Three muscular men of fair complexion resisted the palace guards. Putting up quite a battle, the massive men had the advantage, soon gaining the upper hand. Then two more palace guards ran on stage to even the odds. The guards then began lashing the three slaves into a mild submission, as the cheers from the crowd grew louder.

"Pfft, monsters! Treat us like animals." *Sasha* spat, while wrinkling her face in disgust.

"Wow, just look at that strength! These three *Vikinians* would be excellent for heavy loads, or even to work around the field. Let's say we start the bidding at three-hundred?" he said.

While he bartered with their freedom, *Naji* turned to me saying. "We've gotta get out of here."

"I know - I know, I'm thinking." I replied hesitantly.

"Don't worry. My men will be here soon enough." *Spectre* stated, not really affecting our concerns; he'd been saying that this entire time, to no avail.

Interrupted by his loud voice, the announcer yelled. "Sold - for six-hundred coin! Thank you for shopping, next up we have..."

Suddenly, *Baseer's* underlings began shoving us onto the platform. While escorting the muscular men down the other side, the guards yanked our chains, pulling us on stage.

"Wait a second...Do these three." *Baseer* said, holding his hand in front of them. Separating *Sasha* - *Naji* and I from the others, *Baseer* quietly spoke with the announcer. The guards then carried on.

The announcer winded himself up and began his sales pitch: "Now, here we have a triumphant trio! Each from a distant land far away. They're in great shape, and filled with youthful vigor. Let's start the bidding at two-fifty! Two-fifty it is! - Two-seventy! - Do I hear three-hundred!"

The crowd roared at the spectacle of us being sold; I wondered how they would feel if they had been sold.

"Three hundred! Can I get a three-twenty - three-twenty - three-twenty-one - three-twenty-two!" The announcer bargained, leaning closer to the audience.

Struggling with my chains, I realized they weren't going to break. Desperately, I thought of our only option.

"Run!" I shouted.

Without hesitation, *Sasha* and *Naji* bumped the guards standing beside them, as we started our escape off the platform. While trying to buy them time I lunged for the other guard, holding him back with my arms.

Bang! A shot fired.
Leaving an orange-sized hole in the floorboard before them, *Sasha* and *Naji* paused to turn around. Holding a pistol in his grasp, *Baseer* was now aiming at my head.

"If you value your friend's life, I wouldn't do that if I were you," He warned.

As *Sasha* and *Naji* looked around, we all noticed the odds were against us. *Baseers* four men along with the palace guards, slithering their whips eagerly. Returning us back to the center of the platform, the guards subdued us by our arms.

"Such a lively bunch! They've certainly got a lot of energy. Let's jump the bid up to four-fifty! Four-fifty - four-fifty, can I get a four-fifty?" The announcer continued with excitement.

"Me! - Over here! - I'll give you 470!" A shockingly overweight man crowd blurted anxiously.

"Sold! To the plump man with... Unique tastes," the auctioneer responded.

The palace guards then rushed us off the platform. Our obese bidder was draped in jewels, standing near four athletic men wearing only skin tight red underwear.

"Yoo-hoo, over here." He said, twinkling his fingers in our direction as the palace guards handed us over.

"Where is the help that *Spectre* guy said was coming? I knew he was a fraud," *Naji* lamented.

"You three look scrumptious. You're going to love it at my palace," the buyer stated with a heavy lisp. Clapping his hands he turned to his servants, he haughtily commanded, "Boys? Prepare for departure. I want these two in uniform and inspection ready...The girl stays with me."

He moved over to a bizarre, ornately decorated golden throne that was built spread out wide like a sofa. Laying down, he began fanning himself with a large feather. Nodding their heads, the servants handed *Naji* and I two pairs of crimson colored man-panties, before running to hoist the four corners of their master's wide chair. Patting the seat beside him, our buyer teased,

"Coming sweetie?"

Sasha stepped back immediately frightened, but was pushed forward by the palace guards. "*Amazonian* no want be a slave. She whimpered, facing *Naji* and I as she was forced onto the couch.

v

Eyeing the panties in our hands, *Naji* exclaimed. "There is no way I'm putting this on... Besides, it's not even my size."

Staring at *Naji* with skepticism, I turned to the platform. *Spectre* was now being thrown on stage by himself.

"Here's a tough one folks, with the heart of a lion. Should go well in a breeding stable. Let's start the bid at three-ten!" The announcer continued, "three-thirty, I've got three-thirty! - three-forty, Over here! - fifty, I've got three-fifty!" The crowd barked.

Lowering his head, *Spectre* brandished a smirk. His calm was actually unusual for this situation. All of a sudden, a large shadow was cast over the auction. Looking upwards, I noticed something huge plummeting from the sky. The crowd murmured in speculation, as the announcer put his hand above his eyes, squinting.

"What in *Pangea* is that?" He questioned.

As the silhouette came closer, *Naji* asked, "Is that? Is that?.. A zeppelin?"

140

Cannons then began firing from above, blowing chunks out of the palace. Instantly the audience went into a frenzy, screaming in panic. They dispersed in all directions, confusing the guards. A platoon of sword-wielding figures then repelled from the sky on ropes. Wasting no time, they wreaked havoc on the palace guards. Raising his head, *Spectre's* smile suddenly widened as he winked in our direction. He was then set free by one of the sky pirates, and given a katana.

Seizing our opportunity to escape, I nodded to *Sasha* and *Naji*, shouting. "Let's go! Now is our chance!"

Spectre.

Chapter 9
(7 Days left.)

Slamming into the guard running past me, I elbowed him in the belly then gave him an uppercut. Pushing him to the floor, *Naji* swung around, clocking another guard with a backhand. Reaching into their scabbards, I tossed *Naji* a sword, then cut his chains allowing him to then smash open mine.

As we rushed towards *Sasha*, I saw her already sizing up the pompous lard sitting beside her. Raising from her seat, she strained for a moment while pulling on her chains.

"What - what - what are you doing? Please sit down? We have to get out of here." Our buyer trembled with eyes wide.

Without warning *Sasha* broke free with a loud clang as her manacles dropped to the floor. Grabbing the man's arm, she yanked him from the couch with her impressive Amazonian strength and began swinging him around vigorously. While picking up speed, he gave a high-pitched scream. She let him go, sending him headfirst into a barrel of bananas. An overstimulated gorilla on a leash rushed towards him.

Jumping down from the couch, *Sasha* grabbed a nearby javelin. Looking at the men wearing the underwear, she stated, "No more slave! Free now!" As they stared at each other in shock, the four men finally got the message and then disappeared into the crowd. The twin *Cheroki* women with white bangs were also set free. Scurrying like mice, they ran amongst the pandemonium.

Cannons blared overhead, steadily leveling the palace, piece-by-piece. The palace guards were having a difficult time fighting off the small brigade of pirates. Carving a path through the crowd, *Spectre* fought his way towards *Baseer* and his band. Focusing up ahead, I could see *Baseer* making a run for his donkey driven cart.

"Over there! He's getting away with our stuff!" I shouted.

"Free the others. We'll meet back here!" I told *Sasha* and *Naji*, then dashed into the noisy mosh pit.

While pushing traders and merchants aside, I spun a woman holding her child around in a circle and steadied her before continuing my rush. I bumped into a palace guard, quickly jamming my stolen scimitar into his chest and continuing my advance. In front of me, two more guards were up ahead, coming my way. As the one in front took a wild swing, I dodged to the right, then countered with a left hook to his jaw before kicking him to the floor. Hearing a blade slice through the air behind me, I instantly spun around, managing to deflect a penetrating strike. Wasting no time, I pulled back my sword, then plunged it into the enemy's abdomen. Running along, I left them there to be trampled by the stampede of civilians.

Looking to the side, I could see *Sasha* and *Naji* freeing the slaves by breaking their chains. Aiding the pirates, the freed slaves helped turn the tides. Once they armed themselves, most of them chased after their owners.

Finally catching up to *Baseer*, *Spectre* dueled with three of the remaining slave traders from our desert expedition, blocking a high attack, then parrying a spear from his left side. *Spectre* sprang forward delivering a fatal blow, severing the closest one's arm. Like a ballerina he twirled around, deflecting their attacks.

Joining the mix, I entered with a surprise attack, leaving a wide gash on the back of an enemy. *Spectre* then blitzed the last man standing, frightening our opponent into submission. Throwing his weapon to the floor the slave trader turned around, running in the other direction.

"I told you my men would show." *Spectre* said, lowering his blade.

Watching *Baseer* rummage through our inventory, I said. "We're not done yet, look."

Baseer then retrieved my four barrel pistol from the cart. Pointing it in our direction, he slowly approached.

"Well well well. You two have caused quite the ruckus. Good thing I've got all this gold, huh." He said, while bouncing a bag of coins in his left palm. "It's a shame what you did to my men. They were good people - once you got to know them. No matter. With all this gold they can be replaced. I want you both to know, it wasn't personal, just business. I sell goods, that's what I do." He continued.

"I didn't break out of those chains to hear your life story. It's time to pay up," *Spectre* replied.

Baseer then chuckled. "I'm sorry you feel that way, I guess we should wrap this up then." Pulling the hammer back, he raised the gun along its site. When suddenly, a javelin came soaring from behind us, impaling his hand.

"Yaagh!" He screamed in agony, dropping the gun.

Simultaneously, *Sasha* and *Naji* appeared through a mob of wailing noblemen. Surrounding them were the freed slaves who accompanied us during our travel.

"Nice throw *Sasha*. Hey *Baseer*! Look who we found? Some old friends - and boy, do they look angry." *Naji* teased. Watching the unruly mob twist and wrinkle their faces, *Spectre* turned to *Baseer* saying,

"You know what? Despite the fact you herded us like cattle without any food, and all the cruel lashings, you're not so bad. And I can forgive you."

Handing one of the captives his sword, *Spectre* left *Baseer* on the floor, then walked to the cart.
"But, I'm not so sure that these guys feel the same way... Nothing personal, just business," he continued with a smirk.

Picking up nearby weapons, all of the slaves slowly began to encircle him. Kneeling on the floor, Baseer scanned his surroundings, still holding his palm oozing with blood.

"No - wait. It - it - it was a mistake. Please - stop - Ahhh!" He pleaded dearly.

Seconds later the captives pounced upon him like lions on the gazelle, skewering him like a shish kabob.

"Let's grab our things. It's time to get out of here." I mentioned.

Dashing for the cart, we dumped the loot onto the floor, then pilfered our stolen goods. Once we were suited up, one of *Spectre's* men approached.

"There's a large battalion of reinforcements coming from the front of the city. What should we do sir?" He panted. Grabbing his polished katana and a pair of black sunglasses from the cart, *Spectre* replied,

"All right, we're pulling out. Our job is done here, tell the others to fall back to the ship."

"Yes sir!" The pirate yelled, saluting his captain. Fastening his scabbard, *Spectre* put on his square framed shades.

"It's been fun, kid. Hope you find that treasure you're looking for," He said.

"Thanks for the help," I replied with a smile.

Nodding his head, he finished retrieving the rest of his gear. Trotting backwards, *Spectre* added, "Now if I were you, I'd get going. This place is about to get a lot less friendly," as they then disappeared into the crowd.

"Found it!" *Naji* shouted, pulling the treasure map from *Baseer's* mangled body.

Toting our bags we ran for the docks, hoping to find a boat. Just my luck, they were all gone and were sailing off, too far to swim behind. The cannons continued to roar overhead, as the screams grew wilder. Smoke from the rubble and gunfire filled the air.

"More soon come. Where go to?" *Sasha* said, fanning the air.

"Quick, that way!" *Naji* exclaimed, pointing to a brown hot air balloon.

While we sprinted for our escape, the palace reinforcements arrived. Racing for the balloon we encountered opposition, only a few yards away. Feeling a surge of confidence I searched my bag, retrieving my time-tested metal glove. Slipping it on, I quickly balled up my fist.

Instantly, the thin sheet of metal spun clockwise from behind my hand creating a buckler shield, and I was ready for action. Drawing my sword from behind my waist I slung it around, slashing one of the guards across the face. While *Naji* blitzed for the other two guards delivering a shoulder attack, then swung his scimitar from side to side. Following suit, *Sasha* grabbed a fallen spear.

Standing in front of the hot air balloon, we began throwing our things inside the basket. "Oh no, look!" Said *Sasha*.

An army of palace guards had stormed the crowd, laying siege to any pirate or slave in reach. Once onboard I frantically surveyed our vehicle. "Where are the controls - how do we fly this thing?" I questioned.

"Who cares, just do something! We're running out of time!" *Naji* replied.

Suddenly, the three muscular *Vikinian* slaves from the auction floor emerged from the crowd. Coming to the balloon, one of them asked. "What are you all still doing here? Is there room for three more?"

"Sure, but? I can't get this thing to work." I responded.

"Pull the lever above you, that should raise your altitude." The man returned. So pulling the mechanism, I released a burst of fire in the balloon. Slowly lifting us off the ground.

"We're running out of time, they're too close," The *Vikinian* lamented. Then bending down, he began picking up the basket. With all his might, he strained endlessly.

"What are you doing? There's still time, you guys can make it!" I shouted.

Continuing to hoist the hot air balloon basket over his head, he paid me no attention. Then squatting his legs he exploded upward, tossing us High into the air. Rushing to join his two comrades in battle, he then waved farewell, as the trio valiantly dueled dozens.

Climbing in altitude, we surveyed the mayhem below. Palace guards were finally regaining control of the auction, and the captives who weren't lucky enough to escape were enslaved once more. Pearl colored herring gulls plunged into the sea, feeding off the edible garbage lying around the dock. Way up in the sky, I could make out *Spectre's* shiny zeppelin - *the Silver Bullet.* In no time, they pierced through the pillowy clouds like a marshmallow, vanishing without a trace.

"You no say *Sasha* would be slave, traveler man?" *Sasha* said, leaning back into the basket.

"Yeah, I don't remember reading that in the fine print," *Naji* sarcastically chimed in.
Tugging on the lever, I steadied the balloon, lowering my guard with a sigh of relief.

"We should be safe now. I don't think they'll be able to catch us from way up here... So? What does the map say?" I stated while looking over the edge. Fumbling through his pocket, *Naji* opened the wrinkled parchment. Running his finger across the paper, his forehead wrinkled in confusion. "Well, what does it say"? I repeated.

Flipping it over he mumbled. "*Thomas.* You're not going to believe this - heh heh, but?.. I think I grabbed the wrong map."

"What?! Please, tell me you're joking?" I barked.

"I wish I were, see for yourself." He replied, handing me the map.

Snatching the paper from his hand, my eyes scanned from top to bottom. It read : " Discount flier - 40% off all sales at the '*Water Lily*'...Where your happiness is Just a Touch Away." A tiny diagram was in the corner for directions.

"Great, so now we've got no map - no direction - no plan. And worst of all, we've got about seven days left before we're homeless... This just keeps getting better." I said, sliding down onto the floor.

Taking the paper from my hand, *Sasha* read it carefully. "This map no lead to treasure? It lead to *Singaporia*, city in sky. *Amazonian* tell *Sasha* this *Lady Lotus* home... Maybe we follow direction and find traveler mans map?" she proposed.

Naji stood up saying, "*Sasha*, I'm not sure who this '*Lady Lotus*' is, but that sounds like a great idea! We'll take the directions on this flier and follow it to the city. Someone there has got to know the way. What have we got to lose?"

Angrily, I stared him in the eye. But soon realized he had a point. What other options DID we have? Nodding my head, I agreed. "Fine. Lead the way."

"With pleasure, captain!" *Naji* smiled optimistically. Manning the controls of the balloon, he steered us higher into the clouds, following the diagram on the paper. The sun rays grew dim as dusk approached.

Once night had fallen, the air became chilled and the moon glowed a fluorescent white. Being up so high, one could swear it was only a spear throw away. A few hours had passed by and *Naji* had already given up, succumbing to his fatigue. *Sasha* directed the balloon from there.

Looking out at the stars, I said. "It's wonderful isn't it? The view from up here is spectacular."

"Yeah, sky beautiful. *Sasha* no see stars so close from rainforest." *Sasha* replied, beaming her contagious smile.

Moving to the other side of the basket, I looked down below. We were enveloped in a tunnel of clouds. Sheets of fluffy cotton coasted beneath us, and walls of gray fuzz rolled above.

"Earlier today you said something about a *Lady Lotus*? What have you heard about her?" I asked.

Staring out into the distance, *Sasha* answered, "Little. Sisters say *Lady* small, but have big power. She run city by herself, no need man. Bandits all over come see."

Holding my arms, I rubbed my chin replying. "Interesting."

All of a sudden, an ear shattering boom echoed around us. A bright flash of light sent fear coursing through my veins, forcing me to duck by reaction. Curling up near the floor, I huddled close to *Sasha*. Slowly rising to my feet, I realized it was nothing more than thunder and lightning.

Laughing lightly Sasha took my hand, helping me up. "Traveler man safe, just weather," she reassured me.

"Yeah, it was just the weather - heh heh. I - I wasn't scared or nothing," I stated, peeking over the basket.

As my eyes lingered on the dimples in her caramel cheeks, she began to giggle. Rain ushered forth from the clouds, drizzling over the edge of the balloon. Holding my palm out in the open, a puddle of cold water quickly formed.

"Looks like a storm's brewing," I said.

Seconds later, two terrorizing bursts of thunder clapped throughout the sky. Instantly *Naji* awoke, startled by the streaks of lightning streaming across the clouds. Looking right to left, the sky had become pitch black and the clouds a dark shade of purple.

"Where the hell are we?" *Naji* asked, scratching his head.

While looking down at the compass from my pocket, the needle spun erratically. Pointing in many directions. No surprise there, I thought.

"I'm not sure. But it looks like a thunderstorm," I replied.

BOOM! BA -BA - BOOM!

Thunder roared as blue lightning pierced the sky, leaving a streak like shattered glass. Gusts of strong winds swept us to and fro, causing the basket to spiral. Shortly after, the turbulence increased immensely & rain heavily poured down, pelting the sides of the balloon and spraying us in gusts.

Bracing for impact I bent low, clamping on to the railings inside the basket. I couldn't see fifty feet in either direction. *Sasha* and *Naji* rocked from side to side as we were tossed about.

Suddenly, a bird appeared from the clouds below. And then another. Before I knew it, there was a flock of white birds flapping their black spotted wings up ahead. Desperately trying to escape the weather, they screeched frantically. Some were so frightened, they even began to attack each other.

"Are those eagles!?" *Naji* questioned.

"No! *Gyr falcons*!" I informed.

Flapping their wings closer to the balloon, I could tell these were not average birds. Their bodies were double ours in size, and their wingspans were easily twenty foot. It was clear these were giants.

"This just keeps getting better!" *Naji* exclaimed.

"Caw - Caw!" The birds screamed as the thunder and lightning raged on. A handful of birds then slammed into the sides of the balloon, each pecking at the basket.

"Thunder scare birds!" *Sasha* exclaimed, readying her spear. "If balloon pop, we fall!"

Pulling my pistol, I replied. "She's right. We've got to drive them away from the balloon!"

BANG!

Firing a round in the air, I tried scaring them away. *Sasha* leaned over the edge and swung her spear from side to side, only inciting their riot. Ferociously, the birds lunged their giant beaks into the carriage, biting whatever they could. *Naji* managed to finally retrieve his rifle, then discharged a couple shots at our aggressors. Startling the birds, they pushed off the balloon as a defense maneuver. Except for one, which took a bullet to the wing.

Screeching in pain, it slowly dropped beneath the clouds, leaving us with one less problem to worry about- or so I thought. Enraged by the loss of a flock member, they called to each other adamantly. Swooping in, the falcons all came from multiple sides.

Swinging their beaks and swiping their talons, the birds pummeled our basket. Ducking from one corner to another, I crawled throughout the basket. Then as I raised my gun to fire, it was knocked loose by violent winds, tossing me around. Staring one of the birds in the eye, I tensed up before it's fatal strike.

In that instant a spear intercepted the attack, as *Sasha* slid in between us. With daring courage beyond that of most warriors, she spun the tip of her spear, distracting the bird, before impaling its eye. Quickly withdrawing her weapon, she turned towards the other *Gyr-Falcons* behind us. Squirming its neck out the basket, the wounded bird flew off in the opposite direction.
With a rapid shot, *Naji's* rifle bucked vibrantly, gashing the foot of an adversary. *Sasha* aided by piercing its stomach, then pushing it outside the basket with her spear. Reaching for my sword, I leapt forward with a flurry of wild swings, sending the other birds a clear message.

"Caw - Bacaw!"

The falcons up ahead signaled to the others while flying away from the hot air balloon. They soon caught up with the rest of the flock, flapping their wings towards a silver lining in the clouds. Kneeling down, I retrieved my pistol.

"Where do you think they're going?" I asked.

Lowering his rifle, *Naji* walked to the edge and replied, "I don't know, but look... The rains are stopping."

In the distance, the thin clouds began to part, revealing a magnificent orange hue on the horizon. The once dark and gloomy landscape was now returning to its natural color. Before long, we were engulfed in layers of cirrostratus clouds. Reaching my hand over the railing, I could feel a cold mist forming between my fingers, a once-in-a-lifetime experience. My trance was broken by the sudden realization that we weren't alone in this magical cloudscape-

Drifting above the clouds there she was...

Model - 1.

5 ft.

Chapter 10
(6 Days left.)

High above the clouds, a layer of fog served as the floor beneath us. A massive piece of land hovered before me in the sky, like an iceberg floating through water. A mountain range rose to the top, where manmade structures hung from the side of a cliff. A towering pagoda overlooked the peak.

Singaporia: The city in the sky.

It was truly a sight to behold. As we came closer, the trimmings on the buildings became visible. Golden pillars and cherry blossoms sat under the triangular red-tiled roofs. An array of zeppelins cluttered the sky, most docked on the landing bridges.

"Look at this place. It's unreal," *Naji* uttered in awe.

Coasting along the edge, our hot air balloon scaled the floating island. Thick branches sprouted from the cliffside, some holding the buildings in place.

Pointing to a crowded platform, *Naji* blurted. "There's a spot!"

Pulling the lever above our basket, the warm air inside the balloon was released, lowering our altitude. Moments later we safely landed, avoiding the other vessels. Climbing over the basket's woven rim, we grabbed our gear and headed for the city's entrance.

The port authorities and guards were stationed in separate units. Overseeing the city from tall guard towers, they carried rifles strapped to their shoulders and sheathed rapiers. The symbol of a white lotus was painted onto their chainmail shirts, with hundreds of interlocking rings.

Walking onto a noisy narrow street, the sweet aroma of fried foods carry the four blocks.
It wasn't hard to tell that the city was overcrowded. A herd of people roamed in all directions, under the paper lanterns strung about like spiderwebs. The fitted flagstone walkways held mold in the cracks, probably from years of water sitting in puddles between the stones.

"Let's try to keep a low profile." I advised.

"From who? Look at this place. It's like a hub for sky pirates. One of these guys has got to know something that will lead us to the *Lost City*," *Naji* replied.

Looking around, I realized he had a point. The gentleman surrounding us were of a different caliber. Scruffy guys with tattoos and eye patches, carrying swords. Vagabonds and ruffians of all colors, shapes, and sizes showed each other their scary faces. It was a real fashion show.

Just then, *Sasha's* stomach rumbled."*Amazonian* no scared of man. Need food, belly empty," she groaned.

"Now that sounds like a plan, I second that," *Naji* returned hastily.

Passing a few fireworks stands, I noticed a man eating a bowl of noodles in front of a wide building. Tall red painted wooden doors towered over the walkway.

"Let's try this one." I mentioned.

Entering the small courtyard, beautiful lotus flowers were carved around the red stone wall. Opening the doors, we stepped inside and were greeted by a hint of myrrh tickling our nostrils. Minstrels were playing a tranquil melody on their *Liuqin* by the corner. Petite women tiptoed across the marble floor, escorting pirates through the many sliding paper doors only used for blocking nosy eyes.

Coming to the counter, *Sasha* commented, "*Sasha* no think this place sell food."

An elderly woman wearing her gray hair in a bun, bowed her head to us from behind the counter. "Welcome to the *Water Lily*. You three look weary. No worry, we take good care of you. Come, follow me," she said pleasantly.

Confused, I looked around the room, replying, "Umm,We were actually looking to buy some food. You wouldn't mind pointing us in the right direction, would you?"

"Oh, you look for food, yes? No worries, we give you plenty to eat. My girls make you so plump, you never leave. Come, see for yourself." The old woman responded, squinting her eyes with a smile.

"Thanks, but no thanks. We were really just hoping to find some - " I restated, until *Naji* chimed. "Wait - Wait - Now wait a minute *Thomas*, let's see where this goes. I'm up for the SPECIAL PLATTER." Elbowing my side.

Ready to leave, *Sasha* and I started for the exit.

Suddenly, a figure stepped out from the room behind us. Holding a bottle of rum in his hand, he chuckled. "Heh heh, you naughty girl. Don't worry, I'll be back. Just let me grab a refill."

"*Spectre*? Is that you?" I blurted.

Following the sound, he turned around then threw his hands up in surprise. "Hey, I remember that voice! Glad to see you're alive!"

It was none other than the *Spectre* himself, wearing a red silk robe, with golden lotus patterns. Dropping my gear, I walked to greet him with a handshake. "Well, aren't you a sight for sore eyes."

While shaking his hand, I spotted a familiar silver ring with a black and red stone in the middle. Back in *Bloomsfield,* Hyatt had also worn an identical ring on another finger.

"What brings you to *Singaporia*? You didn't strike me as the brothel type." He replied.

"We were on our way to continue our adventure, when we realized that we grabbed the wrong map. The directions led us here," I responded, scratching my head.

"Oh, you don't say," He replied.

Suddenly, my belly rumbled like a purring cat, reminding me of our quest for food.

"Well, it was nice meeting you again. Now if you'll excuse us, we were on our way to get some grub," I returned, holding my stomach.

"Nonsense, stay a while! After what those desert guys put us through? We deserve a break. Come on, you've earned it," *Spectre* bargained.

Catching the starving look on *Sasha* and *Naji* faces, I humbly declined. "Nah, we should really get going."

"We've got plenty of food in here. I'm not taking no for an answer," *Spectre* insisted, while pushing us inside.

Sliding open the doorway, a short woman dashed in front of us giggling uncontrollably. Chasing behind her was a rugged fellow with a scary face. As I looked around, I noticed the room was filled with women in their underwear, and a crew of about a dozen thugs wearing matching red robes and fuzzy slippers. A buffet of fine meats, fruits and vegetables were laid across a table in the middle of the large room.

"Sorry, I didn't know you had company. We can come back later," I said, backing out the doorway lightly.

"Don't be so modest, enjoy yourself," *Spectre* returned, scooting us inside.
"Of course we'll stay awhile. This is my kind of party." Naji added, sporting a devilish grin.
Spectre then walked past us with his arms stretched in front of him, feeling his way inside the room.

"Hey guys, listen up! These are those kids I told you about, remember? From the desert? It's cool, they're with me!" He announced. Raising their mugs, *Spectre's* men greeted us with a hearty cheer, before diverting their attention to the flirtatious concubines accompanying them.

"You're in good hands, kid," He continued.

Dropping his gear by the door, *Naji* made his way to the buffet, then began cramming handfuls of plump, pink shrimp down his esophagus. Right behind him, *Sasha* fell upon the assorted fruits like a bird of prey. Nearly dehydrated, I headed to the bar for a refreshing drink.
One of *Spectre's* men sporting a snake tattooed across his face held out his hand stopping me.

"Hey kid, ya drink rum?" he asked.

Shaking my head, I told him, "No."

then passed me a clear bottle; the fumes from inside made me slightly light-headed, as I'd never tried alcohol before. My father would drink a glass of whiskey every now and then, but he wasn't an alcoholic, so it was pretty rare to find a bottle around the house. But nonetheless I felt adventurous, so I decided to take a sip.

Cough - Cough - "Blagh!"

I choked once the liquid fire hit my insides, scratching my throat along the way.

"I think I'll just stick with some milk." I said, returning the bottle.

"Hahaha, suit yourself kid." The pirate laughed.

Grabbing a tin flask full of milk, I fell back onto a leather sofa. Turning the flask upside down, I savored every drop. In a nearby chair, a woman sat on *Spectre's* lap. Sitting perfectly still, he stared me down, only instead of his eyes it was his ears that were locked onto me. He finally asked. "What are you kids doing so far away from home anyway? Where are your parents?"

Watching *Sasha* and *Naji* devour piece after piece of what was once a turkey, I answered, "Like I've said before, we're searching for the *Lost City of Old*. I'm hoping to use the coin from whatever treasure we find to save Zep-Tec and my family's workshop from an evil landlord. I'm an Inventor, *Naji's* a traveler, and we met *Sasha* during our stay in the *Amazonian* rainforest. We were piloting a prototype aircraft, until it crashed in the mountains near the *Saharia*. Shortly after, that's when we met you. My parents?... They passed away years ago."

"Sorry to hear that. My old man died before I was born. And my mother? Heck, once I became a sky pirate she didn't want anything to do with me. Heh heh, some life huh?" *Spectre* responded.

"What made you turn to piracy? You don't seem like a bad guy." I questioned.

Rubbing the fine silk threads on his robe, he replied. "Well *Thomas*, why not? It's a life of adventure, freedom; no restrictions. It's answering to your own rules, and not some made-up laws. Besides, my older brother and I made an oath: that one day, we'd make it out of the slums, you know? Make a name for ourselves... Looks like your friend over there's getting the hang of it."

He pointed in the general direction of *Naji, who* was sandwiched between two scantily-clad women, dancing between them. Twirling his shirt above his head, he shouted,

"Yahoo! Partaaay!"

Anyone with eyes could tell that *Naji* was an individual who challenged tradition. He avoided authority; he was unpredictable but not totally random.

Shaking my head, I returned. "He was dropped on his head as a child."

Spectre chuckled then took a swig from a nearby bottle of rum. "Ahh, sailing the skies - looting crooks. It doesn't get any better than this, kid."

Holding her belly, *Sasha* waddled over like a pregnant walrus. "Ughh, *Amazonian* no feel good. No want see food ever again," she moaned in her native tongue, falling face-first into the couch.

As she laid sprawled across my lap, I rubbed her back. "Well, you guys did eat enough for a whole village. You'll be okay," I said with a smile.

Spectre took another swig, giving me a smirk before saying, "Well don't you two look comfortable.. I think you would make a nice couple."

"Who us? Really?" I questioned awkwardly.

Watching the hair sway over her face, it was then I consciously admitted that *Sasha* was far more attractive than any of the girls back home. And ever since she had tagged along, I felt a growing connection between us, giving me butterflies every time we locked eyes. There was no denying it; I was developing a crush on *Sasha*. But with everything happening around us these past few days, how could I tell her how I felt? It would only complicate things.

"Who knows? Maybe some day? Heh heh." I replied sheepishly, hoping to change the subject.

Pulling the *Water Lily* flier from his pocket, *Naji* crumbled it up.

"Well, we don't need this anymore," he said as he threw it aside. The crumpled ball rolled into *Spectre's* foot.

Picking it up, *Spectre* unfolded it. "Hey, where did you get this flier? This feels like the one in my pocket." He asked.

Leaning on his side, he dug through his back pocket, then pulled out a tattered brown parchment. Opening it wide, he said. "Wait a second? This isnt mine?"

Noticing the markings on the parchment, *Naji* shouted. "The treasure map, that's it! How did you get that?"

Scratching his head, *Spectre* gave *Naji* the map as he walked over.

"Good question? Must have grabbed the wrong paper back at the auction," he returned.
Scooting *Sasha* to the side, *Naji* dropped down in between us.

"Sweet, now we can get a move on. It says here that there should be some kind of a cavern nearby. If we hurry, we can still make it!" he rambled.

"*Amazonian* ready. Help find treasure," *Sasha* returned, clenching her fists with enthusiasm.

"Wait? That balloon we're flying isn't going to cut it. It's too slow," I agreed, then thought for a second.

"Yeah, you're right," *Naji* replied.

"So what we do, traveler man?" *Sasha* asked.

While I was biting my fingernails in deep thought, *Spectre* answered, "You'll be taking my ship."

"What? The *Silver Bullet*? Isn't there a bounty on that thing?" *Naji* questioned.

"Bounty-shmounty, she's the fastest bird in the sky. Unless, you'd rather ask all the other nice pirates to let you use their ships? I'm sure they wouldn't mind using you as figureheads," *Spectre* jested.

"We appreciate your offer but... Why would you want to help us?" I asked, trying to sense his motives.

165

Shaking his bottle of rum, he responded, "I like your style, kid. You're genuine, a real diamond in the rough. Your father's invention pretty much shaped the new world, so for that I thank you... Besides, if the legend is true? There will be more treasure than any of us can carry. Not to mention one of those *Power Crystals*. Rumor has it, they're an unlimited power source... I'd hate to see it fall into the wrong hands," the more he spoke, the bigger his grin grew, displaying the gold tooth in his mouth.

"Unlimited power, huh? Sounds expensive," *Naji* responded, rubbing his chin.

"I don't believe in magic," I returned.

Reclining further into his seat, *Spectre* continued, "Oh this ain't magic, kid. It's the real deal. So?.. What do you say?"

Looking at *Sasha* and *Naji*, I gauged their reactions. Spectre's intention seemed honest, and he WAS hospitable. But during my stay in Edenia, I learned to never trust a pirate. So with few options, I made our decision.

"All right, count us in. But only as crew members, Not as slaves. No funny business." I said with a stern voice, extending my hand.

"Hahaha, aye-aye captain!" *Spectre* teased, while shaking my hand. "Relax, you're in good hands."

With that he stood up, yelling, "All right, listen up! A change of plans! Our new mission is to get these three to the *Lost City of Old*! This is *Thomas*, he'll be my second-in-command, whatever he says goes, capeesh?!"

"Aye-aye, captain!" His men sounded in unison, their frothy mugs held high. Immediately after, the man with a serpent tattoo mumbled,

"But sir? Isn't that story an old wives tale?"

"Perhaps, but we'll never know until we find out. Now everyone, roll out!" *Spectre* replied.

"Yes sir!" The man returned with a salute.

After changing out of their complimentary silk robes and fuzzy slippers, *Spectre* and his men grabbed their gear and loaded up. *Sasha, Naji* and I made one last stop at the buffet, shoveling whatever food could fit into our luggage. The lovely woman from the *Water Lily* affected melodramatic sadness to see the crew leaving so soon. They pleaded like whimpering puppies, but eventually ceased.

Moments later we filed out, leaving the brothel. As we squeezed through the crowded twisting streets, *Spectre* informed us that his ship was at the port up ahead. Coming to a large gathering of civilians we soon paused, trying to walk around the dense crowd. Fireworks were bursting in the air, and streamers were being thrown over head. A small marching band was playing music, and dancers paraded around the musicians, wearing colorful costumes.

A luxurious woman sat in the center, raised on a golden throne. Wearing a white lotus flower in her long black hair she was basking in elegance, as four city guards carried each corner of the chair beneath her. She waved to the people, side to side.

"That must be her. The *Lady Lotus,*" *Sasha* explained.

Instantly, I was mesmerized by her beauty.

"Come on, kid. There's a shortcut just up ahead," *Spectre* stated, nudging my arm.
Right at that moment, a soothing voice called out:

"*Tenshi*?! *Tenshi Akari*?! By *Shenzo's* ghost, is that really you?"

As I turned around, the woman on the throne was staring in our direction.
"Let me down." She politely said to her guards.

Stepping down, her long white dress appeared to glide over the floor when she walked. Red flowers outlined in gold were patterned all over her long-sleeved gown. She then approached us with her entourage.

"I overheard the *Silver Bullet* was back in town. I knew it had to be you." *Lady Lotus* said.

Dropping his gear, *Spectre's* eyes widened, as he trailed the sound of her soft voice.

"*Mei-ling*? It can't be? How many years has it been?"

Coming closer, they embraced each other with a passionate hug. The parade now encircled us. Stunned by her elegance, Spectre's men looked on in confusion.

"Wait? You know the *Lady Lotus*?" *Naji* asked, hypnotized by her glamor.

"Know her? How could I forget?" *Spectre* replied, holding her hand.

"You never told us you were royalty, Captain," One of *Spectre's* men added.

The *Lady Lotus* giggled joyously, responding, "He's not royalty. But we were once engaged."

"Funny, you never struck me as the married type. What happened?" I asked in surprise.

Spectre sighed deeply, then began to explain, "Back when my brother and I left home, we joined up with a group of freedom fighters from the local villages nearby. That's when I met *Lockjaw. Mei-ling* and I were already going steady, and I wanted to propose but didn't have the coin for a ring. So I tagged along on a joint expedition searching for the *Jeweled Mountain*. We were told it sat on a large cache of precious stones. Now, no one had ever really seen one of these *Power Crystals* before. So I figured, a piece of one would make one hell of a gift.
Only problem was, once we thought we had found it, *Lockjaw* & his boys stole the damn thing right from under me, leaving us for dead."

Lady Lotus responded, "*Tenchi*, I had no clue. When you left, things just weren't the same. I packed my things and moved here to *Singaporia* with my uncle. At the time he was still the king, with no successors. Shortly after, he fell ill and passed away, bestowing the kingdom unto me."

She then gently caressed *Spectre's* cheek saying. "You don't have to impress me, Tenchi. I've liked you just the way you are."

"I'm a man of my word and a promise is a promise. That's the pirate's code," he returned, lowering her hand with his.

Giving up, *Lady Lotus* bowed her head, regaining her elegant composure and poise.

"I guess some things never change. One of these days, you'll realize it's the small things that matter in the end... There will always be a place for you here," she said, raising her head.

"Thank you, *Mei-ling*. It was nice meeting you again. Now, we should get going. Duty calls," *Spectre* declared. Picking up his gear, he signaled his men for departure.

"Rumors say the *Red Ring's Division 5* has been sniffing you out.. Be careful!" *Lady Lotus* warned while returning to her crowded throne.

Raising an eyebrow, I recalled *Hyatt* saying something similar. Who or what was the *Red Ring*? And why did they want *Spectre*? Curiosity crept through my mind.

Then with one hand, *Spectre* waved farewell as we moved through the celebration.

"Hmph. They're going to need more than that," I heard him mumble.

The parade resumed, and minutes later we came to a busy dock; the port was packed with zeppelins of all sizes; small boats, galleys, frigates, you name it. Walking up a thin wooden plank, we boarded a sailing ship. The steel single mast boat was about seventy-five feet long and twenty feet wide. Square sails danced beneath a red helium balloon keeping it afloat. It was none other than the fabled *Silver Bullet*.

"All right, all hands on deck! I want this thing in the air, pronto!" *Spectre* yelled to his men.

Sounding off in unison, his men shouted. "Aye-aye, captain!"

"Come on, kids. I'll show you to your quarters," He said.

All of a sudden, a monstrous BOOM screamed from behind. Instantly I spun around, as an enormous vessel sailed up behind us. A blood red flag hung from the mast, waving the emblem of a black sun. Armed to the teeth with an arsenal of cannons, the giant warship blocked out the sun.

Kaboom Kaboom! They began firing.

In a matter of seconds they turned the port into a war zone, relentlessly tearing through any vessel in their way. Round after round, zeppelins were blown to pieces as they burst into flames, spiraling out the sky to a fiery grave. Immediately, other ships began returning fire.
Shrapnel and debris wounded the innocent, as chunks of metal and wooden splinters rained below causing a frenzy. From all directions pirates manned their stations, turning it into a battle royale.

Swooping into the air, the *Silver Bullet* was able to avoid inevitable collisions as the brawl heightened.

"What's going on!?" I asked. Raising the dark sunglasses to his forehead, *Spectre* gritted his teeth and replied,

"We're about to find out…"

Stephens.

Chapter 11
(5 Days left.)

The *Silver Bullet* zigzagged through cannon smoke, as we raced to safety. Other vessels fired their weapons furiously, while a barrage of heavy cannonballs were slung around. Taking a sharp right, *Spectre* steered us into a nosedive as the ship dodged falling debris.

Sky pirates held onto ropes with one hand, using their other hands to yank the cannon cords, fire exploded from blackened barrels, launching iron balls into the splintering hulls of other ships. One after another, vessels plunged from the sky. Working in unison, *Specter's* men stuffed fresh cannonballs into smoking breeches while lining their trajectory.

Taking damage from the stern, our ships swayed to the side. *Spectre* curved us around portside, as his crew rained heavy fire down below at an enemy ship. As it burst into pieces, we spun around with an inverted turn.

"Raise the sails!" *Spectre* yelled, spinning the wheel to the right. "Enemies starboard!"

Dashing across the ship, his crew pulled and tightened the ropes. Then once the wind caught the sails, the *Bullet* picked up immense speed, leaving the other ships behind.

Naji leaned close to me, hiding his mouth with his hand. "Umm, are you sure he should be flying this thing!?" he whispered loudly.

Leaning over the banister, I stared behind, awestruck at the ensuing carnage. A gigantic galleon hovered over the port of *Singaporia*, making light work of all other ships around.

"Who are those guys?" I questioned.

"*The Baron of the sky* himself," *Spectre* replied.

"Don't worry. He'll never catch the *Silver Bullet*.. Although, I wonder how they knew we were here… The last time I saw him, we gave 'em' the slip at the coal mines near the *Jeweled Mountains* some years back," *Spectre* stated, while putting enough distance between us and the battle. "No worries. Now, back to the task at hand. What direction does that map point?" He asked, returning to the wheel.

Unfolding the treasure map, *Naji* replied, "To a cavern just north of here. On the other side should be the *Lost City*."

"Then full sail ahead! I want that cavern in sight before sundown! Let's get a move on!"
Spectre yelled as his men sprang into action.

Sasha and *Naji* grabbed their gear then headed for our personal quarters. While watching the floating city of *Singaporia* disappear in the distance, I looked at my pocket watch thinking, "Maybe there still IS a chance. Maybe we CAN find the treasure! …I just hope this ship is as fast as he says it is."

While in the lower deck, we sharpened our melee weapons and loaded our guns. *Spectre's* cargo hold was stockpiled with all kinds of rum, spice, and gunpowder. About fifty tons in all. Although this had been my first time on a real pirate ship, I wasn't surprised. After eating the leftovers from the buffet, I decided to take a quick nap.

Hours later I awoke in a hammock, with the map covering my face. Sliding onto my feet, I folded the paper then headed for the ship's top deck. Once top side, I spotted *Sasha* and *Naji* standing near the bow beneath the moon's light. The lustrous glow from stars overhead complimented the *Silver Bullets* chromed reflective metal coat.

Leaning over the edge, *Sasha* said. "Traveler man, come see."

Wiping the sleep from my eyes, I joined them up front. Peering over the side of the ship, I noticed there was now ground beneath us, but it seemed dry and desolate; a gray wasteland covered by scorched trees and decayed bones.

"Where do you think we are?" *Naji* asked.

"I don't know, but wherever it is, no one has been here for a long time," I responded.

As the ship advanced, the temperature suddenly changed and a heatwave ushered in. The air became humid and the sky fell into a black overcast. Steam was escaping through vents from the cracks below. Feeling the *Silver Bullet* rock to the side, I could hear something scratch against the underbelly of the hull.

"What was that?" I questioned.

Running starboard, *Sasha* replied, "Look, tall spikes."

Looking out ahead, we were now entering a valley filled with large jagged spikes. Some were twenty to thirty feet tall, protruding from the seared earth.

"Watch out!" *Naji* shouted, pointing forward.

Mustering all of his strength, *Spectre* spun the wheel to the right, barely avoiding one of the rough spires. Slamming into the side of another spike, *Spectre* cautiously maneuvered the ship. The steam eventually grew so thick, it formed a layer of mist. Boiling geysers began spewing from the crevices in the ground impairing my vision, I was hardly able to see ten feet in front of me.

"Maybe we should wait until the fog clears? We can't see anything," I said to *Spectre*.

"Nonsense, I can see just fine. I'm getting you to that treasure, kid. One way or another," He returned, wiping beads of sweat from his forehead.

As I felt my way back to the bow of the ship, a faint crimson glow loomed up ahead. The closer we got it became harder to breathe, as the glow magnified. Suddenly, a thunderous boom rumbled in the distance, startling the crew. We all stopped in our tracks. Walking to the front of the upper deck, *Spectre's* jaw dropped.

"What in *Pangea* was that?!"

With the crew members looking over the edge, a large glob of red goop fell from the sky. Followed by another. Then soon it began raining down, as magma poured all around the ship. A blotch landed on the flagless crow's nest, melting one of *Spectre's* men into a screaming puddle.

"It's lava!" *Spectre* exclaimed.

"All hands - evasive maneuvers - full sail!" He shouted.

Scurrying like mice, the crew ran about the ship, preparing the mast. Hoisting the sails up high, the *Silver Bullet* gained a boost of speed. Weaving between geysers, the ship is zigzagged around spires large enough to capsize us.

Drops of perspiration slowly trickled down the side of my face, from the intense heat. The crimson glow from the lava above gave the fog an evil reddish tint, as a pyramid shaped silhouette became visible in the distance.

"Look, over there!" *Naji* yelled, port side.

Sasha and I ran beside him. Squinting my eyes, I asked. "Is that a - "

All of a sudden, another terrifying boom rumbled ahead. Exploding high into the air, lava gushed from the top of the silhouette. A volcano was erupting. Bolting to the other side of our flying boat, I yelled to the crew.

"Watch out!"

Mountains of lava poured down, singeing holes in the ship. While dodging the magma, another one of *Spectre's* men was hit by a ball of fire, instantly boiling his skin. Flailing helplessly the man wailed in agony. The ship then crashed into another spike, jerking us sideways. Stumbling backwards, the disfigured man fell overboard.

"We're sitting ducks out here! You have to do something!" I yelled at Spectre.

"Down there! Big cave!" *Sasha* pointed over the edge.

Spinning the wheel like a hamster, *Spectre* pulled the ship into an upward arc. "Looks like we've got no other choice!" he shouted.

Tilting forward, the *Silver Bullet* then fell into a sharp nosedive as lava rained down around us. Aiming for a gaping hole in the rubble below, the space was wide enough for the ship to squeeze through. The cave was angled diagonally, forcing us lower into *Pangea's* crust. To my surprise, the steam cleared the more we descended. Walking to the bow, one of *Spectre's* men hung a dim lantern on the front of the ship.

"Well, that was close." *Spectre* jested.

"Close?! Two of your men were just burned alive!" *Naji* shouted.

"Then let's make sure they didn't die in vain. Isn't that right, men!?" *Spectre* barked, as his crew sounded off valiantly. "Aye-aye, captain!"

Elbowing my arm, *Naji* murmured, "These guys have a death wish."

The crackling rumble from the volcano soon became inaudible, as the chaos seemed to have subsided. An eerie silence swept over the damp cave as only our voices could be heard.

"That's weird. Where did all that lava go?" I asked.

Moving to the railing on the upper deck, *Spectre* leaned one arm against the banister.

"I've told you. The *Silver Bullet's* the fastest ship in the sky. Besides, we can use this peace and quiet to gather our thoughts," he boasted.

"I've got a bad feeling about this place... Something's not right," I replied, looking into the dark abyss.

"Now, let's see if we can get some light around here! All this darkness is giving me the willies," *Spectre* commanded.

"Aye-aye, captain! " the crew chimed.

Then reaching into their pockets, a few guys pulled out some flares, snapping them in half. As the flares sparkled, they raised them high, illuminating the cave. As the low light cast shadows into the dark corners, I realized obscured stalagmites hung from the ceiling.

"Ahh, much better." *Spectre* said, taking a deep breath.

My curiosity had gotten the best of me, while my eyes were fixed on the stalagmites.

"Hey, look up there. I've never seen rocks like that before," I said, gaining *Naji's* attention.

"Now that you mention it? They do look a little strange..." *Naji* replied, squinting his eyes. Picking up a small rock left over from the volcanoes soot, I heaved it up at the ceiling.

Sasha trembled, "Traveler man? Me no think those rocks...Those look like - "

In a flash an army of bats five feet in height swarmed down from above. Screaming in terror, we all scattered in separate directions. "Hold on!" *Spectre* shouted, getting behind the wheel.

Dropping to the deck, I crawled to the mast keeping my head low. Swatting my hand from side to side proved useless for these oversized *Chiroptera*. Squeaking and chirping, their loud echoes filled the cave, possibly alerting whatever else laid asleep below.

Drawing my gun, I aimed straight then unloaded three rounds. Scaring a group of them away, one bullet ripped through the wing of a bat, sending it into a spiral headfirst for the wall. Swinging their swords, *Spectre* and his men were able to maim a few of the flying rodents. As we blasted our pistols, it sent them into more of a panic.

Using her martial prowess, *Sasha* jousted her spear impaling one of the vermin then tossing him overboard. *Naji* fired his rifle rapidly, while running from cover to cover, quickly dropping two bats out the air.

Seizing the opportunity, one of the bats swooped down, grabbing one of *Spectre's* men within its claws. As he struggled to get free, the giant bat carried him out of the cave, never to be seen again.

Spectre went into a frenzy, slashing the flying rodents to pieces. Then, taking us deeper into the cavern, the *Silver Bullet* eventually outran our unwanted guests.

After plunging in altitude, the cave leveled off into a narrow straight path. The atmosphere down here was different, as the temperature dropped to a cold chill.
As the path grew smaller, we soon came to a body of water with a purplish tint. Bringing the ship to a standstill, *Spectre* looked ahead saying,

"The roof is too low to sail. Looks like we've got to take her on the water."

"Why water purple? Not safe?" *Sasha* asked, hanging over the side.

"I'm not sure, but I don't want to stay and find out," I replied, holstering my pistol.

"Yeah, I'm with you. It's freezing down there," *Naji* added, rubbing his shoulders.

Spectre spun the wheel, saying, "All right, here we go," as he steered the ship into the water.

Feeling the resistance of the waves as we entered the grotto, our vessel rocked side to side. Gliding along the current, the ceiling was only twenty feet from the mast. The murky water seemed to stretch for miles in each direction; it was an endless subterranean ocean.

Walking towards *Spectre, Sasha,* and *Naji,* I stopped before the upper deck.

"This water goes on forever. How are we going to get out of here?" *Naji* asked.

"We'll sail forward until the wind stops. We're bound to hit something, right?" *Spectre* answered, leaning over the wheel.

"Uhh, that doesn't sound like much of a plan," *Naji* returned.

Feeling a cold breeze run over my neck, I shivered, saying,

"Right now we don't have much of a choice. Let's just keep heading north; maybe we'll find a way out of here." Then digging through my pocket, I watched my compass needle spin every which way but up. "No use', I thought.

The crew eventually lowered their weapons and returned to their normal tasks. Lending a hand, we helped throw the slain bats overboard, while the others began

cleaning the debris. As the cadavers took a swim, I stared into the purple ripples unable to see anything beneath.
Turning around, I reached for another corpse, when all of a sudden a loud splash came from behind.

Immediately, I looked into the water and noticed the bodies being pulled under, one by one.

"Hey guys, check this out!" I exclaimed.

Rushing portside, the crew hung over the edge.

"What is that? Did I hit something?" *Spectre* responded, looking around aimlessly. The bats began to bob up and down in the water, until they were yanked below. Blood soon stained the surface as a series of bubbles started rising to the top.

"Maybe water shallow?" *Sasha* said apprehensively. The water soon bubbled all around the ship.

"It might be, but there's something down there," I informed everybody. Suddenly, fish began leaping from the water and into the air. Small framed with dark beady eyes, they chattered their vicious teeth hungrily.

"Piranha!" *Naji* yelled, dropping his blade.

Stepping back, I grab my sword as the others prepared for trouble. An entire school of fish, each with razor-sharp fangs sprang from the depths below. Jumping five, ten, even fifteen feet out of the water, they leapt inside the boat. Swinging my sword erratically, I sliced through a handful of piranhas. *Sasha* and *Naji* slashed their way to the staircase, leading to the upper deck. Splash after splash, the fish rained into the boat, sending the crew into a panic.

Falling back, I swung my blade fiercely at the mob of fish ahead. Jumping onto a crate, I grabbed hold of a rope, swinging myself onto the upper deck. Steering the ship, *Spectre* dodged the fish with poise, while avoiding dozens of biting teeth. Catching one in his hand, he tossed it aside saying,

"We're getting close! I can feel it!"

While twirling her spear like a whirlwind, *Sasha* managed to skewer a large group of fish, then shake them off the end of her stick. Then in an amazing feat, she launched the spear like a javelin, sailing it into a piranha inches away from *Naji's* face.

Spinning around, *Naji* cut through two piranhas with a swing from his scimitar as *Sasha's* spear zipped past his face. Then rolling across the floor, he rose with an upward slash, tearing through two more piranhas.

Sitting on the staircase railing, I slid down to the top deck, ducking the flying fish as I passed by. A few managed to clamp down on one of *Spectre's* men, quickly devouring chunks from his body. Running in terror, he fell to the floor as more piranha soon joined in- eating him alive.

As I fought my way to *Sasha* and *Naji*, one of the crew members fired a cannon.

Kaboom!

It roared, sending a cannonball into the middle of the cavernous ocean. Startling the fish, they all then turned around and began swimming in the other direction. "Great job, sailor. Way to think ahead." *Spectre* stated, removing a fish still clamped onto his butt.

Finishing off the remaining piranha on board, we stabbed them in the head, one by one.

"Is everyone okay?" I asked, out of breath.

Stepping over chum, *Naji* lowered his scimitar, replying, "Yeah, I'm cool. A little smelly though."

"*Sasha* okay," *Sasha* returned, yanking her spear from a piece of wood.

Wiping the fish guts off of my clothes, I looked at *Spectre* on the upper deck. He held his view in a fixed position with his mouth wide open.

"Hey, *Spectre*? Are you alright up there?" I asked curiously.

Slowly raising his hand, he pointed his finger to the bow saying. "It's not over just yet..."

Looking behind me, I could see the remaining crew members cautiously inching backwards toward the stern. A massive tentacle with hundreds of suckers towered before the boat. A rusty pink color, it wiggled daringly. The tentacle raised up to the ceiling, then suddenly came smashing down with all its force.

"*Kraken*!" *Spectre* yelled while spinning the wheel. Bearing to the right, our ship avoided the attack. "All Hands - battle-stations!" He commanded.

Moving to the other side of the ship *Sasha, Naji* and I ran for safety. *Spectre's* men immediately began loading the cannons. Raised once more, the Kraken swung his tentacle horizontally.

"Get down!" *Spectre* barked while diving to the floor.

Without hesitation we hit the deck, crawling in panic. The tentacle then came bludgeoning overhead, destroying a piece of the mast. Dashing to their feet, *Spectre's* men opened fire on the monster, lodging cannonballs into the tentacle. The creature then let out a loud gurgle deep from beneath the water, as it went limp.

Steering as far away as possible, *Spectre* swerved our vessel along the growing waves. Seeing a swirl appear in the water ahead, our ship was slowly reeled into the current. One after another, more tentacles sprouted from the purple abyss.

"Fire at will!" *Spectre* ordered, as he fought with the steering wheel.

Swinging from the left, its tentacles flailed as they crashed through the water. Swaying between the *Kraken's* arms, the *Silver Bullet* managed to carve through the waves. Twirling into a whirlpool, we began losing our footing as we slowly slid across the deck. Grabbing hold of the mast, I leveled myself while reaching for *Sasha* and *Naji*. Still turning the wheel, *Spectre* bore a look of determination upon his face.

Kaboom! *Spectre's* men then launched another round of cannon fire.

Wounding a couple more of the *Kraken's* tentacles, they quickly submerged as the creature groaned once more. Infuriated, another tentacle surfaced just feet from the boat. As it lunged with its suction cups, I let go of the mast, diving for *Sasha* and *Naji*, then holding them down with my arms. Sailing right over our heads, the enormous tentacle swept up one of Spectre's men. Curling him like a snake, the *Kraken* pulled him under the water kicking and screaming.

Kaboom! The cannons continued.

After thrashing us from side to side, the currents from the whirlpool loosened up, allowing *Spectre* to steer us out of danger. Seeing a light up ahead, I shouted,

"There! That must be the way out!"

Putting distance between us and the giant octopus, the ship maneuvered out of the tentacles' reach. As the light grew brighter, we finally came to an opening, leading back to the surface. Spinning the wheel, *Spectre* raised the ship out from the water and into an ascending pathway.

"Hang on!" He shouted, as the ship spiraled up through the cavern. Propelling upwards, the crew put what was left of the mast at full sail.

Launching from the mouth of the cave, we were suddenly blinded by sunlight...

Lock - Jaw.

Chapter 12
(4 Days left.)

Shielding the sun's rays from my eyes, I covered my face with my hand. My eyes eventually adjusted to the orange sun looming over the sky. The warmth from its radiance was rejuvenating, after being in that chilling cave. The *Silver Bullet* continued to climb towards the clouds, once we exited the cavern. As *Spectre* leveled out the ship he laughed heartily,

"Hahaha! It doesn't get any more fun than that! Great job kids, you handled yourselves like real champions."

Facing *Spectre*, I scolded, "So, what? Your men died as martyrs?"

"No. As legends," *Spectre* returned. "The obstacles we face today are what makes us who we are tomorrow. Now, I gave you my word that we'll get you to that treasure, and these men are loyal to the end... It's an honor to call myself their captain." *Spectre's* crew then lowered their weapons to salute their Captain, bumping their fists to their chests. Walking to the side of the ship, *Spectre* peered over the edge saying. "Now, where the hell are we?"

As I looked over the side, I saw a lush jungle set below. Bright green trees and sparkling streams filled the landscape, and flocks of colorful birds grazed with the sky. Some with long necks and long legs, rhythmically soaring with a statuesque pose. I also saw that the mouth to the cavern was camouflaged within the mountain range behind us.

Retrieving the map from my pocket I unfolded it, saying, "It says here, that on the other side of the cavern should be- "

When *Sasha* suddenly interrupted, "Look! More floating islands!"

Turning my head towards the bow, my jaw dropped.

There they were. A sky cluttered with majestic floating islands, each different in size. Plants of neon shades and vivid colors decorated that terrain. Endless streams turned into waterfalls, overflowing from the sides of the islands. The serenity was beautiful and soothing... A much-needed breath of fresh air.

Getting behind the wheel, *Spectre* steered the ship.

"Are they real? Tell me this isn't a dream," I mumbled in awe.

"Oh, it's real all right. Haha, we made it!" *Naji* replied, giving me a hug.

Ecstatically we hopped in circles as the islands hovered around us. Then overcome with emotion, I pulled *Sasha* into our circle. Impulsively placing my hands on her cheeks, I kissed both of her cheeks in joyous celebration.

"I'm glad you came along! We never would have made it without you *Sasha!*" I exclaimed, still jumping up and down.

Instantly *Sasha* began turning red, blushing with a smile. "Yeah - umm - welcome, traveler man," She said, clearing her throat.

While gliding between the inexplicably buoyant chunks of land, *Spectre's* men admired the scenery, leaning over the sides of the ship.

"Keep your eyes peeled, men. We're looking for an old city," he commanded.

Suddenly, the sky echoed - Kaboom!

Jolted by the sound, we stopped in our tracks.

"What was that?" I asked.

"I don't know? But it sounded like a cannon?" *Naji* suggested.

Walking to the sides of the boat, we joined the crew, scanning the sky. Seconds later, another loud crash came, rattling our ship.

"We're under attack!" One of *Spectre's* men bellowed.

Pointing starboard, *Sasha* shouted, "Over there!"

Then as I looked to my right, a familiar warship appeared from behind one of the floating islands. Nearly one hundred feet long and twenty feet wide, a row of three dozen cannons lined each side of the ship. A bloodthirsty crew of about sixty shouted from the top deck. Heading straight for us, they unloaded their cannons.

Kaboom - Kaboom!

Cannons roared as cannonballs slammed into our hull, rocking our ship side to side. Spinning the wheel, *Spectre* barked,

"All hands- Battlestations!" Soon raising the ship's altitude. Scurrying to their positions, the crew prepared for trouble.

Swinging between the floating islands, *Spectre* tried his best to avoid the enemy. Hot on our tail, the warship was able to predict our next moves, then beat us to the punch. While playing cat-and-mouse, the warship slowly closed the distance. In a panic, one of *Spectre's* men fumbled with a cannon ball while loading the cannon. Within the time it took to recover, the warship had already capitalized - firing a series of rounds.

Kaboom - Baboom - BOOM!

Debris and wooden shrapnel flew across the ship from the explosion. Their cannons blew a gaping hole in the deck. Dazed by the attack, I was knocked to the floor. While stumbling to my feet, a handful of scruffy pirates came swinging on ropes, boarding our vessel.
Landing on deck, they were instantly hidden by the smoke from the debris. Drawing my sword from behind my waist I clenched my fists, activating my shield.

"Everyone on guard! Intruders are on the ship!" I shouted.

Seconds later, the sound of metal sliding from scabbards echoed amongst the chaos.

"Chaaaarge!" The enemies screamed at the top of their lungs. As we met them head-on, I dashed into the smoke with a wild swing. Parrying my first attack, one of the enemy pirates countered with a kick to my chest, pushing me back into the mast. As the pirate heaved his mace for the kill, *Naji* intervened with a piercing strike to his abdomen. Falling to his knees in pain, I finished him off with a fatal blow to the neck.

Jumping over a crate, *Sasha* lunged for an enemy. But he quickly sidestepped her attack, returning with a thrusting strike of his own. Back and forth the two danced in a circle,

191

resembling a game of tug-of-war. Then getting the best of her opponent, Sasha stabbed the pirate in his thigh, slowing him down. Relying on her incredibly sharp senses, she ducked low, dodging a swipe from his falchion. She then thrust her spear into his rib cage. Crumbling to the floor, the pirate cringed as Sasha yanked the weapon from his body.

Spectre's crew bested the intruders, as the smoke finally began to clear. Watching the enormous warship overshadow the Silver Bullet, Spectre spun the wheel in the opposite direction.

"Listen up men! We've defeated them once, we can defeat them again!"

"Them?! Who's them?! Why are these guys chasing us?!" Naji asked.

Tying his black hair into a small ponytail, Spectre growled,

"Lock-jaw."

Turning the ship parallel to the enemy, Spectre let go of the wheel then jumped onto a banister. Grabbing a nearby rope, he drew his katana saying, "This time, we bring the fight to them! First mate, man the ship!"

"Aye-aye, Captain!" The man with the serpent tattoo replied, while running to the wheel.
Grasping swinging ropes, Spectre and his crew swung over to Lock-jaw's warship, storming the deck. Feeling the adrenaline surge through my veins, I grabbed a rope yelling,

"Come on, let's go!"

"Umm, you guys go on ahead. Someone's got to live to tell the story, right? Heh heh," *Naji* said, suddenly showing a sense of self-preservation. After all we had endured during our journey, it was surprising to learn that *Naji* actually valued his own safety.

"It's time we faced our fears. If you don't stand for something then you'll fall for anything... suit yourself." I explained. Standing on the edge of the ship, I pulled back on the rope, as *Sasha* wrapped her arms around me. Seconds later, we were sailing through the air, dodging projectiles from the enemy crossbows and pistols.

Landing near the bow, *Sasha* and I rushed to *Spectre* and his men with a spirited charge. Slashing at the first enemy pirate on my right, I followed up with a shield bash to the next enemy pirate on my left, then drove my blade deep into a third pirate's chest. Spinning clockwise, I sliced open the face of a fourth attacker.

Impaling one flunky after another with her spear, *Sasha* easily cleared the pathway. Using her acute awareness she stepped to the side, barely avoiding the bullets fired at close range by a panicking sky pirate. Hurling her spear, she retaliated by plunging it through his midsection, knocking him off his feet.

We quickly caught up to *Spectre*, who was knee-deep in battle as he dueled three of *Lock-Jaw's* men.

"Ahh, how nice of you to join us Thomas," he stated, while carving through his foes.

Together, *Sasha* and I were able to help *Spectre* and his crew advance through the top deck, slashing our way through adversaries. At that moment, a platoon of *Lock-Jaw's* troops filed out from the lower levels. Within seconds, we were outnumbered, twelve against fifty. Staring at the enemy in a face-off, we stood our ground.

"Traveler man? Too many pirates, what do now?" *Sasha* asked.

Weighing my options, I replied, "Hope for the best…"

Then with a terrifying roar, the enemies charged while giving their best war cry. Bracing for impact, we raised our weapons in defense.

Kaboom!

A canon burst nearby. Exploding in the center of *Lock-jaws* troops, the blast sent them stumbling to the floor.

Kaboom - kaboom!

Two more cannons fired, dismantling their formation. As debris soared through the air I turned my head, shielding my eyes.

"What the hell?!" I questioned.

Standing in front of a canon thirty feet away, *Naji* gave me a thumbs up.

"Oh come on. You didn't really think I'd miss out on the climax, did you!?" he shouted.

His support was much obliged. He pulled the ripcord on another cannon, the blast ripping through the beam of the large warship. Slowly it began to topple over. As the heavy mast collapsed through the top deck, it created a hole wide enough to drag *Lock-jaw's* men along with it down below.

"All hands - back to the ship - now!" *Spectre* yelled.

Spectre's first mate then steered the ship closer, as *Naji* began tossing ropes in our direction. The crew grabbed hold, then swung back on board the *Silver Bullet*.

Noticing *Spectre* heading the other way, I spotted an intimidating figure who appeared on the top deck. Wearing a beige overcoat without a shirt, black pants and brown boots completed his ensemble. His hulking stature was almost overshadowed by the five foot long greatsword he held, engraved with gold. Sporting a metal plate for a jaw, the tanned figure stated,

"At last. We meet again."

"Well well well, if it isn't old rust mouth himself. So tell me? How'd you make it out of the mines? Last I remember, those natives weren't very pleased..." *Spectre* replied, following the sound of *Lock-jaw's* voice. "He heh heh. I must say, you were pretty slick. Painting over the *Power Crystal*, then hiding it amongst the rocks. You know, before those gullible natives had a chance to find it, the cave mysteriously collapsed around them," He teased with a satisfied smile."

"What can I say? Every man has his price... But for your head *Spectre*? I'd pay all the gold in the world," *Lock-jaw* replied in a grizzly voice, pointing his large sword with one hand.

"Well, it's just you and me now." He leapt towards *Spectre*.

"Traveler man, come!" *Sasha* said, grabbing hold of a rope.

"What about *Spectre*? We can't leave him?" I replied, when all of a sudden the top deck began to crack and splinter, as the floor gave way.

"Come!" She reiterated.

Looking back at *Spectre* once more, I wrapped my arms around *Sasha* as we swung on board the *Silver Bullet*. Seconds later the top deck collapsed, crumbling to the levels below.

Swinging from ropes furiously, the two rivals *Spectre* and *Lock-jaw* faced off in an intense battle. *Spectre* swung high as *Lock-jaw* ducked low, following up with a forward thrust. Parrying his attack, *Spectre* brought his katana into a downward strike, only to be blocked by *Lock-jaw's* greatsword. Swinging simultaneously, their swords clashed with a loud clang.

"That's all you got?" *Spectre* challenged.

"Hahaha! How amusing," *Lock-jaw* cackled.

With a flurry of attacks, *Spectre* whirled like a tornado. Deflecting the blows, *Lock-jaw* broke the frenzy with an overhead strike. *Spectre* struggled as he tried to move under the weight from the heavy sword pushing down against him. Seizing the opportunity, *Lock-jaw* issued a front kick.

Stumbling backwards into the upper deck banister, *Spectre* managed to dodge to the left, barely avoiding a powerful strike. He countered with a fast swing, but his blade only cut air as *Lock-jaw* stepped to the side in time.

Lunging forward once more, *Lock-jaw's* sword grazed *Spectre's* rib cage, tearing into his clothes. Returning with an upward slash, *Spectre's* blade skimmed the side of *Lock-jaw's* face, though with sharp reflexes, *Lock-jaw* managed to break *Spectre's* stride with an unexpected move: chomping down on the end of *Spectre's* katana, sparks flew as his steel bottom jaw latched onto the blade, biting down.

After freeing his weapon, they then threw wide attacks landing at the same time with another thunderous clang. Pushing their swords against each other, they locked eyes in an overpowering struggle.

Continuing the cannonball barrage of *Lock-jaw's* ship, *Spectre's* crew ensured that *Lock-jaw* and his thugs could chase them no more. Heaps of wood and shrapnel were blown from the warship.

Seeing our chance to flee, I shouted. "*Spectre*, come on! Now is our chance!"

Feeling the ship rumble, *Spectre* became distracted. *Lock-jaw* then kneed him in the stomach, knocking him backwards. Watching his legendary battleship being blown apart, *Lock-jaw* pointed his great sword.

"For this, you will pay dearly," He growled.

Dashing once more, *Lock-jaw* raised his sword for a fatal attack, but was thrown off course, as his foot collapsed through the damaged floor board. Finding his footing again, *Spectre* addressed *Lockjaw* once more:

"The game's over."

Running to the edge, *Spectre* dove over the side of the warship, free falling through the sky. Watching in suspense, I ran to the rail of the zeppelin seeing *Spectre* plummet. Stretching our hands for his, the crew and I failed to reach him in time, as his fingers slipped through my hand.

"Nooo!" I yelled.

We could only watch as he flailed helplessly, plunging to certain death. An unsettling feeling rose in my stomach. There was nothing we could do!

Spectre suddenly stopped flailing for a moment, seeming to focus. What was he doing? He stuck one arm and one leg out, and his trajectory changed: he rolled through the air at an angle, and I thought I began to see what he was doing. He suddenly shot his other hand out and his trajectory changed again, this time unbelievably, moving now in a horizontal arc underneath the ship. I ran to the other side of the deck to look over the edge, but I had lost him in the fire lit clouds. Where was he? Had my eyes deceived me? It had looked as if he was somehow flying!Where had he gone?

Suddenly a long frayed rope fell out of the cloud bank directly in front of me, draping itself across the railing before it's own weight pulled it back overboard; a thud behind me made me flinch, and I spun around to see Spectre rising out of a hyper badass kneeling stance.

While sucking in a breath of fresh air, a wave of relief washed over me. I tried to say something but he just patted me on the shoulder and returned to his position command.

"All right, get us out of here!" He ordered.

The Silver Bullet began veering to port, climbing in altitude. Re-aiming the cannons, Spectre's men launched two more volleys at the enemy as we sailed away. Slowly capsizing, Lock-jaw's warship was crippled and coming to a standstill.

All of a sudden, an unexpected blast emerged from behind.

Kaboom!

Turning around, a cannonball came soaring straight for our vessel with a loud crash.
Smashing into the stern, the collision destroyed our tail rotors, flinging them into the sky. Instantly, our ship began tilting forward as we began losing control.

"What just happened?! I thought we won?!" *Naji* asked.

Staring over the side of a boat, *Sasha* pointed behind us. "Look!"

A tall silhouette loomed behind the smoke, as the warship fell apart. Standing amongst the rubble of his fallen vessel, *Lock-jaw's* menacing cackle could still be heard from afar. The red and black flag above the splintered mast danced with the wind.

As we slid towards the bow, the ship steered for a nearby floating island. "We're going down! Everybody hold on!" *Spectre* shouted.

Scurrying across the ship, I latched onto the mast, while *Spectre* and the crew held onto the sides of the ship. *Sasha* clamped onto the railing leading to the upper deck, as *Naji* tied a rope around his waist.

Coming in fast, the zeppelin crashed into a jungle, veering into a slide. Tearing through trees and other vegetation, debris was slung back at us giving whiplash and whelps. As we rattled around the ship, I was tossed from side to side. The keel of the ship bumped into a fallen tree, and I was thrown from the ship as we came to a stop.

Everything went black.

When I awoke, sunlight shone through the trees, piercing my eyes. Birds sang beautiful melodies as the warm breeze shook the leaves on the trees. Rising to my feet, I held my side in pain. *Naji* and *Sasha* were standing near the *Silver Bullet*, giving *Spectre* and his crew a hand with repairs.

Limping over, I said, "I can't believe we survived...What's the status of the ship? Can we fix it?"

Holding a hammer, *Sasha* replied. "It appears the boat's currently dysfunctional, but *Spectre* believes he can re-fabricate it. We could certainly use your assistance."

Nodding my head, I grabbed an extra hammer then began hitting nails into the side of the ship. Looking from the corner of my eye, I observed *Sasha,* thinking to myself that there's something different about her. Did the crash-landing trigger a latent intellect switch, hidden inside her brain?

"Is it just me, or is *Sasha's* grammar getting really better?" I said to *Naji*.

Wiping the sweat from his brow, he stopped. "Yeah, I guess she's finally getting the hang of it. I just wish I could say the same for *Angela*.. Our mom can be so primitive sometimes."

"Mom?" I replied, lowering my hammer confused. As I turned around, a woman wearing a coat of animal fur was sharpening a wooden spear. While raising her head, I noticed the striking resemblance of my mother. "Mom?!" I exclaimed.

"Ah, traveler man wake. Good see you." She said, with a smile.

"Is that really you? How - how did you get here?" I questioned, walking closer. Rising from the boulder she sat on, *Angela* waved her hand.

"Come, time for hunt. Find fish for dinner," she said, before entering the bushes behind.

Following her path, I stepped through the shrubs coming to a wide river. Standing in the middle, *Angela* was up to her knees and water.
Like a statue she loomed over her prey, waiting for the perfect moment to strike. Then with cat-like reflexes, she thrusted her spear into the clear water in front of her. Cleanly piercing a fish, she pulled it out of the water.

"Wow, that was amazing!" I exclaimed.

"That nothing, you should see father." *Angela* replied, sliding the fish off of the shank.
She then pointed up ahead to a man wearing fishing gear, standing at the edge of a waterfall. Curiously, I stepped into the water, wading towards him through the reeds. The man turned around while dangling a fishing line in the water.

"Come on over, son. There's plenty to catch," he said.

Recognizing that face anywhere, I realized he was none other than *Ferdinand Von Zeppelin*, my father.

"Dad!?"

Embracing him with a warm hug, I rambled, "I'm so glad to see you! I've got so much to say! Okay, first I got the *Model - 1* to work, but we crashed it into a mountain with giants! They weren't very friendly so we had to leave and ran to the desert! From there, we were captured. Oh, did I mention when we met an *Amazonian* named *Sasha*?!"

Handing me a fishing pole, Dad laughed joyously, "Okay, okay. Settle down son, Heh heh. You can tell your mother and I the rest when you get to the *Lost City.*"

Shifting my head in confusion, I questioned, "Huh? How do you know about the *Lost city*?"

Trudging through the water, Mom walked over to Dad.

"*Lost City* just ahead. Down waterfall," she replied, taking his hand. Oddly though, they both began walking backwards the edge of the cliff.

"Wait? What - what are you guys doing?" I asked. Ignoring my question, they continued stepping closer, continuing to smile at me.

"We love you, *Thomas,*" My mother said, as they went over the cliff. Dashing for the edge, I tried to stop them, managing to grab hold of my father's hand.

Staring into my eyes, he whispered. "The compass..." then let go of my hand, falling backwards down the waterfall.

"Wait! Come back!" I yelled.

Refusing to lose my parents once again, I decided to jump over the cliff as well. Falling through the air, I soon landed in a large body of water, crashing with a loud splash...

Cough - cough - cough I choked while spitting up water. Propping myself onto an elbow, I laid on a tuft of grass. *Naji* was kneeling before me, holding a metal canteen with water.

"You alright, man?" he asked.

Frantically, I looked around searching for my parents, then soon realized it had only been another dream. Disappointed, I let out a drawn out sigh.

"Yeah.. I'm all right."

Throwing another cup of water in my face, Naji then extended his hand. "*Cough - cough* What was that for?" I blurted.

"Just making sure." he replied, helping me to my feet.

The sun had declined, casting an orange pastel over the sky. Beautiful plants of all shades gleamed exuberantly, pulsing with color. Flowing streams could be heard over the flock of exotic song birds chirping in the canopy. This neon jungle was truly a fantasy.

Spectre and his crew stood beside their fallen ship, with *Sasha*.

"Good, you're alive. I thought we were going to have to bury you when you started calling everybody mom and dad in your sleep," *Spectre* said as we approached. How did he know it was me walking up? After everything I'd seen him do, I don't know why I even asked that question.

"Glad see you, traveler man," *Sasha* welcomed me, with a soothing smile.

Assessing the ship's damage, I responded, "Thanks guys. What's the status of the ship?"

"What, this old thing? She's been through worse. Seventy-five by twenty foot frame, cast in solid steel; this baby can take anything," *Spectre* returned, resting his hand on the ship.

"Yeah, except a shot from a cannon," *Naji* mumbled.

Spectre continued, "The balloon on top of the ship is torn and the mast is a little banged up, but I'm sure my crew and I can fix it."

"Great, then we'll help," I said, walking towards the ship. Raising his hand, *Spectre* stopped me.

"Oh no you don't. I appreciate the offer but, you've got a *Lost City* to find. It's going to take a few days to get her running again, and you three have come too far to stop now." "How are we supposed to find the *Lost City* without a ship?" *Naji* inquired.

"It looks like you're on foot from here," *Spectre* answered.

Placing my hand under my chin, I pondered over our situation. Brown *howler monkeys* with pale faces could be heard nearby from the trees.

"He's right, there's still time. What's a few more miles right?" I said.

"*Amazonian* ready. We find treasure," said *Sasha*, grabbing her spear. *Naji* and I nodded in agreement then grabbed our things.

"That's the spirit. Hey listen, I wanted to thank you guys for your help back there... It takes real courage to stand up in face of danger the way you three did... It's been an honor," *Spectre* stated, pumping his fist to his chest as a solute.

We then returned his salute. "See you around, *Spectre*," I replied.

Turning around, we headed into the jungle following the sounds of running water. Without a vehicle, time was against us in a race to the finish.

As night fell, the vibrant colors on the floating island came to life. Plant buds began to blossom and wiggled strange phosphorescent blue stamens. Bright emerald green lizards with turquoise throats illuminated our pathways. A pleasant fragrance secreted from an array of large glowing flowers... This place was far from ordinary.

"I've never seen anything like this before: it's amazing," I said, gazing through the woods.

"Well, how often have you seen a floating island?" *Naji* replied, stepping over a large branch.

"Traveler man, look... Is that *Lost City*?" *Sasha* asked, peeking through some shrubs up ahead.

Swatting a few flickering butterflies out of my way, I soon caught up to *Sasha*. Moving the bushes aside, we spied an old ruin. This was quite surprising, because walkways were less common in these denser areas of the luminescent jungle.

Stained white, the moss-covered structure bore old engravings of *Atlantian* alphabets and fallen statues. Tall pillars surrounded the perimeter, each collapsed or broken in pieces. Although entangled in vines, I got the feeling that this stronghold was not the *Lost City of Old*.

"Sorry *Sasha*. But I don't think there's any treasure in there," *Naji* informed.

While walking into the forgotten courtyard, I stopped at a stone fountain. A statue of a long-bearded man wielding a trident stood fixed on the top. "It's got to be around here somewhere," I stated.

Dropping her gear beside the fountain, *Sasha* stretched her arms high, saying,

"*Amazonian* tired, need break...What think happened to ruins? Where all people go?"

Rubbing the mossy surface of the stone columns, I answered, "Good question! It looks like this place has been abandoned for decades."

Wandering around the dark entrance, *Naji* eyed the carvings on the walls. Stepping inside the eerie building we heard him say,

"Whoever they were, they sure were conceited. There are sculptures of naked guys all over the place."

"Maybe they were all turned to stone? You know, like the story of *Medusia*," I teased, leaning back onto the fountain.

Standing before a wide hole from a collapsed wall, *Naji* retorted, "Hmph, yeah right. I think it was something more spooky... Maybe they were all murdered."

Suddenly, a red glow began shining from behind *Naji*. Stealing my attention, the glowing light grew brighter, soon resembling a pair of large eyes.

"*Naji* - there's something behind you!" I yelled.

Folding his arms, he replied, "What's next, *Percia and the Giant Snake*? Give it a rest, *Thomas*. We're supposed to be looking for the treasure."

Readying her spear, *Sasha* noticed it as well. "Traveler man no joke - Turn around!" She added cautiously.

Frustrated, *Naji* let out a sigh as he finally spun around. "Oh come on. It's probably just a barn owl or something - "

Naji then tensed up, becoming stiff as a board. "G - g - guys?" He trembled, stepping back slowly.

An enormous viper with horns above its eyes began slithering out from the stone ruins. Flicking its tone, the giant serpent swayed its head before *Naji*. Waddling like a penguin, *Naji* turned around and screamed,

"Run!"

As he bolted past us, *Sasha* and I grabbed our gear following suit. The giant viper lunged at us with its fierce fangs missing by inches. Biting down onto the stone fountain, his jaws crushed it to pieces.

"Why didn't you say that thing was behind me!?" *Naji* barked, dashing through the courtyard.

"We did! You didn't listen!" I retorted, jumping over rubble. Swinging side to side, the snake smashed through statues, hissing viciously. It's red-and-white diamond pattern glistened under the moonlight. Striking once more, it slammed into a stone column as *Sasha* and I managed to move aside. Splitting up, we brought the snake to a standstill.

Out of breath, we each hid behind separate pillars. Activating my shield, I unsheathed my sword then peeked around the column. Surveying the area, the viper wiggled its tongue menacingly.

"If we split up, he can't get all of us!" *Naji* yelled, holding his rifle.

The snake then began weaving between the pillars, sensing our body heat. Coiling around a column, it raised itself high, gaining a 360 degree view of the courtyard. Hovering over *Sasha*, the viper lunged for the kill.

"*Sasha*- Run!" I shouted, as my heart pounded.

Looking up, she rolled to the side in time, as the snake struck the ground behind her. Zigzagging through the courtyard, *Sasha* went into a full stride. the Viper trailed behind her slithering on a parallel path, hoping to cut her off. As it raised its head for a fatal strike, I intervened by stabbing into its side.

Screeching in pain, the snake swung its tail around, flinging me to the floor. Tumbling into a pile of rubble, I quickly rose to my feet dashing for cover. Returning for *Sasha* the snake crept low to the floor, extending its forty foot long frame. Peering from behind a pillar, *Naji* fired a round from his rifle.

Bang!

Alerting the snake to his position, he dashed for another pillar. Aggravated by the cat and mouse games, the viper began crashing through the pillars. Frantically moving from one pillar to another, we soon ran out of hiding places and energy.

"We can't keep this up!" I said while breathing hard.

Leaning forward, *Naji* panted, "If we stay here, we're going to die!"

"*Amazonian* hear water! Follow stream!" *Sasha* said, searching for cover.

Looking for the viper, I leaned around the white column. "You two go on ahead, I'll make a distraction!" I stated. Nodding in agreement, *Sasha* and *Naji* ran through the courtyard heading for the jungle.

"Be safe!" *Sasha* yelled while looking behind her.

Without confrontation, the snake allowed them to escape, as it hissed passively. Slowly the viper turned its head, pinpointing my location. Then, walking out into the open, I stood before the behemoth. Mere weeks ago, I would have been cowering behind a rock, just like another privileged citizen safe behind the polished city walls of *Edenia*. But during our perilous journey, I found a new courage hidden deep inside myself. The new perception I've gained being outside my comfort zone has helped me to realize the difficult situations the rest of the world has been forced to endure.

"All right, now it's just you and me," I said, banging my sword against the shield.

Simultaneously, the serpent and I charged for each other with a bloodthirsty war cry. As it bared its fangs, I lifted my shield preventing the attack. Thrusting my blade into the roof of its mouth, the creature jerked back, poised for another strike. Opening its jaws, the viper launched forward. Rolling to the side I avoided the attack, dragging my sword across its face.

Hissing ferociously, the snake shook his head in a daze. Sprinting alongside its endless body, I leapt onto a fallen statue then vaulted myself on top of the vipers back.

Regaining his composure, the serpent spun around, giving chase once more.

Running down its back, I sheathed my sword to draw my pistol. Squeezing the trigger, I fired a handful of rounds into the vipers back, before jumping down to the floor. The massive serpent wreathed in pain, as it wiggled erratically.

Seeing my opportunity, I hightailed it across the courtyard and into the jungle, following *Sasha* and *Naji's* footsteps. While hurtling over branches and ducking under vines, I felt like a parkour master scurrying along the forest floor. Desperately chasing the sound of running water, I couldn't help but admire the fluorescent carapaces sparkling all over the trees.

Suddenly, I heard a loud thud from behind... then another. Pausing for a breather, I turned around to watch the trees in the distance toppling over in a straight path. Seconds later, the sound grew louder as a giant silhouette quickly approached. Quickly noticing the same pair of red glowing eyes from before, I spun around darting for the stream.

Trampling the trees and wildlife, the enraged viper crushed anything in its wake. I soon came to a field of colorful plants with luminescent spores blowing in the breeze. Dashing through the tall shrubs, I located *Sasha* and *Naji* up ahead standing knee-deep in the stream. Chasing behind me, the humongous snake made its way through the field.

"Run!" I shouted, waving my hands.

Naji's face suddenly wrinkled in confusion, as he asked,

"What the hell man!? It's still alive!?"

210

Jumping into the stream, I trudged towards them shouting, "Does it look like I can kill that thing?! Of course it's still alive!"

"Umm, traveler man look?" *Sasha* informed, as we suddenly approached another obstacle. A four-hundred foot tall obstacle.

"Is that a waterfall? Tell me that's not a waterfall?" *Naji* asked while slowing down his stride.

The vicious viper mowed through the plant field making its way onto the stream, about a hundred yards away. Slithering side to side, the snake sped in our direction.

Out of options, *Sasha* surveyed the area saying, "What we do, traveler man?"

Staring over the edge behind me, I suddenly felt a wave of deja vu, "The compass..." A thought echoed in my head.

Recalling my dream from earlier that day, I pulled out my father's compass watch, flipping it open. To my surprise, it wasn't spinning around aimlessly like it usually did. This time, it was pointing in only one direction, as the small gem-encrusted in the middle began radiating a faint blue... Down the waterfall.

"Snap out of it! We need a plan!" *Naji* yelled, violently shaking my shoulders.

As the viper quickly closed in the distance, I turned to *Naji* and said. "I've got it! We jump."

"Oh no, I'm not jumping off that thing. I'll take my chances with the snake," He replied, waving his hands in protest.

"That can be arranged. See you at the bottom!" I returned.

Taking *Sasha's* hand, we then leapt off the cliff with our legs swinging. Looking behind him, *Naji* saw the viper open its mouth wide, a dozen yards away. Immediately, he spun around and dove off the cliff, yelling, "Wait for me!"

Chapter 13
(3 Days left.)

Falling hundreds of feet through the air, my heart raced like an olympic sprinter, nearly leaping from my chest. The loud roar from the rapids crashing below took my mind away from the chilling breeze blowing past me. Flapping like little birds, *Sasha* and I plunged into the crystal pool beneath us.

Making a giant splash, our hands were separated. Schools of tropical fish dispersed from around us, creating a tunnel. Paddling through the water, I kicked off the glistening rocks, swimming to the surface. Seconds later, another splash echoed behind me, as *Naji* slammed into the water.

Breaching the top of the waves, I burst forth gasping for air. Looking to my left, *Sasha* popped up as well, latching onto a rock, but was immediately swept away by the rough currents. While bobbing through the waves, I swallowed a mouthful of freshwater as I was pushed up and down. Flowing downstream, we now headed for a cluster of rocks.

Ramming into a boulder, I was bumped around from one to another. *Naji* soon surfaced a little ways behind, holding his rifle above his head. Grabbing hold of a passing log, I frantically called to the others,

"Give me your hand!"

Treading the violent waves, *Sasha* pushed herself from rock to rock, making it to the log. *Naji's* head soon went under, as he splashed about.

"Help!" He screamed, masked within the white foam.

"*Naji!*" I yelled, extending my hand.

Looking at *Sasha*, we shared a worried look while the waves crashed over our heads. Frantically, I scanned from left to right, but *Naji* was nowhere to be found. He had now been under longer than expected and now I feared the worst.

All of a sudden, a hand sprung from under the water, latching onto the log. *Sasha* and I began pulling a gunky forearm up from the current, revealing a man with gooey green hair. Coughing up water, the creature removed a glob of seaweed from over his face.

"Cough - cough. Miss me?" He said with a smile.

Punching *Naji* in the arm, *Sasha* looked behind us saying. "Look! The water calm that way!"

Up ahead, the current branched off into two directions. One raging and turbulent, the other narrowing into a stream covered by trees. With no hesitation, we chose the safer route.

"Quick, paddle to the fork!" I shouted.

Splashing through the water, we managed to steer the wooden log against the current. The fierce tides clashed endlessly, as we tackled the waves. Lunging her spear, *Sasha* managed to fix it between two rocks, enabling us to pull ourselves to safety.

Entering the stream, the water eventually calmed to a gentle nudge. Finally getting a break, we coasted the shallow waters winding beneath the fluorescent trees. Minutes later, the log washed up on shore.

Stumbling to my feet, I collapsed onto the riverbank then rolled onto my back. Unfolding the treasure map for my pocket, I laid it out to dry.

"Huff Huff. Maybe you were right. We should have stayed with the snake," I said, while catching my breath.

Crawling on all fours, *Sasha* hung her head low.

"*Sasha* tired of adventure. Want go back home," She panted.

Knocking the water out of his ears, *Naji* mumbled, "I got it - Let's jump. Pfft, some plan."

Slowly rising to his feet, he continued: "We're soaking wet - were exhausted - we only got three days left - and worst of all? We STILL haven't found the - " As he suddenly came into a pause.

While ringing the water from my clothes, *Naji's* whining finally made my blood boil. Becoming aggravated, I barked.

"What?! You still haven't found what?! This whole trip all you've done is complain about this and that! If you didn't crash my plane in the first place, none of this would have ever happened! You're so irresponsible! I'm sick of you always dragging me down with you, then expecting me to fix your problems! Sometimes - sometimes - I wish Mom and Dad had never found you!"

With sudden shock upon her face, *Sasha* empathetically asked, "...Traveler man don't mean that... Does he?"

Gauging the look in her eye, I could tell my outburst may have been uncalled for. A slight wave of remorse tingled through my body.

Dropping his jaw, *Naji's* eyes widened as he pointed his finger:

"Look."

"What?! What is it this time?!" I responded, continuing my rant.

Picking up the map, *Naji* said once more. "No, behind you."

"Don't change the subject, you need to hear this!" I shouted.

Stepping in between us, *Sasha* turned me around then said,

"Traveler man, look…"

Once I settled down, my heart suddenly skipped a beat. Wiping my eyes, I couldn't believe what I was seeing. Stepping forward, my mouth opened wide.

"The *Lost City of Old*… We found it." *Naji* stated.

Tucked away deep in the jungle, the forgotten city towered over a grassy plain. Stone temples and fallen homes lay scattered in pieces. The debris littering the walkways disguised croaking poison arrow frogs. As we advanced into the streets, I could tell the ivory carvings on the rubble were once a spectacle of the fabled city. Weathered by time, the remains were now covered by vines and overgrown plants. *Golden Orioles* with rich yellow bodies and black wings peeked from the canopy fluting songs; a rare sight to see. This vast empire had been cloaked for centuries.

"This doesn't look like the picture on the map? Maybe it's the wrong place?" *Naji* concurred, while we wandered around the city.

"It's been lost for thousands of years, what's it supposed to look like?" I returned, kneeling down to observe the designs on the stones.

Stepping over a few rocks, *Sasha* came to the only building that was still intact.

"Traveler man, look this one," She suggested.

Joining her, *Naji* & I ascended a wide stone staircase. Walking to the top, we stood before a large circular door. Carved from a solid block of stone, the heavy door seemed unwieldy. Decorated in foreign calligraphy, it was at least a foot thick.

"How we open?" She questioned.

"There's got to be some kind of secret lever around here. You know, like in that book *Indiania John*," *Naji* replied, rubbing his hand against the stone surface.

"This isn't a fantasy novel. I'm sure we just have to put some muscle into it," I said, standing in front of the round door. Grabbing onto the door I tried pulling it open, while *Naji* continued touching the inscriptions. Looking around, *Sasha* accidentally stepped on a loose tile, triggering a loud mechanism. Suddenly, the large door began rolling to the side, rumbling the ground beneath us.

"...Or that works too. Great job, *Sasha*," *Naji* stated.

Watching the vines that covered the door fall to the floor, we each shared a look of surprise.

"Whatever is waiting for us on the other side could change our lives forever. Stay sharp." I warned.

"Yeah yeah, don't bore us to death. This place has been lost forever. Anything back there died a long time ago. Now, let's go find that treasure," *Naji* chimed, darting into the temple ahead of us.

Sasha and I both sighed in unison, shaking our heads.

Entering the temple was exciting and a bit scary at the same time. Dust particles danced around us as we ripped through old spider webs. The ancient stone walls were engraved with beautiful inscriptions and symbols. The pictures seemed to depict a large serpent swimming alongside a fleet of boats - and others of a great battle, with a *phoenix* fighting a dark figure. Smooth tight-fitted stones were covered in concrete, as even the tiles on the floor showcased intricate kaleidoscope designs. Coming to the end of a hall, we reached a short staircase leading down below.

Consciously we descended the stairway, ducking the draping vines. At the bottom of the stairs we entered a wide foyer. Three hallways now laid before us, with a tall vase in the middle sitting inside an empty fountain.

Walking towards the center, I observed the fine engravings upon the vase. A green gem about the size of my fist was protruding from the stone embroidery.

"The room splits into three, should we split up?" I asked, surveying the other halls.

"Might cover more ground?" *Sasha* responded, looking down the hallway. Pacing circles around the vase, *Naji* eyed the gem.

"Nah, we shouldn't spread ourselves too thin. It's best if we stick together," he said, anxiously.

So taking his advice, I replied, "Yeah, you're right. Let's let the compass decide." Digging into my pocket, I retrieved my silver watch and to my surprise was held in awe by the luminous light now glowing from the needle.

As it pointed down the hallway, the tiny shard fixed in the center now radiated a bluish hue, brighter than before. Curious by the discovery, I then pointed my finger suggesting, "Let's go this way."

All of a sudden, the floor began to rumble like before. Large stone doors began closing over each of the pathways, including the one we'd come through. Startled, we looked around in a panic.

"What happened, traveler man?" *Sasha* questioned.

Following his impulse, *Naji* was trying to stuff the emerald into his pocket. "What?" He mumbled.

Sand then began pouring from secret holes in the wall, as the stones crashed to the floor. Within seconds, it was up to our shins.

"You just Had to touch it, didn't you?" I groaned.

"Oh don't act like you weren't thinking it." *Naji* explained, spitting sand from his mouth.

Now fighting against the gushing sand, we struggled to stay on top. More and more stones soon came loose, revealing cracks where the sand seeped through. As the sand began to quickly rise above the base, I realized the ceiling was only another ten feet away... We were goners.

"Look, small opening!" Blurted *Sasha*, pointing to a hole in the wall. Leaving us with no choice, we were forced to give it a try.

"Come on, hurry!" *Naji* shouted.

Crawling on her knees, *Sasha* wiggled into the small opening, but was soon stuck halfway as sand filled in on the sides. *Naji* and I pushed her legs frantically, while the rising sand forced us to crouch. Giving her one last shove, we desperately held our breath as the sand climbed to our necks.

Suddenly we fell forward as *Sasha* finally gave way. Sliding down a dark chute, I was thrown against walls on the inside. Free falling headfirst, *Naji's* high-pitched screams were easily mistaken for *Sasha's*. As we fumbled through more spider webs, we eventually landed in a pitch black room. The sand broke our fall. Rolling onto my stomach, I moaned,

"Ugh...Is everyone alive?"

"*Amazonian* fine. Get off of foot." *Sasha* responded, yanking her leg from under my torso.

"Yeah, I'm good...So is the emerald," *Naji* replied.

Standing on my feet, I began wiping the sand from my clothes. "From now on, give us a heads-up before you steal anything, okay?" I demanded.

"Will do, captain. Now, let's see about getting some light in this coffin," *Naji* remarked, rummaging through his gear.

Pulling out a flare, he snapped the top, activating a dazzling flicker. "Ah, that's better. Where the hell are we?" he asked.

Scanning the dark room, I could hardly see ten feet away. We stood on a bed of sand, with a wall just behind us. Tapping my shoulder, *Sasha* pointed to her right.

"Who's that?" She asked.

Turning my head, there laid a dried up skeleton, sword and shield in hand with its plain bones decorated with cobwebs.

"The poor guy must have starved to death," I concurred, stepping closer.

When suddenly, something shuffled up ahead.

"Shhh - did you hear that?" *Naji* whispered.

"Yeah, it sounded like something moved over there." I replied.

Slowly drawing my sword, it happened again. The sound of something scurrying could be heard up ahead in the darkness.

"There it goes again. What do you think it is?" *Naji* questioned.

Pausing momentarily, we leaned forward, staring into the void... Only hearing silence.

After a few seconds, I lowered my guard saying,

"Whatever it was, it stopped. Come on, let's find a way out of here."

Without warning, a 7 ft creature lurched from the darkness. Frightened, I stumbled backwards onto the floor. Activating my shield, I raised my hand to cover my face in fear.

Clang! The metal sheet vibrated.

As I peeked around the shield, a stinger swayed before me as a jet black scorpion slowly crept out from the shadows. Pulling its tail back, the creature struck once more. Immediately I rolled to the side, avoiding its attack.

"Get back!" I yelled, springing to my feet.

Readying her spear, *Sasha* took a defensive stance, while *Naji* pinpointed his target.

Bang!

Whizzing through the air, the bullet ricocheted against the scorpion's glossy carapace barely leaving a scratch. Placing the rifle strap around his neck, *Naji* quickly drew his sword stating. "Well, that's out of the question."

Charging forward, the scorpion clamped its pincers. Left and right it poked with a flurry, trying to pinch down. Spinning her spear, *Sasha* desperately blocked the attacks. The shiny monster then lunged with its tail and *Naji* fenced with the scorpion's deadly stinger. Back and forth they danced, as the fiend kept the upper hand.

With *Sasha* thrusting the spear into the creature's face, it let out a loud screech before swatting her to the ground. Squirming for a second, the scorpion soon regained focus. Removing *Sasha's* spear with its pincers, it snapped it in half. Aiming for the *Amazonian*, the creature then began creeping closer, raising its tail high for a deadly strike. Jumping in the way, I took the fierce blow to my shield.

Clang!

Sliding across the sand, I scurried to cover *Sasha* as the scorpion pressed the attack. Swinging my shield erratically, we crawled backwards dodging it's large mandibles.

With a wide swing, *Naji* managed to sever one of the creature's thick legs from behind. As it stumbled around, the scorpion raised its arms high, screeching like before. A green ooze dripped on the sand, radiated by a toxic glow. In a flash, the creature swung its long tail in a circle. Using his reflexes *Naji* ducked low, managing to roll underneath.

Naji made his way over to *Sasha* and I. Agitated, the scorpion clamped its claws, slowly stalking our direction.

Hearing the arachnid skitter across the sand, we quickly backed ourselves against the wall. "What do now, traveler man?" She asked, as they moved behind me. Taking a defensive position, I raised my shield.

"This time, I'm not sure…" I trembled.

With a vengeance, the scorpion cocked back and launched its stinger forcefully, instantly demanding we dodge to the side.

Barely evading the attack, its dangerous stinger smashed a gaping hole into the stone wall. Noticing a hallway on the other side, *Naji* began pushing *Sasha* through.

"Go - now's our chance!" he shouted.

Facing the scorpion, I swung my sword to buy them some time. Banging against the shield, it continued reaching for me with its pincers.

While avoiding the claws, I managed to ram my blade into a soft spot in its armor. Wiggling backwards, the bleeding scorpion was now distracted.

Turning around I climbed into the hole, sucking in my stomach for leverage. *Sasha* and *Naji* grabbed my arms, helping to pull me through the wall. Rushing to my feet, I backed away from the hole-

-and not a moment too soon, as the scorpion's elongated stinger stopped just inches away from my face, before retracting back into the darkroom. Stepping away from the hole, beads of sweat rolled down my forehead.

"Huff Huff. That was way too close," I panted.

Staring down both sides of the hall, *Naji* said, "It looks like the other side has collapsed. I guess we've got to go this way."

"Right. Let's keep moving," I agreed, sheathing my sword.

Walking down the mysterious hallway was nerve-wracking. With each passing step, the eerie silence played tricks on my mind. Since the beginning of our adventure, we've had one unfortunate event after another. So this time, I was anticipating our next encounter. Was it going to be a ghost, claiming we've stolen its family heirloom? Or maybe a bloodthirsty mummy, searching for revenge? The hand-carved inscriptions on the walls didn't tell the tale, but it definitely fueled my imagination.

While daydreaming I stepped upon a loose tile, triggering a mechanism. Instantly, a school of darts zipped by

in front of us from secret crevices in the wall. We had waltzed into another trap.

Endlessly, the darts wizzed in all directions. Flying with no apparent pattern, it left us with no time to figure one out. Raising my shield, I waved to *Sasha* & *Naji* shouting. "Get behind me!"
Dashing through the hallway, we kept our heads low. Bracing my buckler to the left, darts ricocheted off its steel exterior before dropping to the floor.

I then leapt over a heap of rubble blocking the path, as the cloud of darts swarmed like bees. Balling up behind the shield, I continued to provide cover for our party, swinging the sheet of metal from side to side. The end of the hall was now in sight. Sprinting for the exit I fell to the floor, sliding for home base.

Coming in right behind me *Sasha* and *Naji* followed suit, as the darts finally came to a stop. We came to another small foyer branching off into three more directions. With the exception of the path on our right, that had caved in.

"The path is divided into separate routes, and we can't go back the way we came... Any ideas?" *Naji* asked.

Placing her hand upon *Naji's* shoulder, *Sasha* teased with a smile, "Yeah. You touch nothing."

While standing in the center of the room, I surveyed both hallways.

"The hall up ahead seems to lead downstairs. The treasure's got to be down there," I said.
"Then it sounds like a plan..." A deep voice echoed from the pathway on our left. Startled, we drew our weapons ready for an attack.

Seconds later, five rough-looking pirates appeared from down the hallway. Holding firearms, they pointed them in our direction. Shuffling behind them, a securely chained prisoner was pushed down to his knees, as the prisoner raised his head.

"*Spectre*?" I mumbled.

A tall figure then came into focus behind him, clapping his hands for emphasis. He spoke:

"Great job finding the *Lost City* all on your own. I must say, you kids are smarter than you look... How about you come work for me? The *Red Ring* could use people with your talents!"

Hearing such a half-hearted statement was an insult to my intelligence. Dropping his jaw in surprise, *Naji* said, "Lock-jaw? How did you- "

When I then stepped in front of him, interrupting, "Thanks, but we don't want whatever it is you're selling, metal mouth."

Grabbing *Spectre's* chains, he hoisted him onto his feet then walked him in front of his flunkies, "Pity. You've all got so much potential. But it seems you're destined to be nothing more than scallywags," *Lock-jaw* stated.

Raising my sword, I gritted my teeth growling, "Let him go."

"Heh heh, you're in no position to make demands. Now, hand over your weapons," *Lock-jaw* returned, chuckling lightly.

"No way *Thomas*, it's a trick," *Naji* whispered behind me.

Punching *Spectre* in the abdomen, *Lock-jaw* knelt him back down to his knees. Drawing an old gun from his belt, he pointed the flintlock pistol to the side of *Spectre's* head. A silver and onyx & red ring glistened on his finger, catching my eye.

"Drop them...Or your friend here gets it." *Lock-jaw* threatened.

Spectre looked up at us, giving a smirk and saying, "*Cough-cough* Don't trust him, kid. I'm not worth it."

Clicking back the hammer on his pistol, *Lock-jaw* and I locked eyes. Then dropping my sword to the floor, I said to *Naji,* "Lay them down."

Staring at me with confusion, *Naji* paused for a second before dropping his sword and rifle.

"Okay, but I hope you know what you're doing," He whispered.

Instantly, the pirates walked over and retrieved our weapons. "You three are going to be our personal slaves, and the first order of business? Finding that treasure. Legend has it, one of those ancient *Power Crystals* are laying around here, and I'm curious to know if its power is real. Now, let's get a move on, shall we," *Lock-jaw* stated, placing his pistol into his belt.

Shoving us with their guns, *Lock-jaw* and his men forced us through the hallway leading downstairs. As we walked down the staircase, I turned to *Sasha* saying, "I'm

228

sorry we dragged you into this Sasha... You deserve better friends."

Holding back her beautiful smile, she replied, "Traveler man kidding? *Amazonian* never had so much fun in life. *Sasha* go back home with BIG stories."

Walking beside *Spectre*, *Naji* asked, "I thought these guys were dead? Their ship was in pieces, how did they find you?"

"Turns out that warship was stronger than we thought. He was able to steer the damn thing near our crash site, shortly after we fell from the sky. By nightfall we were surrounded." *Spectre* explained, with his hands bound behind him.

"That's enough out of you two! Pipe down!" One of the ruffians crowed, while pushing *Spectre* and *Naji* with the butt of his rifle.

Suddenly, the sound of another mechanism triggered. A loud 'Shink!' echoed up ahead, as a bed of sharp spikes sprang up from the floor tiles, skewering one of *Lock-jaws* men.
Instantly, we all stopped in fear of activating another trap. Then after realizing the coast was clear, *Lock-jaw* stated,

"Tread lightly men...This place is booby-trapped," as we continued our stride.

Walking through layers of cobweb, a large heap of rocks in our way proved more difficult than the task of finding the treasure itself. Some required us to shimmy between obtuse boulders, while others called for a more subtle climbing approach. Dry weeds lying on the floor crunched underfoot with each step.

Tat's when I heard the click from another mechanism - a thorned log came swinging from a trap door in the wall. Bludgeoning another one of the pirates, the wooden log rammed into his chest with a hard -

Whack!

Leaving his blood dripping from the thorns bursting from his back. Pausing momentarily, *Lock-jaw* said. "Hmph, more treasure for us... I want you to lead." While pointing in my direction.

"Who me? No way, didn't you see what that thing just did!?" I refuted, waving my hands.

Nodding his head to his men, they grabbed hold of *Sasha* as she struggled to get free. While raising their weapons, *Lock-jaw* demanded with an evil smirk. "You lead... Or the girl dies."

"This guy's really starting to grind my gears." *Naji* mumbled, balling up his fist.

Without much of a choice, I responded. "Fine! Just let her go."

Nonchalantly raising his hand, *Lock-jaw* commanded, "Let the girl go...No funny business you three." Pushing *Sasha* forward, the pirates chuckled as they released her.

I took the forefront, moving us along...

Cautiously trying to avoid triggering another trap, I paid close attention to the details of the temple. Making sure to step lightly and keep our hands off the walls, we eventually exited the hall, entering another room.

Upon walking inside, a tall ceiling was easily noticeable thanks to a ray of light illuminating the floor. A dusty skeleton holding a leather satchel sat beside a star-shaped podium fixed in the center of the room. Bearing a hole at the top, the podium was elegantly inscribed in calligraphy. We had finally come to a dead end. Only a giant slab of marble laid ahead.

"Perfect. I should have known that it was a hoax. Where is the treasure?" *Lock-jaw* lamented, stepping forward.

Examining the giant slab, I noticed indentions concave to the surface.

"Hey guys, check this out. There's something strange about this rock," I called to *Sasha* and *Naji*.

While rubbing the smooth texture, *Sasha* concurred, "Something missing."

Avoiding the skeleton, *Naji* inspected the carved rock in the center.

"That's not all. Look at the writings on this podium... They don't connect like all the other writings around the temple," he stated.

Becoming irritated, *Lock-jaw* sat on the podium folding his arms.

"Whatever it is, I'm losing my patience," He growled, while leaning his foot against the base. Suddenly, a small piece of the podium chipped off and fell to the floor. Looking down, he kicked it to the side saying, "Guess this place is older than it looks," causing his goons to snicker.

"What's this?" *Naji* questioned, while picking it up.

Walking beside him, I analyzed the object. "It looks like the piece of a tile," I replied.

Kneeling before the podium, *Lock-jaw* stepped aside as *Naji* started to wiggle some of the inscribed tiles. Suddenly, they all began falling down, fourteen in tall. Lifting them higher, *Naji* squinted his eyes for a better look.

Having a stroke of genius I blurted, "I've got it! What if all these tiles fit together on that slab? You know, like a puzzle?"

"I think you're onto something, kid." *Spectre* responded.

"For your sake. I hope so," *Lock-jaw* threatened, giving me a sinister look.

Gathering up all the tiles, *Naji* and I brought them over to the giant piece of marble. As we placed one onto the smooth surface, it was then snatched from my hand, sticking to the slab like a magnet. This grabbed everyone in the room's attention and everybody stopped what they were doing to see what came next. Then one by one we stuck the tiles on the slab, completely filling the smooth area. Taking a few steps back, *Naji* and I waited anxiously for the treasure to appear...

Until nothing happened.

"Well?" *Sasha* remarked.

"I don't get it. It should have worked," I said, scratching my head.

Looking at the strange puzzle, *Naji* leaned his head sideways,

"Maybe we've got it the wrong way," he said.

While digging through the skeleton's bag for treasure, one of *Lock-jaw's* men pulled out an old tattered book, tossing it aside on the floor. Sliding across the floor, it soon stopped at *Spectre's* feet.

"Thomas, take a look at this," *Spectre* said.

Walking over I picked it up. The initials of R.B. were branded on the hide cover. I then began flipping the pages, soon coming to a conclusion.

"This journal is filled with information about the *Lost City*. Names of the kings, dates, agriculture. Look, there's even a codex in the back," I explained.

Getting an idea, *Naji* returned, "Maybe we can use the codex to translate the inscriptions on the tiles?"

"It's worth a try," I agreed, as we eyed the rectangular tiles. Wasting no time, we scanned through the pages in hopes of cracking the code.

About an hour had passed by the time we finally deciphered the transcript. *Lock-jaw* and his henchmen lounged around, keeping close watch over us. We eventually discovered the fourteen tiles were written in ancient *Mid East* calligraphy. They read:

- Sincerity - Certainty
- Ignorance - Love
- Acceptance - Obedience
- Deception - Hate
- Truth - Knowledge
- Doubt - Rejection
- Compliance - Resistance

After reviewing it for a few minutes, the puzzle still remained a mystery. No matter how many times we rearranged the words, nothing happened.

"Ugh. There has to be something we're not seeing," I groaned.

"That's impossible, we changed that thing a hundred times... Maybe it's broken?" *Naji* replied, flipping through the book.

Drawing his pistol, *Lock-jaw* growled,

"I've had enough of these games. It's been over an hour and you have yet to produce any results. Perhaps you've been stalling this whole time?..No worries. Now's my chance to get rid of all of you, once and for all."

As he aimed his pistol, *Spectre* then stood in front of us.

"They just need more time. Leave' em alone, brace-face. Besides, it's me you want," *Spectre* reasoned. Revealing a devilish grin, *Lock-jaw* lowered his weapon.

"Hmph, who knew you had such compassion for complete strangers? You're a disgrace to the *Red Ring*. We should have replaced you and *Division 3* a long time ago," *Lock-jaw* stated.

"My brother *Aku* is overzealous. His thirst for power is out of control. If you give him that *Power Crystal*, he'll lead the *Red Ring* into the darkness...You wouldn't understand," *Spectre* explained stoutly. "In the past few days I've known these kids, they've really shown me a lot. They've shown me it's never too late to follow your dreams, and not to let anything stand in your way."

After hearing his statement, I was deeply moved. During our journey together, I had never pictured *Spectre* as a person with such wisdom... Then again, staring down the wrong end of a barrel would change anyone's perspective.

"Oh, how touching. But what you don't understand is that I'm not finding that *Power Crystal* for him... I'm finding it for myself. Then finally, I can bring the world to its knees, under MY rule," *Lock-jaw* informed with a sinister glare.

"Now, have fun dying alongside your new comrades... Have at them." He continued, while giving his men the command to execute. Raising their firearms, his troops took aim as we braced ourselves for impact.

"Wait - tiles are opposite!" *Sasha* blurted suddenly.

Gaining our attention, we all turned around. "What are you talking about?" I asked.

"Traveler man put tiles wrong way. Must put them opposite," she continued, walking closer to the giant slab. Confused, I re-examined the puzzle, taking *Sasha's* advice into consideration. After a few seconds, I began rearranging the tiles once more.

"What are you doing? I think these guys are serious this time." *Naji* whispered behind me.

"Who cares? They'll kill us if we don't try anyway. Besides, I think *Sasha's* right... Maybe some of these words negate the others." I responded, continuing to move the puzzle.

Made curious by our defiance, *Lock-jaw* questioned:

"What's the meaning of this?"

After putting the last tile in place, I stepped back to double-check the puzzle. It now read:

- Knowledge - Ignorance
- Certainty - Doubt
- Sincerity - Obedience
- Truth - Deception
- Love - Hate
- Compliance - Resistance
- Acceptance - Rejection

All of a sudden, a mechanism triggered behind the marble slab, revealing a small slot in the middle. Astonished, I thanked *Sasha,*

"You're a genius, how did you know?"

"*Sasha* didn't. Puzzle just make sense," The *Amazonian* replied, shrugging her shoulders. While inspecting the hole in the center of the puzzle, I concurred,

"Looks like there's more... something must fit in there. Anyone seen more tiles laying around?"

Lowering their weapons, the pirates turned side to side scanning the floor for a missing tile. Even *Lock-jaw* gave his assistance, checking under the skeleton with his foot.
As we looked around, *Naji* noticed the ray of light shining down from the ceiling. Standing beside the podium, the beam casted a reflection off of *Spectre's* dark sunglasses.

"I got it!" He exclaimed.

Walking to the podium, he studied the indentation on the top. Rummaging through his pockets, *Naji* pulled out the green gem he pilfered earlier, placing it onto the podium.

Suddenly, the light was redirected through the emerald and into the small slot on the marble slab. Activating another loud mechanism, the ground began to rumble. Splitting into two sections, the puzzle slowly rotated to the sides, opening a stone door...

Scorpion.

5 ft.

Chapter 14
(2 Days left.)

Once the floor stopped shaking, my engineering mind was rapt with awe. The ability required to fashion nested hinges strong enough to slide the marble door was mind-boggling. It's excellent construction showed a skilled craftsmanship long forgotten.

"It seems you kids are good for something after all. Now, stop standing around and find my treasure," *Lock-jaw* stated, cold heartedly. Shoving us with their rifles, *Lock-jaw's* goons forced us inside. On the other side of the door sat the entrance to a small cavern. A set of winding slippery stairs were carved into the rock walls, leading down into a damp eerie void.

Upon our descent, I could feel the cool breeze of wind blowing past me. Shortly after, we reached the end of the staircase. Standing at the underbelly of the cave, the uneven surfaces of the walls were smooth but filled with tiny holes. I could tell the fungus and mildew in the crevices had been festering for a long time.

Stalactites from the ceiling hung about 50ft in the air. A raggedy wooden bridge was suspended before us, leading towards another part of the cave. Complete darkness laid below obscure ledges, with no telltale signs of the possible death that lay beneath us.

"Well, what are you waiting for? Go on," *Lock-jaw* anxiously commanded.

Unsure about the bridge's safety, I said to *Sasha* and *Naji,* "This thing doesn't look sturdy, watch your step."

Tapping my foot on the first floorboards, I swallowed a lump of spit before making my advance. As I tiptoed onto the bridge, the wooden planks creaked with each step.
The cold wind rushing against my face, made the hairs on the back of my neck stand. One by one we all moved on to the bridge, lowering it ever so close to what laid below.

Hearing *Naji* tremble before him, *Spectre* reassured, "Whatever you do, don't look down," when all of a sudden, a loud snap echoed behind us.

"Ahhh!"

A voice from behind screamed as the sound soon trailed away. Looking behind me, one of the pirates in the back was now missing. Stepping on a loose floorboard, he must have fallen through a hole in the bridge. As a result, the bridge momentarily swayed up and down, causing us to latch onto the braided ropes for security. Regaining stability, I cautiously tiptoed the remainder of the bridge.

Once we made it onto the other side, *Naji* dropped to the floor. Embracing the rough surface with wide arms.

"Oh thank God," He prayed, while kissing the ground.

Spectre stumbled to a halt as *Lock-jaw* growled, "On your feet. You've got work to do."

"What is this, *Rushian Roulette*? Three of your men just died," *Naji* replied, rolling over onto his butt.

Yanking *Naji* up right, the pirates began shoving us through the passage ahead. Away from the bridge, the cave narrowed into another tunnel. The hewn limestone walls glistened with an oily sheen, as the smell of chalk stained the air.

We then came to a wide set of steps, descending a few feet into a chamber. Upon entering, I instantly noticed a difference in the architecture. The room was sprawling with old antiques and scrolls, scattered all over a few tables and the floor.

Maps draped across the course walls, fixed above a collection of fine vases and pottery. Walking to a cluttered table, I thumbed through some old papers and books.

"Looks like another dead end. Where's the treasure?" *Naji* stated, spinning a globe beside the wall.

"Good question. Whoever these people were? They were excellent navigators. These calculations are accurate. Longitude and latitude, star patterns. There's even a section in here about algebra and chemistry. If the city's been lost for thousands of years, how could they have known that?" I returned, flipping through the old notes.

"There's a diagram of what the city once looked like drawn here as well. It looks like there were tall spires and arched bridges, with *Power Crystals* levitating around the buildings," I continued.

"Sound beautiful," *Sasha* replied wistfully.

Standing in front of a desk, *Naji* moved the beads on an abacus saying,

"That treasure's around here somewhere, maybe there's another hidden door."

"Then find it, before I lose my patience!" *Lock-jaw* barked, twisting his mouth in anger.

Spreading out, we began rummaging through years of research, tearing cobwebs from the furniture. *Lock-jaw* and his two remaining cronies lent a hand while keeping a close eye on us.

For about ten minutes, we searched through every scroll, drawer and vase finding nothing but dust bunnies and spiders. Sitting down in a chair beside a desk, I skimmed through the old journal from the puzzle room, reviewing the commentary, reading aloud.

"It says here, the *People of Old* reigned over the *Lost City* for millennia. But during the evil conquest of *The Dark One*, they fled their villages and stumbled upon a marooned group of *Pangea's* first men, and were embraced by their civilization. Their wealth and intellect went unmatched by anyone of their time. And their generosity was strange to these people."

"Pfft, generous enough to leave a cave filled with giant scorpions and loaded traps," *Naji* responded, curiously sticking his hand inside of a tall vase.

Leaning forward, I placed the book on top of the desk continuing, "It says the city was a lush oasis, with hanging gardens and palaces overlooking the *Atlantian* ocean. Gentle silver lakes complemented its exuberance, and various fruits were always in easy grasp. The intricate masonry was a testament to their vast knowledge of science and the stars above them."

"I know we're probably going to die, but is there a point to all of this?" *Naji* asked, while surveying a map on the wall, causing *Spectre* to reply,

"Yeah. What are you getting at?"

Putting my finger to my lips, I hushed them, "Shhh, just listen," then turned to another page before continuing. "This group of survivors were a righteous people, firm on upholding the truth. But the descendants of *Pangea's* first men came from a long line of soothsayers and magicians, as their forefathers were acolytes to *The Dark One*. However, the *People of Old* believed in a *Cosmic Creator* and the energy it bestowed into the *Piku* trees. Fearing the destructive tendencies of *Pangea's* first men, these survivors harnessed the *Piku* tree's energy in attempts to purify darkness from their society. But the conceit and arrogance from *Pangea's* first men eventually became corruption, as they continued their misguided rituals, eventually convincing them to pledge allegiance to *The Dark One,* once more."

"So? What happened next?" *Naji* said, suddenly intrigued.

Flipping to the next page, I continued, "So? I think these ruins are the fabled city of *Atlantia*. The *Atlantians* must have built this temple with all of these traps, to HIDE the treasure from *The Dark One, ho*ping that he would never find it." Standing beside me *Sasha* leaned back, sitting on the desk.

"What happened to city?" She asked.

"It says the ancient people mysteriously vanished without a trace. And as legend has it, *The Dark One* sent a great plague to ravage the natives... Obliterating their entire civilization," I explained.

"Well, that was a beautiful story. Now, where's the loot?" *Naji* returned with sarcasm.

Knocking over vases and throwing papers to the floor, the pirates were becoming aggravated. Facing *Naji*, I stood up with a look of insight, then said,

"You know what, I think I get it now. Maybe we've had it wrong this whole time?"

Turning over tables and antiques, *Lock-jaw* and his vandals began trashing the room.

"It's obvious there's nothing down here except a stack of old books. The treasure was a hoax," *Lock-jaw* said to his thugs.

"What are you talking about, kid? Now is not the time to go all looney on us," *Spectre* replied, staring at me.

Picking up the book off of the desk, I pointed my finger in the middle.

"Maybe the missing clue is the same message that the *People of Old* gave to *Pangea's* first inhabitants. That all of this energy flowing around us, even in the *Piku* trees, was meant to connect us and bring us all together, As One... Look, there's more translation on the next page."

Squinting my eyes, I continued, "But I can't pronounce the sentence."

Snatching the tattered journal from my hands, Naji stated, "Here, let me try," then began sounding out the words in his head.

Unsheathing their swords, *Lock-jaw* and his swashbucklers approached us. Drawing my four barrel pistol, he bore his typical evil smile. "Well scallywags, your journey has come to an end. It's time you landlubbers walk the plank."

Aiming the pistol, *Lock-jaw* sadistically teased, "Heh heh, Any last words?"

Raising our hands to our shoulders I realized, maybe this WAS it? Maybe our journey HAD come to a disappointing end? Staring down the barrel of my own creation, I turned to look at my friends. One last time.

Unaware of the threat at hand, *Naji* continued to review the contents of the book.

"Hey *Thomas*, I think I got it. This is written in an old *Saharian* calligraphy. It reads : La-ilaha-illallah!" He pronounced.

Hearing *Lock-jaw* pull the hammer back on the pistol, a loud mechanism suddenly triggered behind the wall. Feeling the room begin to rumble, we bent low fearing another trap. Grabbing hold of the furniture, I stumbled into a vase trying to regain my balance.

"What happened, traveler man? We dead yet?" *Sasha* shouted over the rumbling.

A long map on the wall then glided to the floor, as a bare patch of limestone behind it began sinking deep into the ground, revealing a secret room. Once the tremors subsided, I arose to my feet.

"Is everyone all right?" I asked.

Struggling to get up with his hands restrained, *Spectre* groaned. "Uggh, what's better than having shackles cut off your circulation."

Running fingers through her hair, *Sasha* looked ahead then gasped. While tracing her eyes, I noticed a golden shimmer coming from the secret room. Stashing my pistol

245

between his belt, *Lock-jaw* and his men stepped inside with mouths wide.

"Hey guys? You're gonna want to see this…" *Naji* stated, entering behind them.

Sasha and I shared a look of curiosity. As we followed *Naji* into the new chamber, I was instantly captivated. A room so deep it could pass for an olympic swimming pool laid before us, filled with all kinds of treasures. Weapons, jewelry, artifacts, gold and silver coins, rich fabrics, polished gems, you name it. The exuberant sparkle reflected off the glossy walls, like a disco ball. Piled in mountains, the treasure sprawled across the floor in the large heaps, at least ten feet high. It was all here, and shining radiantly.

Up ahead, a glowing blue stone sat above an altar. Getting an idea, I decided to open the compass from my pocket. It was then that I realized the two stones were one and the same, as the needle now pointed directly towards the pedestal. It was the *Power Crystal*.
Basking in the ambience, we walked down a small flight of stairs carved into the side of the wall.

"Is - is this real? Tell me I'm not dreaming," *Naji* exclaimed.

Grabbing two handfuls of golden coins, I examined them closely validating their authenticity.

"Nope, you're not dreaming. And yes, this is real," I said with a smile. I then threw coins high into the air, shouting. "We did it! We found the treasure!" As the golden coins came raining down. Jumping around, *Sasha*, *Naji* and I began to celebrate.

Belly flopping into a pile of jewels, *Naji* swung his limbs back and forth, making angels. Holding *Sasha's* hands, we hopped around in circles kicking coins into the air. Awestruck, *Spectre's* mouth drooled as he walked between the cornucopia laid before him. Stuffing coin into their pockets, the two pirates wasted no time.

Lock-jaw palmed a lump of coins, then slowly poured them back into the cache. Wrinkling his face diabolically, he formulated a plan mumbling.

"The crystal wasn't a myth?"

Turning around, I heard the sound of a hammer click. Facing *Lock-jaw*, I clearly saw that he was aiming my pistol once again. "Sorry to rain on your parade, but we'll be taking the treasure now." He informed us.

"What?! You can't do that!" *Naji* shouted , while sitting up.

"Yeah, worked hard for this!" *Sasha* exclaimed, balling her fists.

"Hahaha, that's touching. Now I really appreciate all your help. But it seems you are no longer useful," *Lock-jaw* returned, with a smirk. Then aiming the pistol, he fired a shot - Bang!

All of a sudden, the room began to convulse. *Lock-jaw* lost his footing and the bullet veered and ripped through my left arm, ricocheting off the treasures behind. Instantly, I felt a surge of fire course through my arm. Falling to the floor, I tensed up in pain from the gunshot.

"Grrr, now what?!" *Lock-jaw* questioned while looking around.

One of his pirates now held the small glowing *Power Crystal* they'd removed from the altar. While trying to stuff it into his pocket, the pirate realized he'd triggered another mechanism, which caused the tremor.

"Heh heh, Sorry boss," he apologized with a look of shame.

Suddenly, the entrance to the room began to close. Geysers of rushing water started bursting through the walls as the room quaked. Rolling to the side, I escaped *Lock-jaw's* line of sight while he was distracted. Large rocks then came crashing down all around the room.

Grabbing an antique golden helmet, *Sasha* clocked *Lock-jaw* across the face, causing him to fumble into a pile of treasure, dropping my four-barreled gun. As *Sasha* dashed behind another pile, *Lock-jaw* quickly drew his other pistol and fired rapidly.

Bang - Bang - Bang!

The bullets ricocheted, as they missed her by inches.

"Grrr!" He roared.

Naji then managed to free *Spectre* from the chains binding him. *Sasha* helped me onto my feet, and we grabbed some weapons out of the treasure pile. The water in the room was now starting to rise, soon reaching our feet. Picking up a jeweled sword, I met one of the henchmen head-on.

Clang!

Blocking an attack with my shield, I countered with a low swing, forcing him to jump over it. Once he landed, he swung his flail for my midsection, but I parried with the right side of my blade. Instinctively, I returned with a slashing attack, slicing his throat.

The other pirate quickly approached, as *Sasha* stepped before me. Swinging left and right, he unleashed a flurry of vicious attacks. Dodging to the side, *Sasha* was having trouble defending herself with the tiny golden dagger she had chosen. Thrusting her knife through the air, it was easily tossed to the side each time it hit the pirates club. Evening the odds, I leapt forward with a wide swing, but was blocked effortlessly, due to my limitation of now using one arm. Kicking me into a pile of treasure, the pirate then gave *Sasha* a backhand to the floor. Lifting his sword for the final strike, the private chuckled.

Bang!

A shot echoed, jerking his body forward. The pirate stared at the gaping hole in his chest before toppling over. *Naji* then appeared from around a heap of golden coins, holding my four-barreled pistol.

"The place is flooding! At this rate, we're gonna drown!" He exclaimed.

While holding my bleeding arm, I quickly assessed that the water had risen up to our thighs, hindering our mobility.

"We've got to find a way out of here! Quick, get the *Power Crystal!*" I replied.

"Not so fast!" A grizzly voice threatened. Aiming his flintlock pistol, *Lock-jaw* slowly approached from behind, now holding the glowing *Power Crystal* in his off hand. "What? You thought I was going to let you off that easily?" He taunted.

249

"Now's not the time, metal mouth. We've got to find an exit, or we're ALL going to die." I responded, waist-deep in a cold pool.

"It's too late, boy. In a couple of minutes we'll all be fish food, lost for another thousand years just like the treasure." *Lock-jaw* stated, while looking around to survey the damage.

"Are you really that vengeful? You would lose everything trying to settle a score?" I tried to reason, shaking my head.

"Hmph, only one way to find out. Now, show yourself *Spectre*! Or your friends sleep with the fishes!" He replied while grinning dastardly, still pointing the large flintlock gun at me.

As he prepared to pull the trigger, another voice shouted over the rushing waters:

"Leave them alone, *Jaws*!"

Seconds later, *Spectre* then revealed himself from behind a pile of shimmering coins, wielding a golden katana. "Sorry I'm late. I had to find the right blade."

As the water reached our abdomens, *Lock-jaw* said,

"There you are. I was afraid you'd gotten cold feet."

Pointing his weapon, *Spectre* replied,

"This ends now..."

Watching the pressure about to burst on *Spectre* and *Lock-jaw's* lids, I paused to reflect on the situation. Here I was, fighting a leader of perilous pirates, the most wanted man this side of *Pangaea*. With only one day left to come up with 100,000 coin, I was in too deep to run away now.

Staring *Spectre* in the eyes, *Lock-jaw* tossed his pistol into the water.

"I can feel the *Crystal's* power surging through my body. You were never fit to lead *Division 3*... So be it." He replied, while raising his large sword.

Wading through the water, *Spectre* and *Lock-jaw* climbed opposite sides of a mountain of treasure. Eager to settle the score, they charged simultaneously, kicking up golden coins in their wake.

With the water almost up to our necks, *Naji* exclaimed,

"Hurry, there's not much time!"

Splitting up, we began searching the confines of the room. Desperately trying to find an exit, we felt around for any loose rocks or hidden switches, but the rising water continued bursting through the walls. Within moments, the rushing water had flooded most of the area, forcing us to seek higher ground.

Swinging his katana to the left, *Spectre* followed upward with a quick slash. Dodging to the side, *Lock-jaw* countered with a hard cleave, as the two blades clashed with a loud sound. *Lock*-jaw came back with an overhead strike, but his weapon fell short, smashing into the pile of treasure, as coins scattered. Following up with a series of thrusts, *Spectre* pressed the attack. Weaving between the sword's jabs, *Lock-jaw* managed to avoid his attacks, then lunged his blade down the center line.

Parrying the greatsword, *Spectre* returned with a stunning fist to *Lock-jaw's* rib cage causing him to stumble backward. Then, suddenly harnessing the power of the *Crystal*, *Lock-jaw's* muscles began to bulge.

He then used his enhanced combat reflexes to predict his opponent's next attack. While swinging wide, *Spectre* was then caught off guard by a handful of coins thrown into his face.
Lock-jaw then ducked his attack, as boulders fell from the ceiling. Elbowing *Spectre* in the stomach, *Lock-jaw* swept him off his feet with the broadside of his blade, *Spectre* crashing into the water with a splash.

"Such power! I can feel it coursing through my veins!" he roared, as his eyes began glowing in a neon blue.

Ascending the pile of treasure, I tried to intervene with a crippling strike to *Lock-jaw's* throat, but he easily countered as he deflected the blow, kicking me off the mound. Raising his sword above his head, *Lock-jaw* pounced on *Spectre* with a spring attack. Relying on his mobility, *Spectre* rolled to the side barely avoiding a critical blow. The large blade plunged into the gold, with a loud clanging thud.

"We have to stop him before the *Crystal* gives him too much power!" I shouted.

Immediately, *Sasha* scaled the shimmering mountain and fell upon him with a surprise attack. With a dazzling display of speed and agility, she managed to pierce *Lock-jaw's* tough skin. However, the *Crystal's* limitless energy willed him to backhand her into the water. Ignoring the minor flesh wounds, they instantly began to reconstruct, as wispy swirls of blue energy filled the puncture.

"Ha ha ha! I'm Invincible!" He yelled vehemently.

Hopping onto his feet, *Spectre* and *Lock-jaw* proved their weapon finesse while exchanging a flurry of blows. Locked in a heated battle, they peered into each others' souls.

Stepping to the side, *Lock-jaw* then forced another powerful strike.

All of a sudden using his deadly aim, *Naji* seized the opportunity and fired a precise shot into *Lock-jaw's* spine, giving *Spectre* enough time to dodge the deadly attack.

"Graahr!"

Lock-jaw bellowed as he dropped the glowing *Crystal* from his hand into the water. Staggering for a second, he looked down at the wound, expecting it to heal. Then without hesitation, *Spectre* plunged the sword into his solar plexus, finishing him for good.

Stumbling back a few steps, *Lock-jaw* mumbled,

"Touche..." before slowly falling off the mound of treasure and into the water with a loud splash.

A boulder then dropped from the ceiling and landed on top of him, while the room continued to split asunder.

"Cough - cough. We're not going to make it!" I said, spitting up water.

With only a yard of breathing room from the roof, we were running out of time. "It's not supposed to end like this! We proved the myth, we found the treasure!" *Naji* responded.

"Not every story has a happy ending, kid," *Spectre* replied, swimming towards us.

"But we're too young to die! I'm handsome, I've got good teeth - hell, I haven't even had my first kiss yet!" *Naji* confessed in fear.

Rolling his eyes toward *Sasha*, he slowly leaned in. Puckering up for a smooch. Repulsed, *Sasha* stuck her hand into his face stating, "No thanks. *Sasha* not dead yet."

With less than a foot of breathing room, *Naji* stated,

"Look *Thomas*, before we die, I just wanted to thank you for always being there for me, even when nobody else would... I know I've dragged you through a lot of trouble over the years, and that dealing with me can be difficult. But you've always stuck it out with me 'til the end... You'll always be my brother and I love you. Thanks man."

While treading water, I was moved by *Naji's* tear jerking performance. The trials we endured during this expedition had made us both better men, as young as we still were. And Naji was now more patient and humble than ever before.

"Look, about what I said before, I didn't really mean it. I was just angry. I'm glad Mom and Dad took you on that day. I mean, who else would I have that drives me crazy right?" I explained with a smile.

"Hey, what are brothers for?" *Naji* returned.

Taking our last deep breaths, the water finally submerged us. I looked down through the clearness, seeing *Lock-jaw* pinned under a rock, his lifeless henchmen drifting beside him in the water's current. The reflections from the golden treasure were astounding. Yellow sparkles glistened through the water as coins and jewels spun in the swirling eddies.

Swimming through the room, we searched the walls diligently. Then tugging my pant leg, *Sasha* pointed to the altar. While swimming over, I noticed a stream of bubbles escaping from under the bottom. Quickly rallying *Naji* and *Spectre*, I returned with their help. Grabbing hold, we began to push against the stone altar, inching it slowly. Once the hole was wide enough, *Sasha* squeezed through as we followed suit.

The hole led us into a small underwater tunnel that snaked beneath the *Lost City of Old*. Almost running out of air, we managed to find a hump in the tunnel, creating a small air pocket above us. Stopping for a breather, Naji gasped.

"*Huff Huff - cough*. How far do you think this tunnel goes?"

"Huff Huff - Who knows? It's too late to turn back now," *Spectre* returned.

"But what about the treasure? What about the *Crystal*? What if it's another trap?" *Naji* questioned.

Catching my breath, I answered, "Right now, I don't think there's much of a choice."
Suddenly, the tunnel began to rumble and quake. Chunks of rock crumbled around us, falling over our heads. A roar could be heard brewing from behind, causing the water to ripple.

Something huge was coming.

Ducking the debris, I shouted, "We've got to go! Come on!"

Diving under, we continued our way through the tunnel, as rocks cluttered the path and sank to the bottom, making it difficult to squeeze through. I began to fear the worst, as my lungs constricted from lack of air. A mild headache then set in.

The roar became louder and more intense by the time we finally came to a bright light. Closing the distance, the mouth to the exit widened and the ground soon became shallow. Stumbling to the exit *Sasha* suddenly paused.

"This not good," she relayed.

Just steps behind her, *Naji* came to a halt. "Huff - huff. What? What is it?"

"See for self," she replied pointing outside the tunnel.

Trudging through the water, I held my bleeding arm, soon standing before the exit. Looking out ahead, I could see nothing but clear skies and floating islands scattered on the horizon. Realizing there was nothing beneath us, our situation had taken another unfortunate turn. We were stranded.

Holding on to the wall, *Spectre* peered over the edge saying. "It looks like the cliff side of a mountain. We must be on the bottom of the island. You know, like an iceberg."

"So what are we supposed to do? Tie our shoelaces together then swing to the top?" *Naji* asked, pacing back and forth.

"That's an option," I answered, staring down below.

Hearing the earth begin to rumble once more, we swayed with the tremors. The frightening roar of the water pressure building up, raised at the hairs on the back of my neck.

"Whatever it is, we better hurry. Because here it comes," *Spectre* returned. With nowhere left to run, we braced ourselves for impact.

Seconds later, a fierce wave came spiraling through the tunnel. Washing me away, the current swept us out from the cave.
The built up pressure managed to launch us fifty feet out into the air. Spinning around helplessly, my heart jumped from my chest. We were free falling through the clouds, with nothing beneath us for hundreds of miles.

The winds ripped past my face, as we picked up immense speed. *Sasha* and *Naji* continued to flail about in circles, kicking and screaming. *Spectre* tried his best to steer toward one of the islands by flapping his arms, but failed desperately. Knowing death was imminent, I shut my eyes out of fear. Letting my body go limp, I fell backwards... this was it.

All of a sudden, my back hit something soft that bounced me in the opposite direction. Within moments I came back down, landing on something warm and rubbery. Rolling onto my stomach, I realized I was no longer falling. Seconds later *Sasha*, *Naji* & *Spectre* came bouncing down as well, as the mysterious surface broke our fall. Standing up, we looked around in confusion. We were in a cloud, and all we could see was the hazy outline of each other and the alien surface we had landed on.

Speculating about the outcome, *Naji* questioned, "Umm, where are we?"

"I'm not sure, but whatever this thing is? It's saved our lives," I responded, scratching my head.

Kneeling down, *Sasha* rubbed the surface. Inspecting it closer she said. "This look familiar. *Sasha* seen before." Taking a better look, I noticed the bright red material and the roped nets overlapping the surface.

"Yeah, you're right. It kind of looks like those balloons above a zeppelin," I concurred.

Out of nowhere I heard the sound of *Spectre* laughing heartily.

"What's so funny?" I asked curiously.

His head poking up over the edge, he replied, "Hahaha. Welcome aboard, kid!"

Dumbfounded, *Sasha, Naji* and I shared a puzzled look. Walking to the edge, I carefully shimmied down a net with my right arm, as the other arm was still in pain. I followed *Spectre* down the side. Upon reaching the bottom, we climbed down onto the top deck of a ship; it was The *Silver Bullet* herself. Stupefied, we looked around with wide eyes. Immediately, one of *Spectre's* men saw my bleeding arm then began to wrap it in a bandage, applying pressure.

"How - how did? But, I thought the ship still needed repairs?" I stuttered, watching his crew tend their posts. Taking off his sunglasses to wipe them, *Spectre* answered,

"Oh, it did. But I had the boys make some last-minute adjustments."
Shaking my head, I returned. "But didn't *Lock-jaw's* crew capture the *Silver Bullet* when they captured you? How did your crew escape *Lock-jaw's* men?"

"I'm a man of many mysteries," He said with a knowing grin. "So? Where to now?"

Staring at *Sasha* and *Naji*, I lowered my head, disappointed that I let them down. After coming all this way, we had nothing to show for it. Stepping closer, *Sasha* placed her hand on my shoulder with a smile. The once sheltered *Amazonian* now wore the scars of perilous adventures. She was now free to shape her own destiny, and live life on her own terms. Eager to embrace what laid ahead.

"Who cares we didn't keep treasure. Traveler man still find *Lost City*," she consoled.

Naji then walked forward, handing me my four-barreled gun.

"Yeah, you had a dream and you saw it through. Besides, we've still got one more day to come up with the coin. I'm sure we'll think of something…"

My morale boosted, I accepted their encouraging words. Giving *Spectre* a smirk, I commanded:

"Take us home."

Standing behind the wheel, *Spectre* yelled to his first mate,

"All right, I want all hands on deck! Set the mast full sail! We're headin' home!"

The man with the serpent tattoo on his face quickly gave a salute.

"Aye-aye, Captain!" he shouted, as the crew ran about the ship, preparing for departure.

Sasha and *Naji* had moved to the side of the ship, watching a flock of macaw parrots soar in the distance.

Heading to the bow, I leaned over the banister, thinking to myself. We did find the treasure, proving that the legend was true. We braved the tallest of mountains - trekked across the *Saharian Desert*, hell - we even battled ninjas! Even though no one would probably ever believe us without the gold, isn't that what an adventure is all about? During this journey, I've met a group of total strangers that have since become my closest friends. And like my father once said, "There's nothing like family."

The *Silver Bullet* soon picked up speed, once the sails were raised. Shooting off into the clouds, we followed the sun rays lining the horizon... What a voyage.

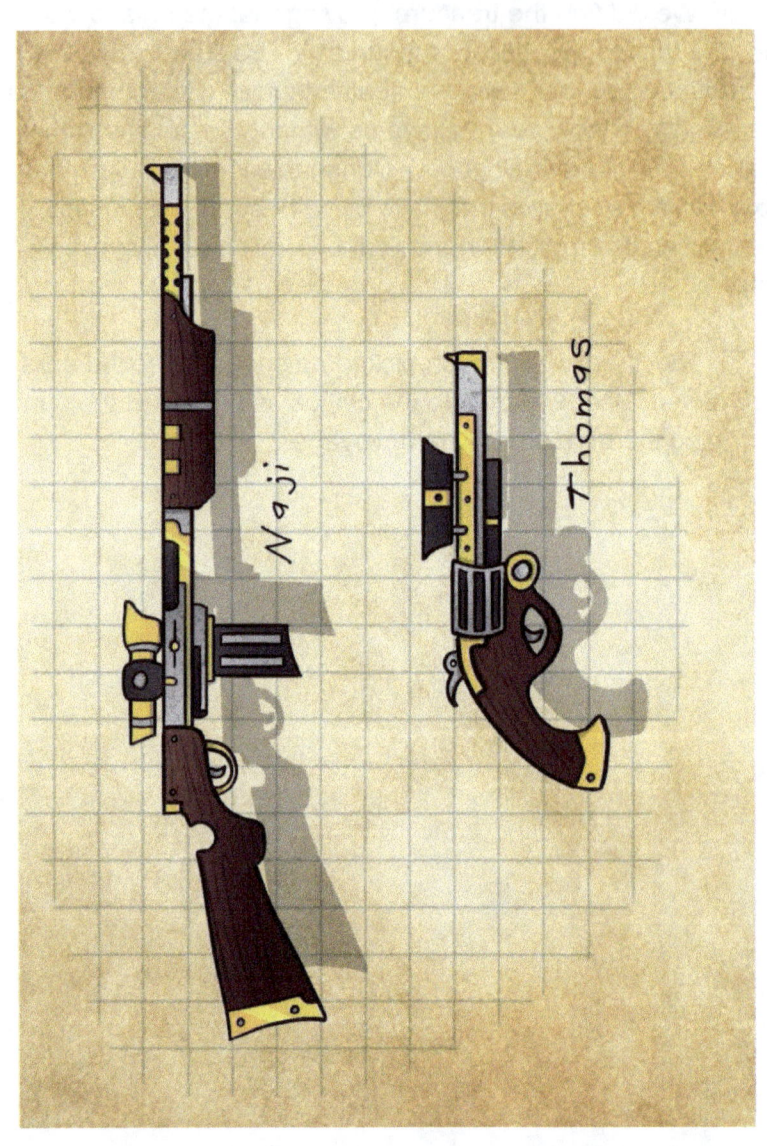

Naji

Thomas

Epilogue

One month later...

Since our return, the sling around my left arm had become a major conversation starter amongst my peers. They were fascinated by the bullet wound, so I made up a cool story. I figured no one would have believed me if I told them the truth anyway.

While turning the handlebars on my bicycle, I glided through a mob of pedestrians. The beautiful city of *Edenia* was now under construction, so more people than normal clustered the cobblestone streets. With my legs stretched in front of me, the steam powered engine on the *Type - M* propelled me without any pedals. I called it the "*Mo-Ped*", (short for "Motorized Pedal"). In no time, I gained much unwanted attention. The privileged people here never did get the hang of having a good time.

Up high, a few zeppelins drifted along the clouds, casting giant shadows down below. Lowering my head, I rode underneath a steel girder four workers were carrying. Recently *Mr. Stephen's* had learned of my steam engine's success, and wanted a similar model for his prototype, a steel trolley designed to accommodate travelers as they made their way throughout the local regions of *Pangea*. The schematics showed the machine had separate cars, running over specialized tracks. The noisy banging and welding from inside the steel mill kept the neighbors up at night, as they complained about the smell of iron in the air.

Coming up ahead was an old building with a steeple. Pulling into the front yard, an army of little monsters swarmed around me. Jumping up and down, they showed me their fierce teeth while pulling on my pant legs.

"Okay okay, I'll give you whatever you want. Just please, don't hurt me!" I shouted, as if fearing the worst. Going into the compartment behind the *Type - M's* back seat, I pulled out a large basket of freshly baked bread. Handing it over, the ruffians pilfered them one by one. After stuffing their little faces, the children then returned to their playground under a large evergreen.

"Thank you, Mr. *Z*!" They yelled.

"Anytime kids, now play nice." I laughed while waving my hand.

That old building was once the *Deacon Blues* orphanage for wayward souls, until an anonymous tip came from a reputable buyer. Informing them of the *Deacon's* mistreatment of his wards and of the illegal sweatshop he'd been running. Authorities immediately investigated and found out that the *Deacon* himself was wanted for multiple counts of tax evasion and coin laundering. He was sentenced to twenty years in prison.
I later purchased the property and expanded its walls. After replacing the steeple with a giant playground slide, I turned it into a real orphanage.

Climbing back onto the *Mo-Ped*, I whizzed through *Edenia's* wide streets, finally heading home. The sweet smell of cinnamon buns from the bakery awakened my senses.
Upon entering my driveway, there were *Mo-peds* parked all over, just under the new *Zep-Tec* billboard. Walking inside I was greeted warmly by the new staff.

"Good morning, Mr. Z," They said in unison.

Returning the greeting, I waved my hand replying, "Good morning, ladies and gentlemen. How is our new project coming along?"

Handing me the blueprints, my top employee *Sylvester* responded,

"The *Model - 2* is coming along just fine, sir. She'll be ready for a test run as soon as we recalibrate the fuel line."

"Great job, guys. Keep up the good work," I replied.

While scanning the schematics, I thought to myself, "Mr. Z? ...I guess that's got a nice ring to it."

After the *Silver Bullet* safely returned from our expedition, an anonymous donation was offered to purchase *Zep-Tec*, and my family's workshop. Leaving only a white lotus flower in an envelope, the buyer immediately signed the deed over to my name. Days later we all returned to the floating islands, but decided to leave the *Lost City* & its treasure the way it was. We agreed to keep it the fable it was, for the next set of adventurers. Although, we did manage to recover *Lock-jaw's* body from the rubble and divided the bounty on his head, four ways.

Spectre finally settled down with *Mei-ling,* the queen of *Singaporia,* and has been granted the honorary title '*Baron of Sky*', now that *Lock-jaw* was defeated. He and his men soon retired from the life of piracy, and now live on the floating city as Royal Guards to the queen.

Sasha went home, to become the new *Amazonian* princess. After abolishing the execution of males, she used her share of coin to educate her native people, and introduced some modern technology into their society. We currently visit each other on the weekends.

Naji was given control of the *Silver Bullet*, refurbishing its frame with a new 12-cylinder steam engine. After hiring a new crew, he abandoned his former lifestyle and set sail, vowing to preserve the other rare treasures across the world.

As for me? I enlisted the help of the best welders, mechanics, and technicians in town. *Zep-Tec* has since expanded the family workshop by ten acres, and even installed our own assembly line for new inventions, locking us into a multimillion coin deal with the steel mill.

Tightening the last lug nuts on the engine block, the workers slammed the metal hood closed. Wiping their hands with greasy rags, they stepped back, giving me a thumbs up. Returning their gesture, I lowered the goggles over my brown pilot's helmet & flipped a series of engine switches. The *Model - 2* aero-plane sputtered loudly before reaching its normal rotation. The dual propellers on separate wings spun rapidly, creating a familiar hum. I was now ready for takeoff.

Steering the plane out from the garage, I approached the runway, watching my father's silver compass watch dangle in front of the controls. Moving the steering columns forward, I began speeding down the runway like a bullet. Then tilting backwards, the plane slowly climbed into the sky. Veering for the horizon, I leaned the plane left into a barrel roll, vanishing amongst the clouds.

Then from the top of my shirt, I retrieved a small necklace with a blue shard, holding it up to the sunlight. The sapphire stone glowed from the within as this *Power Crystals* energy swirled inside limitlessly, as if synced by the warmth of my hand. In a matter of minutes, I was no more than a speckle on the horizon.

Gazing into the sunrise with a smile, I figured some stories were better left untold...

The End.

Ryan "Cam-tron" Cameron is an Author - Actor - Animator - & Artist. Born in the *Bronx, NY* 1990 - he was raised in south *Florida*. After moving to *Georgia* during his senior year of high school, **Ryan** unfortunately spent 10 years in the prison system while battling mental health - before being diagnosed with schizophrenia. But during those trying years, **Ryan** was able to refocus and realign with his passion for creativity & storytelling. Upon his release, he exited with a college degree and numerous other certifications. It was then **Ryan** decided to pursue his love for the arts & entertainment.

Thanks for reading.

Liked the story & want to know more?

Get in touch with me or leave a review online.

At **TalesFromPangea.com**
At **Amazon.com** - (Search "**Tales from Pangea**").
At **Instagram.com** - (Search "**Cam.Tronius.Maximus**").
At **Facebook.com** - (Search "**Ryan Cam-Tron Cameron**").